MARÍA

JORGE ISAACS

MARÍA

By Jorge Isaacs

Translation by Rollo Ogden

AN INTRODUCTION BY THOMAS A. JANVIER

TRANSLATOR'S NOTE.

IT is a part of the faithfulness of Isaacs's transcript of life in provincial Colombia that he uses many words which are Cauca localisms. Several of these have been left untranslated, as having no equivalent, either as word or thing, in English—or, indeed, in Spanish. It is always sufficiently clear from the context, however, that they are names of animals, often onomatopoetic, or of plants; and nothing more could be conveyed by a roundabout translation. Special acknowledgments are due Senior Carlos Martinez Silva, LL.D., delegate from the republic of Colombia to the Pan-American Congress, for valuable aid kindly rendered the translator.

R. O.'

INTRODUCTION

IT is a fact, but a fact not adequately appreciated, that American literature was born, and for a long while received its nourishment, in the Spanish colonies. The first book printed on this continent was a Spanish book. It came from the press in the year 1537: and it antedated the " Bay Psalm Book" by three years more than a century. In his scholarly "Bibliografia Mexicana," my honored friend Don *Joaquin* Garcia Icazbalceta has produced a catalogue raisomzé of all the books published in Mexico before the year 1600. His list includes one hundred and sixteen titles—and it ends twenty years before the Pilgrims landed at Plymouth. A little more than seventy years ago Dr. Beristain y Souza published his "Biblioteca Hispano-Americana Setentrional;" a work which, while confined almost exclusively to Mexican authors, contains upwards of twelve thousand titles distributed under nearly four thousand names. S0 far from abating, this extraor dinary literary fecundity has increased steadily during the present century, while the quality of the work produced has been steadily refined: for the genius of letters never has ceased to abide with the Spanish Americans among whom American literature was born.

It is but a part of our unfortunate lack of knowledge of all matters concerning these neighbors of ours that we are so ignorant of what they have accomplished in literature—to say nothing of what they have accomplished in other directions—during the past three hundred and fifty years. Of Mexico, because of the possibility of making cheap excursions thither by rail, a few of us have gained a superficial knowledge: but the names of the republics beyond Mexico—Guatemala, San Salvador, Honduras, Nicaragua, Costa Rica, and onward through Colombia and Venezuela into the vast region of South America—t0 most of us are names only; or, at best, are names which arouse in our minds but vague thoughts of sixteenth-century adventurers, and coffee-growing, and revolutions, and Mr. Church's landscapes, and filibustering expeditions, and the purchase of guano and hides. Of the real people, leading real lives, who dwell in these countries—of their achievements, and of what they have failed to achieve, of their social organization and customs, and especially of the intimate life of their homes we scarcely could know less were they the inhabitants of another world. Indeed, to come to the matter immediately in hand, no apter illustration can be had of this ignorance on our part of interests which are very near to us than that there should be need to explain anything whatever to English speaking Americans in regard to a story that has been the admiration and the delight of their immediate neighbors, dwelling close beside them on the same continent, for more than twenty years. In a business way we do, of course, know something of these otherwise unknown lands and peoples; but the information that comes to us through commercial channels is not of the most edifying nature, and it is highly objective in the matter of its point of view. By a happy coincidence, I find in this morning's press despatches an interview with an enterprising citizen of the United States who is described as being "engaged in the transportation business " in Colombia, and who just now is having built at Pittsburg a brace of steamboats for use upon the Magdalena and Cauca rivers. This person, in his way, probably, is typical; and, from his own stand-point, the views which he expresses concerning the people of Colombia are far from flattering. "The natives are not of an industrious or mechanical turn of mind," he says; and he adds: "At Bogota the people think a great deal more of literary pursuits than of manufacturing." No doubt this same opinion might have been expressed, with an equally just scorn, six-and-twenty years ago, when a certain young poet published in Bogota' a thin volume of verses. Jorge Isaacs, the author of these verses, was of mixed race—the son of an English Jew married to a woman of Spanish blood. He was born in the town of Cali,-in the State of Cauca; but when only a lad—his father and his mother being both lost to him in death—he found a new and, as it proved, a permanent home in the Colombian capital. The Bogotanos, therefore, claim him as especially their own; and "the cradle of his glory," they justly affirm, was Bogota. Isaacs certainly did "think more literary pursuits than he did of manufacturing' as the publication of his volume of verses sufficiently showed. Being not less esteemed for his charming personality than for his genius—as is authoritatively declared by his fellowtownsman, who also was his editor, Senor Vergara. y Vergara—his verses were received by the critical public of this little capital with a warm enthusiasm; and thus, doubtless, Isaacs was confirmed in his purpose to make literature the leading motive of his life.

All this seems very familiar and very real to me. I have never been in Bogota, but once I lived for a while very happily in a certain other small Spanish-American capital that possesses, I fancy, many similar characteristics. There literature, both productive and critical, was, and no doubt still is, carried to a high degree of perfection; and there more than one young gentleman, in my time, suffered his hair to grow to an abnormal length that thus, in true Samsonian guise, he might the better woo the Muse. Because it is a tangible reminder to me of the queer and very pleasant life that I led in this contracted yet self-sufficing literary community, I cherish tenderly a little volume inscribed "Versos. Por Ricardo." I must confess that, for the most part, they are execrable verses, but, because of their association, they are exceedingly dear to me.

How good, or how bad, were these verses which Isaacs published I do not know, for my efforts to procure a copy of the volume so far have been vain. But in regard to his next literary venture no question can be raised touching the genuineness of its intrinsic merit or the perfection of the workmanship displayed in the making of it. Three years later, in 1867, he published "Maria," and so, at a stroke, won for himself enduring literary fame. In the mass of critical comments prefacing the several editions of "Maria" which have been published in Colombia, in Mexico, and in Spain, the attempt constantly is made to draw a parallel between this story and the "Atala" of Chateaubriand and the "Paul et Virginie" of Bernardin de St. Pierre. Save in the obvious points of resemblance which are found in simplicity of theme and beauty of style, this suggested parallel does Isaacs injustice. Chateaubriand attempted to describe a region of which he had no personal knowledge, and, naturally, failed to impart to his work an air of reality. St. Pierre manufactured an absolutely artificial situation, and dealt with it in a vein of sentiment that even his delicately beautiful handling does not always save from lapsing into mere sentimentality. The essential charm of "Maria," precisely the reverse of all this, comes from the absolute knowledge that the author possesses of the life that he describes, whence follows the air of realism that everywhere pervades his work; and his fine literary intuition that enables him wholly to avoid sentimentality, although a most tender and exquisite sentiment ani mates his story from its beginning to its end. Guillermo Prieto says of "Maria," that it is "a reliquary of pure sentiment," and this is a poet's description of a poem in a genuinely poetic phrase. Adding to and intensifying this charm of subject and this beauty of method, there is a solemn undertone of resistless fatality in the story that allies it— as Senor Altamirano well has pointed out—with certain of the Greek tragedies. The sunny landscape in which the action is carried on is made the brighter by contrast with a most sombre background— and this background, by a masterly use of cumulative effect, grows constantly more distinct and drearier as the foreground fades away and is lost. And in it all, the dominant characteristic is entire truthfulness to nature. To quote Senor Altamirano again: here is "truth contemplated by a man of genius and exhibited with an art that conceals itself in simplicity."

But the side of the story which comes nearest to my own heart—because of the warm feelings bred of pleasant memories which it arouses there—is its beautiful and its absolutely truthful portrayal of life in a Spanish-American home. The author shows, without any apparent effort to show it, the gracious relations existing between the several members of these charming households: which are ordered with a patriarchal simplicity, which are regulated by a constant courtesy, and which are bound together by an ever-present lore. Homes of this sort, my own experience has convinced me, are not the exception but the rule in Spanish-America; and this perfectly finished picture of one of them, in its perfectly-described setting of a country-side community, exhibits the genius of the people more accurately than would an exhaustive study of all other phases of their life combined.

I cannot but hope, therefore, that the story of "Maria" will do something more than give delight to its readers by the beauty of its theme and by the excellence of its art. For I am well satisfied that, showing as it does these stranger neighbors of ours as they truly are, it must tend to the accomplishment of a larger and a higher purpose by fostering a desire among us to transform them into friends. This seems to me a most natural conclusion; for my own experience has shown me that they need only to be known in order to be loved. And no happier issue than this could come of the passage of "María" from the hearts of the Spanish-speaking Americans of the south to the hearts of the English-speaking Americans of the north.

THOMAS A. JANVIER.

February 5, 1890.

MARIA

The brothers of Ephraim

Behold, my dear friends, the story of adolescence of the one whom you loved so much and which no longer exists. I have done a long time to wait these pages. After writing I found pale and unworthy of being offered as a testimony of my gratitude and my affection. You are aware of the words spoken that terrible night, putting my hands on the book of his memories: "What you know is missing there: read up what my tears have been deleted." Sweet and sad mission! Read them, then, and if reading suspendéis to mourn, those tears I will prove that I have faithfully.

I

I was still a child when I walked away from the family home to give the beginning of my studies in college Dr. Lorenzo Maria Lleras, established a few years ago in Bogotá, and famous throughout the Republic at that time.

On the eve of my journey night after the evening, came into my room one of my sisters, and without saying a word loving, because the voice sobs embargoed, cut a hair of my head: when he left, had rolled some tears for my own neck.

I fell asleep crying and felt like a vague presentiment that he should suffer many regrets later. These hairs removed a child head; love that caution against such life before death, made during sleep vagase my soul for all the places had gone, without understanding, the happiest hours of my life.

The next morning my father broke my head, wet with many tears, my mother's arms. My sisters say their goodbyes to the rinsed with kisses. Mary humbly waited his turn, and stammering his farewell, gathered his rosy cheek to mine ice for the first sensation of pain.

A few moments later I went to my father, who hid his face in my eyes. The footsteps of our horses in the pebbly path sobs choking my past. The rumor of Zabaletas whose vegas were on our right, is lessened by the minute. We took as a return to the hills of the village, which used to house seen from the travelers desired; I looked at her looking for one of many loved ones: Mary was under vines adorning the windows of the room my mother .

II

After six years, the last days of August I received a fancy to return to native valley. My heart was filled with love of country. It was already the last day of the trip, and I enjoyed the most fragrant summer morning. The sky was a pale blue tint: to the east and towering peaks of the mountains, half mourning still, wandered a few puffs of gold gauze turban as a dancer scattered loving breath. Southward mists floated during the night had wrapped the distant mountains. Gramal crossed green plains, watered by streams whose passage obstructed me beautiful herds, they left their resting places to go into the gaps or vaulted paths tread by flowering and leafy fig trees. My eyes were fixed hungrily half hidden in those places the traveler in the tops of guaduales elderly, in those farms where people had left and virtuous friends. In such moments would not have touched my heart piano arias U. .. Perfumes were so fond aspiring compared to that of her fine clothes, the singing of those birds had no name so sweet harmonies to my heart!

I was speechless at such beauty, whose memory had believed kept in memory because some of my verses, admired by my fellow students, it had pale inks. When in a dance hall, flooded with light, full of voluptuous melodies, thousand aromas mixed with whispers of many garments of seductive women, found those who have dreamed at eighteen and a fleeting glance his burning our front, and his voice makes mute for a moment another voice for us all, and her flowers essences leave behind unknown, then we fall into a heavenly prostration: our voice is powerless, because our ears do not hear his, our eyes can not follow. But when, refreshed mind, her memory returns hours later, our lips murmur in his praise songs, and that woman is his accent, is her look is her light step on the carpet, which mimics that song, that the world will believe ideal. So the sky, the horizon, the plains and the mountains of Cauca make mute who contemplates them. The great beauties of creation can not at once be seen and sung: it is necessary to return to the soul, the memory empalidecidas unfaithful.

Before sunset, I had already seen on whitening on mountainside home of my parents. As I approached her with anxious eyes had groups of willows and orange, through which the cross saw the lights shortly after they were distributed in the rooms.

Finally breathed the smell of the garden never forgotten where I was training. The shoes of my horse sparkled on the cobblestones of the courtyard. I heard a cry indefinable was the voice of my mother to shake her arms and closer to his chest, a shadow covered my eyes: the supreme pleasure was moved to a wilderness.

When I tried to recognize women I saw, I left the sisters girls, Maria was standing next to me, and watched his eyelids wide eyes fringed with long lashes. It was his face that was covered the most remarkable blush when to roll my arm brushed shoulders with her figure, and her eyes were moist, even when smiling loving my first expression, like a child whose cry has died down a touch mother.

III

At eight o'clock we went to the dining room, which was picturesquely situated on the eastern side of the house. Since he saw the naked crests of the mountains above the starry sky background. Desert Auras passed through the garden picking flavors to come play with roses around us. The fickle wind could be heard for a few moments the sound of the river.

That nature seemed to hold all the beauty of the night, as a guest for a friend.

My father took the head of the table and put me on the right, my mother sat on the left, as usual, my sisters and children alike stood, and Mary stood in front of me.

My father, graying in my absence, I headed glances and smiled with satisfaction that her maliciously and sweet at the same time, you've never seen in other lips. My mother spoke little, because in those moments was happier than all those around her. My sisters were determined to make me try the snacks and creams: and blushed her whom I ran a flattering word or a look examiner.

Mary was hiding his eyes stubbornly, but I admire in them the brilliance and beauty of the women's race, in two or three times reluctantly met squarely with mine, her red lips, wet and gracefully imperatives , showed me an instant the prime of his veiled nice set. He had, like my sisters, abundant dark brown hair in two plaits arranged on the birth of one of which looked a red carnation.

He wore a light muslin robe, almost blue, which was discovered only part of the bodice and skirt, for a thin cotton shawl, purple color, covered her bosom to the base of his throat, white matte. Returning braids to the back, where it rolled to bend to serve, I admired the underside of deliciously shapely arms, and hands manicured like a queen.

After the dinner, the slaves rose tablecloths, one of them prayed the Our Father, and their owners completed the sentence.

The conversation then became confidential between my parents and me.

Mary picked her sleeping child in her lap, and my sisters went to the rooms: they loved her very much and fought his sweet affection.

Back in the room, my father, to retire, I kissed her daughters forehead. My mother wanted me to see the room that I had intended. My sisters and Mary, less shy and wanted to see what effect it caused me the care with which it was adorned. The room was at the end of the corridor in front of the house, his only window was to the inside height of a comfortable table and at that moment, with leaves and bars open, went in her flowery branches of roses to finish to decorate the table, where a beautiful blue porcelain vase containing laboriously in his glass lilies and lilies, carnations and purple bells River. The bed curtains were white gauze tied columns wide with pink ribbons, and near the head, by a native delicacy, the Dolorosa was small that I had served my altars as a child. Some maps, comfortable seating and a beautiful set of bathroom completed the outfit.

- What beautiful flowers! I cried to see all that the garden and vase covered the table.

-Mary remembered how much I liked my mother-observed.

I turned my eyes to thank him and his men as they strove to endure this time my gaze.

-Mary-I-will guardármelas, because they are harmful in the room where you sleep.

- Is it true? He answered, for the'll replace tomorrow.

How sweet was her accent!

- So many well there?

-So much, will be replenished every day.

After my mother hugged me, Emma gave me his hand, and Mary, abandoning his for a moment, smiled and I smiled in childhood: that smile hoyuelada was the girl of my loves children, caught in the face of a Rafael virgin.

IV

Slept quiet, like when I dozed in childhood one of the wonderful stories of slave Peter.

Mary dreamed I went to renew my table flowers, and that had brushed out the curtains of my bed with gauzy muslin skirt dotted with blue flowers.

When I woke up, fluttering birds sang in the foliage of orange and pomarrosos, and the blossoms filled my room with its aroma as soon as I opened the door.

Mary's voice came to my ears so sweet and pure: his voice was a child, but more severe and longer list to be provided to all modulations of tenderness and passion. Oh! How many times, in my dreams, an echo of that accent has come after my soul, and my eyes have looked in vain so beautiful that garden where I saw that morning in August!

The girl whose innocent caresses were all for me, it would not be because the companion of my games, but in the golden summer afternoons on the rides would be on my side, in the middle of the group of my sisters would help me to grow their flowers favorite, in the evenings I would hear his voice, his eyes would look at me, would separate us one step.

After I had fixed me lightly dressed, opened the window and saw Mary in one of the streets of the garden, accompanied by Emma: wearing a suit darker than the day before, and the color purple shawl, bound at the waist , fell as a band on the skirt, her long hair, divided into two tresses, ocultábale half of the back and chest: she and my sister had bare feet. He wore a little porcelain vase white arms that held, which was filling with roses open overnight, by discarding the wilted and less humid lush. She, laughing with his partner, sinking the cheeks, more fresh roses in the brimming bowl. Emma Descubrióme Mary noticed, and without turning to me, fell on his knees to hide their feet, the shawl desatóse the waist, and covering the shoulders with him, pretending to play with flowers. The nubile daughters of the patriarchs were not in the most beautiful dawns when picking flowers for their altars.

After lunch, my mother called me to her sewing.

Emma and Mary were embroidering nearby.

He returned it to blush when I introduced myself, remembering perhaps the surprise that I had inadvertently given in the morning.

My mother wanted to see me and hear me constantly.

Emma, more flirtatious and I wondered a thousand things in Bogota, I demanded that describe splendid dances, beautiful lady dresses were in use, the most beautiful women then appear in high society. Heard without leaving their jobs. Mary looked at me sometimes carelessly, or made under his observations to his seatmate, and stand to approach my mother to ask something about the embroidery, I could see her neatly shod feet: his brisk and worthy revealed all pride, not killed, of our race, and the seductive modesty of Christian virgin. Ilumináronsele eyes when my mother said that I wish to give the girls some lessons in grammar and geography, subjects that had but very few notions. It was agreed that we would start to lessons past six or eight days, during which I would grade the state of knowledge of each.

Hours later I was told that the bath was ready, and went to him. A big orange lush, ripe fruit overwhelmed, was flag on polished quarry pond width: floated on the water many roses; semejábase an oriental bath, and was perfumed with flowers in the morning had picked Mary.

V

It had been three days when my father invited me to visit their estates in the valley, and it was necessary to please, on the other hand, I had real interest in favor of their companies. My mother insisted strongly by our early return. My sisters were grieved. Mary begged me not like them, that regresase in the same week, but I was still with eyes constantly during my preparations.

In my absence, my father had markedly improved properties: an expensive and beautiful sugar factory, many bushels cane to supply it, large pastures with cattle and horses, good feedlots and a luxurious room, were the most notable of his Hot landed estate. Slaves, well dressed and happy as far as possible be pregnant in servitude, were submissive and affectionate to his master. I found men who, shortly before children, had taught me to set traps and guatines chilacoas in the dense forests, their parents and they came back to me with unmistakable signs of pleasure. Only Peter, good friend and faithful schoolmaster should not find him: he had shed tears to put me on the horse the day of my departure to Bogotá, saying: "Amice mine, and never see you again." His heart was warned that he would die before my return.

I noticed that my father, without ceasing to be master, affectionate treatment gave their slaves, was jealous of the good conduct of their wives and children petted.

One afternoon, already sunsets, returning from the crops to the factory my father, Higinio (the butler) and me. They talked about work done and to be done, to me occupied less serious things: I thought the days of my childhood. The peculiar smell of freshly felled forests and the pinecones in season: the outcry of the parrots in the bamboo and guava neighbors, the tolling of a distant horn pastor, echoed by the mountains, the castrueras of slaves returning spaciously of the work with the tools to shoulder the afterglow seen through the reeds to shifting all evening reminded me that, abusing my sisters, Mary and I leave some of my mother, obtained by dint of tenacity, we collect solazábamos guavas of our favorite trees, pulling pinecones nests, often with serious injury to arms and hands, and parrots chicks peeping fences corrals.

When faced with a group of slaves, said my father to a young black man of remarkable good looks:

'So, Bruno, is everything in your marriage is arranged for tomorrow?

Yes, my master replied rush his hat and leaning on the handle of his shovel.

- Who are the sponsors?

Dolores and Lord Na Anselmo, if your worship will.

-Good. Remigia and you'll be fine confessed. Did you get everything you need for her and for you to give you the money I sent?

-Everything is ready, master.

- And anything else you want?

His mercy will.

-The fourth Higinio you noted, is it good?

'Yes, master.

- Ah! I know. What I want to dance.

Bruno then laughed, showing his dazzling white teeth, looking back at his companions.

-Just is, you behave very well. You know, he added, addressing Higinio-: fix that, and that they are happy.

- What are their grants before? Bruno asked.

'No,' I replied, we give guests.

At dawn next Saturday and Remigia Bruno married. That night, at seven, my father and I rode to the ball, which we began to hear music. When we arrived, Julian, the slave gang captain, came to take the step and get our horses. He was lavish with her Sunday dress and hung from the waist trim the long machete silver insignia of his employment. A room of our old house had been unoccupied room of work containing utensils, to dance in it. Habíanla surrounded by pallets, in a wooden chandelier hanging in one of the beams, half dozen spinning lights, musicians and singers, aggregate mixture, slaves and freedmen, occupying one of the doors. There were only two reed pipes, a makeshift drum, two alfandoques and a tambourine, but the fine voices of the blacks sang masterfully bambucos such, had in their songs as heartfelt combination of melancholy, joyous and light chords, the verses tenderly sang were so simple, that the more educated *dilettante* had heard that music in semi-wild ecstasy. We entered the room with coats and hats. Remigia then danced and Bruno, she follao blue bolero, cuddy red flowers, white shirt and black embroidered crystal necklace and earrings ruby color, danced with all the kindness and grace that were expected of her figure cimbrador . Bruno, bent over his shoulder cloths yarn poncho, blanket colorful panties, ironed white shirt and a waist again *cabiblanco,* zapateaba with admirable dexterity.

Past that hand, that they call each piece peasant dance, the musicians played their most beautiful bambuco because Julian told them it was for love. Remigia, encouraged by her husband and by the captain, was resolved at last to dance with my father a few moments, but then did not dare to raise his eyes, and his movements were less spontaneous dance. After an hour we left.

My father was satisfied with my attention during our visit to the farms, but when I said I wanted to participate onwards from their labors staying beside him, I said, almost regretfully, we looked at the case of sacrificing for mine their welfare, cumpliéndome the promise that I had made some time ago to send to Europe to finish my medical studies, and travel to be undertaken no later than four months. When you talk like that, his face took on a seriousness solemn without affectation, that it showed in him when taking irrevocable decisions. This happened in the afternoon we returned to the mountains. It began to get dark, and have not been, would have noticed the excitement that its refusal caused me. The rest of the journey was made in silence. How happy I would see Mary again, if the news of that trip had not been brought from that time in my hopes and her!

VI

What had happened in those four days in the life of Mary?

Was she going to place a lamp on a table in the living room, when I went to say hello, and I had missed not seeing her in the middle of the group of the family in the stands where we had just desmontarnos. The trembling of his hand exposed the lamp, and I lent him aid, less calm than I thought to be. It seemed slightly pale, and around his eyes had a faint, imperceptible for those who had seen it without looking. She turned her face toward my mother, who was speaking at the time, so I could avoid examine bathed in the light that we close, I then noticed that in the birth of one of the strands had a withered carnation, and was definitely the one that I had given the day before my departure to the valley. The enameled coral crucecilla she had brought for her, like that of my sisters, the slope of her neck a string of black hair. He was silent, sitting in the middle of the seats we occupied my mother and me. As the resolution of my father about my trip never left my memory, I must have seemed to her sad, as I said in a voice almost floor:

- Did you hurt the trip?

-No, Mary, 'I said, but we both sunny and we walked ...

I was going to say something else, but the accent of his voice confidentially, new light for me that was surprised in his eyes, I was unable to do anything but watch it until, noticing that he was ashamed of the involuntary fixity of my eyes, and finding examined by one of my father (more terrible when some fleeting smile on his lips wandered), left the room in the direction of my room.

I closed the doors. There were the flowers picked by her to me, the Aje with my kisses once wanted to suck all their flavors, looking at them from the dresses of Mary; bañélas with my tears ... Ah, those not well have wept with happiness, weep with despair, if you have spent your adolescence, because so neither shall return to love ya!

First Love! ... Noble pride of being loved: sweet sacrifice everything before us was expensive for the beloved woman, who bought happiness for a day with the tears of an entire existence, we would receive as a gift from God; perfume for every hour of future; inextinguishable light of the past stored in the soul flower and wither is not given to the disappointments, only treasure you can not take away the envy of men; delirium delicious ... inspiration of Heaven ... Mary! Mary! How I loved you! Love you much!

VII

When did my father's last voyage to the West Indies, Solomon, cousin to whom much had loved since childhood, had just lost his wife. Very young people had come together to South America, and one of his trips my father fell in love with the daughter of a Spanish captain bold, after leaving the service for a few years, was forced in 1819 to take back the arms in defense of the kings of Spain, which was shot in Majagual on May 20, 1820.

The girl's mother demanded that my father loved to give it a condition for his wife to renounce the Jewish religion. My father became a Christian at the age of twenty. His cousin is fond in those days to the Catholic religion, without giving their bodies so that did baptize also, knowing that I've done for my father, gave the wife he wanted, he would be acceptable to prevent the woman he loved in Jamaica.

After a few years of separation, they met again, then, the two friends. It was a widower Solomon. Sara, his wife, had left a girl who was at the time three years. My father found him morally and physically disfigured by pain, and then his new religion gave consolation to his cousin, consolations had sought in vain to save relatives. He urged Solomon to give him his daughter in order to educate them on our side, and dared to suggest that Christian would. Solomon agreed saying, "It is true that only my daughter has kept me on a journey to India, would improve my spirit and my remedy poverty: it has also been my only solace after the death of Sarah, but you want it, either your daughter. The Christians are sweet and good, and your wife must be a saint mother. If Christianity gives supreme misfortune in relief that you have given me, maybe I would my daughter leaving unhappy Jewish. Do not tell our relatives, but when you get to the first coast where he is a Catholic priest to baptize and to make it change the name of Mary Esther. " It said the unhappy shedding many tears.

A few days later was to sail in Montego Bay the schooner that my father was driving the coast of New Granada. The ship was rehearsing its white light like a heron wings of our forests theirs before going on a long flight. Solomon entered the room of my father, who had just fix your suit on board, taking Esther sitting on one arm, and slope of a chest containing another baggage girl: this little arms stretched his uncle , and Solomon, putting on his friend, fell sobbing on the small trunk. The creature, whose head had just beautiful bathing in a shower of tears of pain before baptism than the religion of Jesus, was a sacred treasure, my father knew well, and never forgot. A Solomon was remembered by his friend, to jump into the boat he was going to separate them, a promise, and he said in a choked voice: "The prayers of my daughter for me and mine for her and her mother, rising together at the feet of the Crucified! ».

I was seven years old when my father returned, and disdained precious toys that brought me from his trip to admire the girl so beautiful, so sweet and smiling. My mother covered her with caresses, and my sisters were treated to tenderness, from the time that my father, putting it in the lap of his wife, said, "This is the daughter of Solomon, he sends you."

During our playground lips began modular Castilian accent, so harmonious and seductive in a pretty mouth of the smiling woman and a child.

They would run about six years. When I entered the room one afternoon when my father heard him sobbing had his arms folded on the table and rested his forehead on them; near him my mother was crying, and Mary resting on her knees head, not understanding that pain and almost indifferent to the cries of his uncle was a letter from Kingston, received that day, gave the news of the death of Solomon. I remember only an expression of my father that afternoon: "If all are leaving me without being able to receive their final goodbyes, what will I turn to my country? '. Alas, his ashes were to rest in a strange land, without the ocean winds, whose beaches frolicked as a child, whose vastness crossed young and ardent, come sweeping over his grave slab of dried flowers and dust flavors the years!

Few were then those who, knowing our family, might suspect that Mary was not the daughter of my parents. He spoke our language, were friendly, lively and intelligent. When my mother stroked his head, while my sisters and me, no one could have guessed what was there the orphan.

Was nine. The head of hair, yet light brown, loose and playing on his thin waist and moveable; talkative eyes, the accent with some melancholy that had our voices, such was the picture that I took when I left her father's house , and was in the morning of that sad day, under the vines of the window of my mother.

VIII

A night raw Emma called to my door to go to the table. I bathed his face to hide the tracks of my tears, and I moved the clothes to excuse my tardiness.

Mary was not in the room, and vainly imagined that they had done their jobs take longer than usual. Noticing my father a vacant seat, asked for her, and Emma apologized saying that since that afternoon he had a headache and was sleeping already. I tried not to show me impressed, and making every effort to ensure that the conversation was pleasant, spoke enthusiastically about all the improvements that were found on farms that had just visited. But to no avail: my father was more tired than me, and retired early, Emma and my mother got up to go to bed at children and check on Mary, which I thanked them, but I was surprised as me that same feeling of gratitude.

Although Emma returned to the dining room, the desktop did not last long. Felipe and Heloise, who had committed to take part in their game of cards, charged my sleepy eyes. He unsuccessfully requested permission to accompany my mother the next day at the mountain, making retired discontent.

Meditating in my room, I thought I guess the cause of suffering of Mary. I remembered how I had left the room after I arrived and how the impression I made the confidential tone of it was ground that will answer to the lack of tact of one who is suppressing an emotion. Knowing and the origin of his sentence, would have given a thousand lives for him obtain a pardon, but the doubt came to aggravate the distress of my spirit. I doubted the love of Mary. Why, I thought, my heart strives to believe before this same martyrdom? Consider me unworthy to hold such beauty, such innocence. Echéme pride in that face that I had obfuscated to the point of believing by the object of his love, to be worthy of her affection only sister. In my madness I thought with less terror, almost with pleasure, on my next trip.

IX

I got up the next day at daybreak. The flashes eastward delineating the cusps of the central mountains gilded in semicircles on it some light clouds that were unleashed from each other to get away and disappear.

The green valley plains and forests were seen as through a glass the blue, and in the midst of them some cabins white fumes of freshly burnt hills rising spiral, and once the riots of a river. The mountains of the West, with its folds and breasts looked like dark blue velvet robes suspended from their centers by the hands of geniuses veiled by the mists. In front of my window, roses and foliage of the trees of the garden seemed to fear the first breezes that come to shed the dew glistened on the leaves and flowers. Everything seemed sad. I took the shotgun, I motioned to loving Mayo, seated on hind legs, staring at me, wrinkled forehead by excessive attention, awaiting the first order, and stone jumping the fence, took the mountain road. At internarme, I found it fresh and trembling under the caresses of the latest auras of the night. Herons left their roosts in flight forming undulating lines that silvered the Sun, as tapes abandoned to the whims of the wind. Numerous flocks of parrots in the bamboo rose to address the neighboring cornfields, and greeted diostedé up with his sad and monotonous singing from the heart of the mountain.

I went down to the river plain mountainous along the same path by which he had so many times six years earlier.

The thunder of the flood is going to increase, and soon discovered the streams, rushing to rush into the jumps, turned in foams kettles in them, clear and smooth in the backwaters, rolling it over a plush bed of moss rocks, fringed in the bank by iracales, ferns and yellow rods stems, silky seed plumes of purple.

Detúveme in the middle of the bridge, formed by the hurricane with a big cedar, where it had happened in another time. Parasitic flowering hanging from their branches, and shimmering bluebells and down in festoons from my feet to rock in the waves. A lush and proud abovedaba at intervals the river, and through it penetrated some rays of the rising sun as the roof of a broken left Indian temple. May coward on the bank yelled that I had just left, and my request was resolved to go through the great bridge, then take the path before me leading to the possession of the old Joseph, who expected me to pay that day Welcome your visit.

After a short steep slope, dark, and jumps through a dry woodland on recent demolitions Highlander, I found myself in the small square planted with vegetables, where I saw the little steaming set amidst green hills, which I had stopped between forests apparently indestructible. Cows, beautiful for its size and color, bellowing at the door of the yard looking for their calves. Domestic poultry ration morning getting rattled, in the nearby palm trees, which had spared the ax of the farmers, the orioles bustling swayed in their hanging nests, and amid uproar was heard so pleasing to the time the shrill cry of the fowler, Since its barbecue and armed honda frightened hungry macaws that flew over the cornfield.

Antioquia dogs by barking gave notice of my arrival. May, afraid of them approached me pouting. Joseph came to meet me, ax in one hand and his hat in the other.

The small house denounced industry, thrift and cleanliness, everything was rustic, but in a convenient ready, and everything in its place. The room of the house, well swept, bamboo benches around, covered with reed mats and bearskins, lit some paper prints depicting saints and lit with orange spines to walls unbleached had right and left the bedroom Joseph's wife and the girls. The kitchen is small and made of cane with the roof of leaves of the same plant, was separated from the house by a little garden where parsley, chamomile, pennyroyal and basil aromas mingled.

Women seemed dressed more carefully than usual. The girls, Lucy and Traffic, wore purple and chintz petticoats very white shirts with lace ruffs, edged with black braid, under which hid part of their rosaries, necklaces and colored bulbs opal glass. The braids of her hair, thick and jet black color, they played on their backs at the slightest movement of bare feet, care and restless. I spoke with extreme shyness, and his father was the one who, noting that, encouraged them by saying: "Is it not the same child Ephraim, because they come from school and already knew lad? '. Then became more jovial and smiling: we amicably laced memories of childhood games, powerful in the imagination of poets and women. With aging, the face of Joseph had gained much: but let not the beard, his face was something Biblical, like almost all of the elders of morality in the country where he was born, a abundant white hair and shadowed him the toast and broad forehead, and their smiles revealed tranquility of soul. Luisa, his wife happier than him in the struggle over the years, kept in dress fashion something Antioquia, and his constant cheerfulness kept realize he was happy with their lot.

Joseph led me to the river and told me about their crops and hunting, as I plunged into the airy haven from which water throwing forming a small waterfall. On our return we found served at the only table in the house the provocative lunch. Corn rampant everywhere: in the mote soup served in glazed earthenware dishes and golden arepas scattered on the tablecloth. The only utensils covered the cross on my plate was white and bordered in blue.

May sat at my feet with watchful eyes, but more humble than usual.

José mended a cast net while their daughters, but shameful lists, full of care served me, trying adivinarme in the eyes he could miss me. Much has been embellished, and loquillas girls who were women had become informal.

Hurried the thick glass of frothy milk dessert that lunch patriarchal Jose and I went to tour the garden and it was fucking slashing. The was amazed of my knowledge about the fields, and returned to the house an hour later and I say goodbye to the girls and mother.

Púsele the good old at the waist the hunting knife he had brought from reino1, neck and Lucia transit, precious rosaries, and in the hands of a reliquary Luisa she had asked my mother. I took around the mountain when it was noon per edge, according to the survey that the Sun did Joseph.

X

On my return, I did slowly, the image of Mary returned to cling to my memory. Those solitudes, its silent forests, its flowers, its birds and its waters, why I talked about it? What was there to Mary? In the humid shadows in the breeze moved the leaves, in the sound of the river ... Eden was that he saw, but she was missing, was that he could not stop loving her, but not love me. And inhaled the scent of wild lilies bouquet that daughters of Joseph were formed for me, thinking that perhaps I deserve to be touched by the lips of Mary and had weakened into a few hours of the night my purposes.

Just got home, I went to my mother's sewing Mary was with her, my sisters had gone to the bathroom. After answering the Hail Mary looked down over the seam. My mother said elated by my return, for startled at home with the delay, had sent for me at that time. He spoke with them pondering the progress of Joseph, and Mayo off his tongue with my dresses cockleburs that they were caught in the weeds.

Mary raised her eyes again, fixing them in the bouquet of lilies I had in my left hand, as I leaned right in the shotgun, I thought I understood that he wanted, but an indefinable fear, true respect for my mother and my purposes of night, preventing me from offering them. But I delighted in imagining how beautiful would be one of my little lilies on her shining brown hair. For it should be, because it would have collected during the morning and violet blossoms vase for my table. When I entered my room I saw a flower there. If I had found on the table a coiled snake, I would not have felt the same emotion that I caused the absence of flowers: the fragrance had become something of the spirit of Mary wandering around me in the hours of study, which rocked in the curtains of my bed at night ... Ah! So it was true that I loved! So he could deceive both my visionary imagination! And that class had brought for her, what could I do? If another woman, beautiful and seductive, had been there at that time, in that moment of resentment against my pride, resentment with Mary, she would have given him shew condition and beautify all with him. I took it to my lips as if to say goodbye for the last time an illusion dear, and threw it out the window.

XI

I made efforts to show jovial during the day. In the table spoke enthusiastically of the beautiful women of Bogotá, and thank intentionally pondered and ingenuity of P. .. My father was happy hearing me: Heloise would have wanted the desktop lasted until night. Mary was silent, but I found that sometimes her cheeks paled, and that its original color had not returned to them, as well as the roses that have graced overnight feast.

Towards the latter part of the conversation, Mary had pretended to play with the hair of John, brother of three years whom she doted. Endured to the end, but as soon as I stood up, she went with the child to the garden.

All the rest of the afternoon and early evening was necessary to help my father in his work desk.

At eight o'clock, and then the women had already said her prayers always, we called the dining room. As we sat at the table, I was surprised to see one of the lilies on the head of Mary. There was such a beautiful face in her air noble, innocent and sweet resignation, as mesmerized by something hitherto unknown to me in it, I could not stop staring.

Loving and cheerful girl, woman as pure and seductive as those with whom I had dreamed, and knew her, but resigned to my disdain, was new to me. Deified by resignation, I felt unworthy of fixing a look on his face.

Poorly answered some questions that I made about Joseph and his family. My father could not be hide my embarrassment, and turns to Mary and said, smiling:

-Beautiful lilies in her hair you: I have not seen these in the garden.

Mary, trying to hide his embarrassment, faint voice responded:

-Is that these lilies only in the mountains.

Surprised at that time a kind smile on Emma's lips.

- Who sent them? My father asked.

The embarrassment of Mary was already known. I looked at her and she had to find something new and entertainer in my eyes, for firmer accent answered:

-Ephraim bounced around the garden, and found it to be so rare, it was unfortunate that were lost: this is one of them.

Mary-le-I said, if I had known they were so esteemed those flowers, I would have saved ... for you, but I found it less beautiful than the day put in the vase on my desk.

She understood the cause of my resentment, and I said so clearly his look, I feared they hear the beating of my heart.

That night, when the family leave the room, Mary was casually sitting near me. After much hesitation, I finally said, his voice denouncing my excitement: "Mary, were for you, but I found yours."

She stammered some excuse when I stumble on the couch with his hand, held it was a people's movement to my will. He stopped talking. His eyes looked at me astonished and fled from mine.

Pasóse anguish over his forehead with his free hand, and leaned on her head, plunging the bare arm on the cushion immediately. Finally making an effort to undo the double loop of matter and soul that united us in that moment, he began to walk, and as a reflection begun concluding, he said so softly I could barely hear her: "So ... I will take every day the most beautiful flowers, "and disappeared.

Souls like Maria ignore the mundane language of love, but shudder at the first bend caress that they love, like poppy forests under the wings of the winds.

Had just confessed my love for Mary, she had encouraged me to confess humbling himself as a slave to pick the flowers. I repeated with delight his last words, his voice still whispered in my ear: "So every day I will gather the most beautiful flowers."

XII

The moon, which had just raised under a big full and deep sky on the crests of the mountains towering, bleached selvosas skirts lit here and there by the tops of the Yarumos, foams argentando torrents and spreading his melancholy clarity to the bottom Valley. Plants exhaled its softer and mysterious aromas. The silence, broken only by the murmur of the river, was more pleased than ever to my soul.

Leaning his elbows on the frame of my window, I imagined seeing her among the roses among them had caught that morning first, was there gathering bouquet of lilies, sacrificing his pride to his love. It was I who would disturb sleep onwards child of his heart could already speak of my love, make it the object of my life. Tomorrow!, Night magic word that we are told we are loved! Their eyes, meeting mine, would have nothing to hide, she embellish for my happiness and pride.

Never July auroras in Cauca were as beautiful as Maria when I was presented the next day, moments after leaving the bathroom, shaded tortoiseshell hair loose and medium curl, the rosy cheeks gently faded, but in some fueled by the flush times, and loving playing on his lips that smile that reveals chaste women like Mary a happiness that can not hide. Their eyes, sweetest and brightest, showed that his dream was not as peaceful as it had solid. When you approach him on his forehead noticed a contraction funny and barely noticeable, kind of mock severity that used many times to me when after all the light dazzle with their beauty, imposed silence to my lips, next to repeat what she knew both .

It was now a necessity for me to have her by my side constantly, not wasting a single moment of her existence abandoned my love and happy with what they had, and even avid said, I tried to make a paradise of the family home. I talked to my sister Mary and who had expressed the desire to make them some basic studies under my direction: they came to get excited about the project, and it was decided that from that day would start.

They turned a corner of the room in cabinet study; desclavaron some maps of my room, dusted the geographical globe on my father's desk had been hitherto ignored, were cleared of ornaments two consoles to make them study table. My mother smiled to witness anyone rigged derangement that our project.

We met every day two hours, during which I explained to them a chapter of geography, we read some history, and sometimes many more pages *Genius of Christianity*. Then valuing all intelligence could Mary: my sentences were recorded indelibly in his memory, and his understanding was ahead almost always win my explanations child.

Emma was surprised and delighted secrecy in our innocent happiness. How do I hide in those frequent conferences in my heart what happened? She must have seen my look still on his face while his partner sorcerer gave this explanation requested. He had seen her trembling hand to Mary if I put it on some point searched in vain on the map. And if sitting near the table, they stood on either side of my seat, leaned Mary to see something that was better in my book or in the letters, his breath, brushing my hair, her braids, rolling their shoulders, troubled my explanations, and Emma could see her straighten modest.

Sometimes housework called the attention of my disciples, and my sister took charge always go back to fill them for a while then reunírsenos. Then my heart was pounding. Mary, forehead and lips childishly grave almost laughing, left to mine some of his aristocratic hands planted dimples, made to oppress fronts like Byron, and his accent, while having music that was peculiar, became slow and deep to pronounce words softly articulated in vain to prove I remember now, because I have not heard them, because lips uttered by others are not the same, and written in these pages appear meaningless. They belong to another language, which for many years does not come to mind or a phrase.

XIII

The pages of Chateaubriand inks were slowly giving the imagination of Mary. As faith-filled Christian, rejoiced to find beauties for her presentidas in Catholic worship. His soul took the palette that I offered him the most beautiful colors to make it beautiful throughout, and fire poetic gift of Heaven makes admirable men who possess and deifies women reveal reluctantly, gave his countenance charms unknown to me before in the human face. The thoughts of the poet, welcomed into the soul of this woman so seductive in the midst of his innocence, turned to me as a distant echo and harmony that becomes known to move the heart.

One afternoon late as my country, adorned with violet clouds and sudden flashes of pale gold, beautiful as Mary was beautiful and transitory as it for me, her, my sister and I sat on the wide stone slope, from where we could see right into the deep rolling vega bustling river flows, and taking the valley below us majestic and quiet, I read the episode of *Atala, and* two, admirable in its stillness and abandonment, heard sprout my lips all that melancholy agglomerated by the poet to "make the world mourn." My sister, right arm leaning on one of my arms, his head almost bound to mine eyes were still lines that I was reading. Mary, half kneeling near me, my face did not separate from their eyes, and wet.

The sun had altered voice when I read the last pages of the poem. Emma's pale head rested on my shoulder. Mary hid her face with both hands. Then I read this heartbreaking farewell Chactas over the grave of his beloved, farewell so often a sob ripped my chest: "Sleep in peace in foreign land, hapless youth! In return for your love, your exile and you die, you are abandoned to the same Chactas "Mary, leaving my voice heard, discovered the face, and big tears rolled down her. It was as beautiful as the creation of the poet, and I loved her with the love he imagined. We drove in silence and slowly toward the house. Oh, my soul and Mary were not only moved by reading this: they were overwhelmed by the feeling!

XIV

After three days, dropping, an afternoon of the mountain, I seem to notice any shock on the faces of the young men with whom I came across in the interior corridors. My sister told me that Mary had suffered a nervous breakdown, and adding that he was still senseless sought soon as he could soothe my painful anxiety.

Forgetting all caution, I went into the bedroom where she was Mary, and dominating the frenzy that I had done to my heart to clasp back to life, I approached his bed baffled. At the foot of it sat my father noticed me one of her looks intense, and then turning it on Mary, seemed to want me to make a counterclaim to show me. My mother was there, but did not look up to find me, because, knowing my love, pity I pitied as a good mother knows the woman loved by his son, his son himself.

I stood there staring, not daring to find out what his wrong. I was like asleep: his face covered with deathly pallor, looked half hidden by the hair decomposed, which were discovered crushed the flowers I had given in the morning revealed a contracted forehead unbearable suffering, and a slight sweat she moistened his temples: closed eyes had tried to sprout tears shining in the tabs arrested.

Understanding my father all my suffering, stood up to leave, but before leaving he approached the bed, and taking the pulse of Mary, said:

'Everything happened. Poor girl! Exactly the same was afflicted his mother.

Maria's chest rose slowly to form a sob, and to return to its natural state just breathed a sigh. That my father was gone, coloquéme to the bedside, and forgetting my mother and Emma, who remained silent, I took on the cushion of the hands of Mary, and bathed in the torrent of my tears, until then content. It measured all my misfortune was the same evil of his mother, who died very young attacked an incurable epilepsy. This idea took possession of my whole being to bruise.

I felt some movement in that limp hand, which he could not return my breath heat. Mary began to breathe more freely, and his lips seemed strive pronounce a word. He shook his head from side to side, as if trying to get rid of an overwhelming weight. After a moment of rest, mumbled unintelligible words, but at last he saw clearly including my name. I stood, my eyes devouring her, perhaps too I pressed my hands in his, perhaps called it my lips. He opened his eyes slowly, and wounded by an intense light, and looked at me, straining to recognize. Middle incorporated a moment later, "what is?" He said turning away, "What happened to me?" He continued, turning to my mother. We tried to reassure her, and in a tone which had something of a counterclaim, which by then I could not explain, he said: "You see? I was afraid. "

It was, after access, painful and deeply sad. I went to see it at night, when the label established in such cases allowed by my father. Leave of her hand holding me a moment, 'till tomorrow, "he said, stressing the last word as he used to always interrupted our conversation that evening somewhere, was looking forward to the next day that the concluyésemos.

XV

When I left the corridor leading to my room, a mighty gale swung Willows courtyard and approach the garden, I heard tear in the groves of orange trees, where birds darted frightened. Lightning weak, similar to instant reflection of a buckler struck by the glow of a fire, seemed to want to illuminate the dark background of the valley.

Nestled in one of the columns of the corridor, I feel the rain lashed the temples, thought Mary disease, on which my father had uttered such terrible words. My eyes wanted to see her as quiet and serene nights that we not return anymore!

I do not know how much time had passed, when something like the wing of a bird vibrant wine to rub my forehead.

I looked into the woods to follow immediately: it was a black bird.

My room was cold roses window feared trembled as if left to the rigors of the stormy wind: and the vase containing lilies withered and fainted in the morning Mary had placed in him. At this a sudden burst of the lamp went out, and thunder was heard for a long time its growing rumbling, as if it were a giant chariot headlong from the summit of the Rocky mountains.

In the midst of that nature sobbing, my soul had a sad serenity.

Had just struck twelve the clock in the hall. I heard footsteps near my door and soon my father's voice calling me. "Get up," he said as soon as I answered, "Mary is wrong."

Had repeated access. After fifteen minutes found myself perceived to march. My father was the latest indication of the new disease symptoms, while the black Juan Angel retinto quieted my horse, impatient and scary.

Mountain, their shod hooves crunched on the pavement, and a moment later I was down to the plains of the valley looking for the path to the light of some livid lightning ... He was on the request of Dr. Mayn, passing at that time a field season three leagues from our farm.

The image of Mary, as seen in the bed that afternoon to tell me that "tomorrow" that may not come, went with me, and stoking my impatience made me constantly measure the distance that separated me from the end of the journey, impatience which the horse's speed was not enough to dampen.

The plains began to disappear, fleeing in the opposite direction to my career, like huge sheets overwhelmed by the hurricane. The nearby forests believed, looked away as he advanced towards them. Only a moan of the wind between figs and dark chiminangos, wheezing tiring horse and crash helmets that sparkled in the flint interrupted the silence of the night.

Some cabins of Santa Elena were on my right, and left shortly after hearing the barking of their dogs. Herds asleep on the road began to make me moderate pace.

The beautiful home of Mr. M. .. with its white chapel and its forests of ceiba, distance could be seen in the first rays of the rising moon, whose castle which towers and roofs had collapsed over time.

The low Amaime grown overnight rains, thunder and announced me long before I reached the shore. In the light of the moon, which through the foliage of the banks would wave plate, I could see how it had increased its flood. But it was not possible to expect: two leagues had done in an hour, and was still little. I put spurs into the flanks of the horse, with ears that stretched out to the river bottom and looked silently puffing calculate the impetuosity of the waters that plagued his feet hands immersed in them, and as overwhelmed by a terror invincible fast turning back on its feet. I stroked her neck and mane wet and gets through again to that lanzase the river, then raised his hands impatiently, while calling all the reins, he left, fearful that he had missed the botadero2 of growing. The up the bank some twenty yards, taking the side of a cliff; came nose to the foam, and then lifting it, rushed into the stream. The water covered him almost everything, coming to me knee. The waves curled soon after around my waist. With one hand he patted the animal's neck, and only visible part of his body, while the other tried to make more upward curve describing the cut line, because otherwise, lost the lower part of the slope, was inaccessible for his height and strength of the waters, which swung guaduales broken off. The danger had passed. I got out to examine the straps, of which one had burst. The noble animal shook, and a moment later the march continued.

Then I walked a quarter league, went through waves of Nima, humble, airy and smooth, which lit rolled away into the shadows of silent forests. I left left the pampas of Santa R., whose house, amid groves under the ceiba and palm group that raise the foliage on your roof, resembling the moon in the shop of an Eastern king hung from trees an oasis.

It was two in the morning when after passing through the town of P. .., I dismounted at the door of the house where the doctor lived.

XVI

In the afternoon of the same day we said goodbye to the doctor, after dropping almost completely restored to Mary and have prescribed a regimen to prevent recurrence of access, but promised to visit the sick often. I felt an inexpressible relief to hear you ensure that there was no danger, and he double affection than I then had professed, only because as Mary predicted prompt replacement. I entered this room, then the doctor and my father, who was to accompany him in a league of road, were launched.

I was running out of braided hair in a mirror seeing my sister held on the cushions. Flushed away furniture said:

-These occupations are not sick, is not it?, But I'm good. I hope not to cause you a trip as dangerous as last night.

-On this trip there was no danger, he said.

- The river itself, the river! I thought about it and so many things that could happen to my account.

- A three leagues? Does this name? ...

-That trip that you could drown, according to the doctor referred here, so surprised that I had not yet down and talked about it already. You and he have had to return two hours waiting for him to come down the river.

The doctor is a maula horse: and his mule pacienzuda is not the same as a good horse.

The man who lives in the house of Mary interrupted me step-by recognizing your horse black this morning, he marveled that he had not drowned the rider that was launched last night into the river while he had not shouted ford. Oh! No, no, I do not want to get sick. Not the doctor told you that I will no novelty?

'Yes,' I replied, and he has promised not to miss two days in these fifteen without coming to see you.

'Then you will not have to make another trip at night. What would I have done if ...

-I would have cried a lot, does not it? I replied smiling.

Looked at me for a few moments, and I added:

- Maybe I can be certain to die at any time convinced ...

- What?

And guessing else in my eyes:

- Always, always! He added, almost in secret, pretending to examine the beautiful lace pillows.

-And I have to tell you sad things she continued after a moment of silence, so sad, that are the cause of my illness. You were in the mountains ... Mom knows everything, and I heard that Dad told her that my mother had died of a disease whose name could not hear, that you were destined to make a beautiful race, and I ... Ah! I do not know if it's true what I heard ... will not be like you deserve to be with me.

In their eyes veiled shot at her cheeks warm tears dry quickly.

Do not say that, Mary, do not think, 'I said, no, I beg you.

'But I have heard it, and then when I did not know it was me ... Why, then?

-Look, I beg you ... I ... Want to send you afford to say no more about that?

She had left her forehead down on the arm that is supported and whose hand I shook in mine, when I heard in the next room the sound of Emma's clothes, approaching.

That night, at the dinner, we were in the dining room waiting for my sisters and me to my parents, it took longer than usual. Finally they heard in the room as putting an end to an important conversation. The noble countenance of my father showed, in the slight contraction of the tips of your lips and that little wrinkle between her brows furrowed forehead, which had to sustain a moral struggle that had altered. My mother was white, but making no effort to be quiet, he told me to come to the table:

-I did not say that Joseph remembered was this morning to see us and convidarte for a hunt, but when he heard the news that occurred, promised to return early morning. Do you know if it is true that he married one of his daughters?

-Seek to consult you your project-idly observed my father.

He is probably a bear hunt I replied.

- Bears do? What! Fighters you? Bears?

'Yes, sir, it's a fun hunt I did with him a few times.

In my country, 'said my father, I would by a barbarian or a hero.

-And yet, that kind of games is less dangerous than deer, which makes every day and everywhere, for it, instead of requiring hunters to throw to collapse the desatentados by between bushes and waterfalls, requires only a bit of agility and sharpshooting.

My father, still see already in the furrowed face he had before, spoke of how deer are hunted in Jamaica and the fans who had relatives that kind of hobby, distinguishing between them, for their tenacity, skill and enthusiasm, Solomon, who told us, laughing and some anecdotes.

When leaving the table, approached me to tell me:

'Your mother and I have something to talk to you, come to my room then.

A time came to him, my father wrote her back to my mother, who was in the least illuminated the room, sitting in the chair he occupied whenever stopped there.

'Sit down, he said, leaving for a moment to write and looking at me over his glasses, which were white glasses and fine golden setting.

After a few minutes, having placed carefully in place the account book he was writing, approached a seat that I occupied, and quietly spoke thus:

-I wanted your mother to witness this conversation, because it is a serious issue on which she has the same opinion as me.

He went to the door to entornarla and Dispose the cigarette he was smoking, and continued in this way:

-Three months ago are with us and will only last two more Mr. A. .. leaving for Europe, and he's the one you should go. That delay, up to a point, no meaning, both because it is a great pleasure for us to have you on our side after six years of absence to be followed by others, and because I note with pleasure that even here, the study is one of your pleasures favorite. I can not hide, and I do, that I conceived great hopes, for your character and skills that coronarás lucidly the race going forward. Do not ignore that soon the family will need your support, more so after the death of your brother.

Then, pausing, he continued:

'There's something in your behavior that must tell you is not right you have no more than twenty years, and at that age a love could recklessly fostered illusory hopes that all just talk. You love to Mary, and for many days that I know, of course. Mary is almost my daughter and I would have nothing to watch if your age and position allow us to think in a marriage, but not allow it, and Mary is very young. Not only these obstacles are presented, there is one perhaps insuperable, and it is my duty to tell you about him. Mary can drag and drag you to an unfortunate mishap that is threatened. Dr. Mayn almost dares to ensure that she will die young the same disease succumbed to his mother, which yesterday suffered epileptic syncope is that taking increased each access, end by a character known epilepsy worse: so says Dr. . Answer you now, meditating much what you say to a single question, answer as a rational and gentleman you are, and that is not what answer dictated by a strange exaltation to your character in the case of your future and that of your family . You know the doctor's opinion, an opinion that deserves respect for being who gives Mayn, you known the fate of the wife of Solomon: If we consintiéramos it, will you marry today with Mary?

'Yes, sir,' I replied.

- You arrostrarías all?

- All, all!

I think not only speak with a child but with the gentleman that you've tried to form.

My mother then hid his face in his handkerchief. My father, perhaps softened by tears and perhaps also by the resolution that was in me, knowing that the voice was going to fail, momentarily stopped talking.

'Well,' he continued, as that noble resolution encourages you, you will agree with me that within five years you can not be husband of Mary. Not I who should tell her, after you've loved since childhood, loves you today so that intense emotions, new to her, is that according Mayn have made before symptoms of the disease: ie Your love and his need precautions and I demand that henceforth I vow to thee for good, as well as the love, and for her sake, you will follow the doctor's advice, given by if he came here. Nothing must promise to Mary, for the promise of being her husband after the deadline I have outlined, would your more intimate, which is precisely what it seeks to avoid. Are useless for you more explanations: following this behavior, you can save Mary, you can spare us the disgrace of losing.

-As a reward for all that you concede he said, turning to my mother must promise that: not talking to Mary that the threat of danger, nor reveal anything that happened tonight between us. You should also know my opinion on your marriage with her if his illness persists after you return to this country ... soon as we separate for a few years: as yours and Mary's father, would not I pass that link. In expressing this irrevocable decision, not for others you know that Solomon, in the last three years of his life, succeeded in forming a capital of some consideration, which is in my power to serve as a dowry to his daughter. But if she dies before marriage, one must pass by her maternal grandmother, who is in Kingston.

My father walked around the room a few moments. I believe our conference ended, I rose to retire, but he, resuming his seat and indicating mine, and resumed his speech:

Four days ago I received a letter from Mr. M. .. Mary's hand asking for his son Carlos.

I could not hide the surprise caused me these words. My father smiled imperceptibly before adding:

-The Lord of M. .. term given fifteen days to accept or reject the proposal, during which they will come to visit us before they had promised me. Everything will be easy after the agreement between us. Good night, then, 'said putting his hand affectionately on the shoulder: you're very happy in your hunt, I need skin to kill the bear to put it at the foot of my bed.

'All right, I replied.

My mother gave me her hand, and holding mine told me:

'I hope sooner, watch those animals!

So many emotions agitándome had happened in the last few hours, I could hardly realize each of them, and I could not take care of my strange and difficult situation.

Maria threatened with death, and promised to reward my love, through absence terrible promised on condition of love less, I have to temper that powerful love, love forever taken over my whole being, failing to see it disappear Earth as a fugitive beauties of my dreams, and having to appear ungrateful and insensitive onwards perhaps their eyes, only for conduct that the need and the reason I was forced to take! No longer could I hear again those confidences agitated voice, my lips could not even touch the tip of one of her braids. Mine or death, between death and me, one more step to approach it would be to lose it, let abandoned mourn was torture beyond my strength.

Heart coward, you were not able to leave the fire that consumed by evil hidden agostarla could ... Where is she now no longer throb now, now that the days and years pass over me without knowing me you own?

Juan Angel Fulfilling my orders, knocked on the door of my room at dawn.

- How is the morning? I asked.

-Mala, my master wants rain.

-Good. Go to the mountain and tell Joseph not expect me today.

When I opened the window, I regretted having sent the black boy who whistled and hummed bambucos going to go into in the first spot of the forest.

Saw blew a cold wind and shaking intemperate roses and willows swaying, shifting in his flight to another couple of travelers parrots. All birds, fancy garden in the morning happy, silent, and only hovered pellares neighboring meadows, waving her singing the sad winter day.

In brief the mountains disappeared under the gray veil of rain nourished, which could be heard and his growing buzz when approaching whipping forests. Within half an hour, muddy streams and clattering combing scrubland descended the slopes across the river, which increased, thundered angrily, and was visible in the distant revolts yellowish overwhelmed and wavy.

XVII

Ten days had passed since that painful conference took place. Not feeling able to fulfill the wishes of my father on the new kind of treatment that he said I should use with Maria, and painfully concerned with the marriage proposal made by Carlos, had sought all kinds of excuses to get away from the house. Those days I spent locked in my room, and in the possession of Joseph, more often wandering walk around. He had a companion in my walks a book that could not quite be able to read, my gun, never fired, and in May, I was fatigándose. While dominated by a deep melancholy I kept running times hidden in the most rugged, he vainly tried to doze coiled on leaf litter, where the ants evicted or impatient popped horseflies and mosquitoes. When old friend got tired of inaction and silence, which were unfriendly despite his infirmities, approached me, and leaning his head on one of my knees, I looked affectionate, and wait to get away after a few yards distance on the path leading to the house, and in their eagerness to emprendiésemos up once I got to follow him, was propasaba to give some leaps of joy, youthful enthusiasm that, more than forget his composure and senile gravity , leaving little windy.

One morning my mother came into my room, and sat at the head of the bed, which I still had not left, I said:

-This can not be, should not live like this anymore, I am content.

As I keep quiet, he continued:

-What you do not what your father has demanded, is much more, and your behavior is cruel to us and even more cruel towards Mary. I was convinced that your frequent trips were intended to go to Luisa's house on the occasion of love we profess there, but Braulio, who came yesterday afternoon, we did not know that five days ago have not seen you. What causes you sadness that you can not dominate and in the few moments you spend with the family in society, and that makes you constantly seek solitude, as if you were already annoying to be with us?

His eyes were full of tears.

-Mary, ma'am I replied, should be completely free to accept or not the good luck offered Carlos, and I, as a friend of him, I must not give reasonably illusory hopes of feeding should be accepted.

Thus revealed, helplessly, the most excruciating pain that had plagued me since the night I heard the proposal of the Lords of M. .. Nothing had become for me in front of that proposal forecasts the fatal disease doctor about Mary, no need to leave her for many years.

- How could you imagine such a thing? Surprised he asked my mother. Just have seen it twice to your friend: just one that was here a few hours, and one that we went to visit his family.

'But, mother, little time is left to justify or fade what I thought. I think it is well worth the wait.

'You are very unfair, and I regret to have been. Mary, for dignity and duty, knowing you better control, concealed how much your behavior is doing the suffering. I can hardly believe my eyes, I was amazed to hear what you just said. I, I thought to give you a great joy and remedy all letting you know what we said yesterday Mayn goodbye!

-Say you, say I begged sitting up.

- What now?

- She will not always ... not always be my sister?

-Afternoon think so. Or is that a man can be a gentleman and do what you do? No, no, that should not make a child of mine ... Your sister! And you forget that what you're saying who knows you more than yourself! Your sister! And I know he loves you since you both slept on my knees! And is now when you think, now coming to talk about it, scared by the suffering that the poor thing to hide is vain.

-I do not want, even for a moment, give you reason for an upset like that lets me know.

Tell me what to do about what you found in my behavior reprehensible.

-It must be. Do not want to love her as much as you?

'Yes, ma'am, and so, is not it?

'So it would, but I had forgotten that no other mother I, Solomon's recommendations and trust worthy he believed me, because she deserves it and loves you so much. The doctor says that evil is not Mary suffered Sara.

- He has spoken!

-Yes, your father, and reassured by that party, I wanted to do it you know.

- Can I, therefore, again be with her as before? I asked alienated

-Nearly ...

- Oh! She will excuse me, do not you think? Does the doctor has said there is no longer any kind of danger? -I added, it is necessary to know Carlos.

My mother looked at me in surprise before answering:

- And why you had to hide? Remains for me to say what I should do, because the lords of M. .. have to come tomorrow, as advertised. Tell Mary this afternoon ... But, what can you tell it enough to justify your detachment, without violating the orders of your father? And even if you could talk about what you demanded it, you could not apologize because that for what you've done these days there is a cause for pride and delicacy that you should not discover. Here is the result. It forced me to Mary revealed the real reason for your sadness.

'But if you do, if you've been light of believing what I believe, what will she think of me?

Luckily, considering you'll think capable of fickleness and inconsistency most odious of all.

'You are right to some extent, but I beg you not say anything to Mary just mentioned. I made an error, maybe I have suffered more for me than her, and I must remedy it I promise you that I will remedy: I demand only two days to do it properly.

'Well,' I said, getting up to leave, you seeing today?

-Yes, ma'am.

- Where are you going?

-I will pay Emigdio welcome your visit, and it is imperative, because yesterday I sent that to the steward of his father to wait for me for lunch today.

-But again early.

-At four or five.

-Come to eat here.

-Yes. Are you satisfied with me again?

-How not replied smiling. Until the afternoon, then: give the ladies fine memories, from me and the girls.

XVIII

I was already ready to go when Emma came into my room. STRANGE me with smiling face.

- Where are you so happy? He asked.

'I wish I did not have to go anywhere. To see Emigdio, who complains of my inconsistency in all shades, whenever I meet him.

- So unfair! Exclaimed laughing. Fickle? Thou?

- What are you laughing at?

-Because of the injustice of your friend. Poor!

-No, no, you laugh about something else.

'That is,' said my table taking a comb and coming close bathroom. Let me comb me, because you know, Mr. Constant, one of the sisters of his friend is a cute girl. Too bad he continued, aided by combing their graceful hands that gentleman was put Ephraim a little pale these days, because not imagine bugueñas manly beauty without fresh colors on the cheeks. But if Emigdio's sister was aware of ...

'You're very parlera today.

- Yes?, And you very happy. Look in the mirror and tell me if you have not been very good.

- Do visit! I cried hearing Mary's voice calling my sister.

'Really. How much better to go for a walk around the peaks of anchovy Amaime and enjoy ... great and lonely landscape, or walking in the mountains as wound response, swatting mosquitoes, notwithstanding that fills with Nuches May ... Poor thing, that is impossible.

-Mary called I interrupted you.

'I know what it is.

- What for?

-To help you do something you should not do.

- Can you tell which?

-No drawback is waiting for us to go and pick flowers that will be used to replace these, he pointed the vase on my desk, and if I were she would put not one more there.

-If you only knew ...

And if you knew you ...

My father, who called me from his room, interrupted the conversation, which continued, thwarting what could have been since my last interview with my mother had set out to accomplish.

Upon entering the room of my father, he examined the machine in the window of a beautiful pocket watch, and said:

'It's a wonderful thing: certainly worth the thirty pounds.

Then, turning to me, said:

-This is the watch that I ordered to London, look at him.

'It's much better than the one you used-watched consideration.

-But they use very accurate, and very small yours: you must give it to one of the girls and make it for you.

Without giving me time to thank him added:

- Will you Emigdio house? Tell your father that I can prepare the guinea paddock to do the priming in the company, but that his cattle should be ready precisely the fifteenth of the next.

Then I went to my room to take my guns. Mary, from the garden at the foot of my window, gave Emma a bunch of Montenegros, Marjoram and carnations, but the most beautiful of them, because of their size and freshness, she had it on her lips.

-Good morning, Mary, 'I said hurrying to receive flowers.

She paled instantly cut corresponded to the greeting, and carnation came off the mouth. Entregóme flowers, dropping some on the feet, which collected and put at my disposal when their cheeks were rosy again.

- Want-I said to receive the last-change me all they had for the carnation on the lips?

'I have trodden down the head replied to locate it.

Stepped-So, I will give all these for him.

It remained in the same attitude without answering.

- Do you allow me to go pick it up?

He bent to take it and then handed it to me without looking at me.

Meanwhile Emma pretended complete distraction placing new flowers.

Mary Estrechéle the hand that gave me the desired carnation, saying:

- Thank you, thank you! Until the afternoon.

He looked up to see me with the most rapturous expression can produce, when combined in the eyes of a woman, the tenderness and modesty, and tears counterclaim.

XIX

Had I done something more than a league of way, and was struggling to open the door and hit that gave entrance to the hubs of the estate of the father of Emigdio. Having overcome the resistance by its hinges and rusty axis, and even tougher pylon, composed of a stone so large enzurronada, which was suspended from the ceiling, giving passers torment that apparatus maintaining singular closed, I gave lucky not me stuck in the quagmire stony, whose age was known respectable by the color of water.

I went through a short level on which the fox's tail, and the bush friegaplato on Gramal dominated swamp, there browsed some shorn of grinders nags mane and tail, scampered old colts and burros meditated, as sealed and mutilated by the loading of firewood and cruelty of their carriers, that Buffon would have found puzzled by having to classify.

The house is big and old, surrounded by coconut and mangoes, Cinderella and highlighted its ailing roof on top and thick forest of cacao.

No exhaustion of obstacles to get, because I ran into the pens surrounded tetillal, and that's what robustísimas rolling guaduas crossbars on rickety stairs. They came to my rescue two black, male and female: he, without breeches dress that showed athletic back shining with sweat peculiar race, she follao of Fula blue shirt and a scarf tied at the neck and caught with the waistband, which covered his chest. Both wore hats of rush, of little use to those who are taking aparaguan and thatched roof color.

He was the smiling and smoking partner none other than deal with another of foals which had reached a turn in the flail, and I knew what, because I was struck by the view not only black but also his companion, armed of tentacles to bind. In cries and career were when I got out under the eaves of the house, ignoring threats of inhospitable large dogs that were lying under the seats in the hall.

Some litter and sweatshirts and frayed reed mounted on the railing were enough to convince me that all the plans made in Bogotá by Emigdio, impressed with my reviews, had crashed chocheras what he called his father. Instead habíase greatly improved livestock breeding, which were proof of the goats of various colors that stank the courtyard, and just noticed improvement in poultry, as many peacocks greeted my arrival with shouts alarmadores and between Muscovy ducks or swamp, swimming in the nearby ditch, were distinguished by their dignified demeanor some so-called Chilean.

Emigdio was a great kid. A year before my return to Cauca, his father sent him to Bogota in order to put it, he said the good man, on his way to become a good trader and merchant. Carlos, who was living with me at the time and was always aware even of what not to know, Emigdio encountered, I do not know where, and planted it in front of me on a Sunday morning, preceding to enter our room to tell me "Man!, I'll kill the taste: I bring you the cutest thing."

I ran to hug Emigdio, who stood at the door, had the rarest figure imaginable. It is folly to pretend to describe.

My countryman had been charged with hat hair, color coffee, Ignacio gala, his father, holy week in his youth. Whether you come close, it seemed well take it well, the junk was in the back of the neck long and blackened our friend, a ninety degree angle. That thinness; those sideburns enralecidas and limp hair matching the most desolate in its abandonment ever seen, that sallow, descaspando the sunny road, the collar sunk without hope under the flaps of a white vest whose tips hated, imprisoned arms into the sleeves of a blue jacket, pants with wide loops of cambrún cordovan, and deerskin boots alustrado were more than enough cause to exalt the enthusiasm of Carlos.

He wore a pair of spurs Emigdio orejonas3 in one hand and a bulky parcel for me in the other. I rushed to download it all, taking a moment to look severely Carlos, who lay on one of the beds in our room, biting a pillow crying her eyes out, which almost gives me the most inopportune bewilderment.

Emigdio offered to seat in the parlor, and as spring chose a sofa, the sinking feeling poor, tried by all means find something to grab in the air, but in despair, was redone as he could, and once stood and said:

- What the hell! In that Carlos did not enter the trial. Now! Rightly laughing in the street came the glue that I was going to do. And you too? ... Go! If people here are the same demontres. How about the fact that I have today?

Carlos left the room, taking advantage of that happy occasion, and we both laugh and at our ease.

- What, Emigdio! I said to our visitor: sit in this chair, which has no trap. CRIES belt is necessary.

'Yes,' said Emigdio EA4 sitting warily as if he feared another failure.

- What have you done? Laughed more than asked Carlos.

- Hase seen? He was not telling.

'But why? Carlos insisted the relentless, throwing an arm around her shoulders, tell us.

Emigdio was angry at last, and could hardly please him. A few glasses of wine and some cigars ratified our armistice. About the wine was our countryman looked better than they did in Buga orange, and green anisette Paporrina sale. Ambalema cigars seemed aforrados lower than in dried banana leaves and other fig scented with orange and chopped, brought him into his pockets.

After two days, and our Telemachus was suitably dressed and groomed by master Hilario and although its fashionable clothing was uncomfortable and made him see new boots bougies, had to be secured, spurred by vanity and Carlos, to which he called a martyr.

Established in the nursing home we inhabited us, amused us in the hours of our home desktops referring your travel adventures and issuing concept about everything that had caught his attention in the city. On the street was different, because we saw the need to leave to their fate, or impertinence to the saddlers jovial and peddlers, who ran to besiege barely glimpsed, to offer chocontanas chairs, arretrancas, chaps, brakes and thousand trinkets.

Fortunately I had finished all your shopping Emigdio when he came to know that the daughter of the lady of the house, perky girl, despreocupadilla and laughing, he was dying.

Carlos, without stopping in bars, managed to convince him Micaelina had hitherto spurned the attentions of all the guests, but the devil, who never sleeps, made Emigdio chicoleos sorprendiese in one night in his room and his beloved Cabrion when asleep believed unhappy because it was ten o'clock, when he used to be in his third dream custom justifying always rising early, even if it was shivering.

Emigdio seen by what he saw and heard what I heard, I wished for recuperation and ours had seen or heard anything, thought only hasten his departure.

Having no complaint from me, brought me their evening confidences eve of the trip, saying, among many other reliefs:

-In Bogotá there ladies: these are all about ... flirty seven soles. When it has done, what is expected? I'm not saying goodbye to her. Dammit!, There is nothing like the girls of our land, but there are no dangers. You see Carlos: altar made walks *corpus,* lies at eleven at night and is more fullero5 than ever. Let it be, that I know I will know that you don Chomo put the ash. I am amazed to see you thinking only in your studies.

Emigdio since departed, and with him the fun of Carlos and Micaelina.

Such was, in short, the honradote and hearty friend whom I was visiting.

Waiting to see it coming from inside the house, front to rear di I heard screaming while jumping a fence of the yard:

- Finally, maula so!, And believed that you let me waiting. Sit down, I'm there.

And he began to wash their hands, which were bloody, in the ditch of the courtyard.

- What were you doing? I asked after our greetings.

-Since today is a day of slaughter and my father got up early to go to the fields, I was rationing to blacks, a scrub, but I'm unemployed. My mother has a great desire to see you, I will tell that you're here. Who knows if we will make the girls go, because they have become more race course each day.

- Choto! He shouted, and presently a black half naked, monas6 raisins, and a withered arm and scarred.

-Take the canoe that horse and cleanse the sorrel nag.

And turning to me, having noticed my horse, said:

- Carrizo with retinto!

- How well the arm broke down that boy? I asked.

-Putting cane to the mill: they are so gross! Serves not only to care and horses.

Soon began serving lunch, while I was with the Dona Andrea, mother of Emigdio, which almost leaves her shawl without fringes, for a quarter of an hour we were talking alone.

Emigdio was to wear a white coat to sit at the table, but before we presented a black serving tray adorned the pastuso with aguamanos, yet carrying one arm delicately embroidered towel.

Serving dining room, which was limited to trousseau canapés old cow, some altarpieces depicting saints Quito, hung high on the walls are not very white, and two tables adorned with plaster Orchard and parrots.

Truth be told: at lunch there was greatness, but he knew the mother and sisters of Emigdio understood that to disposal. The tortilla soup flavored with fresh herbs from the garden, the fried bananas, shredded meat and cornmeal threads, the excellent chocolate earth stone cheese, milk bread and water served in old and large silver bowls not left to be desired.

When we had lunch glimpsed peering between a half ajar door to one of the girls, and his sympathetic face, illuminated by chambimbes7 black eyes, let him think that hiding must harmonize very well with what could be seen.

I said goodbye to Mrs. Andrea eleven, because we had decided to go to see Don Ignacio in the fields where it was doing rodeo, and use the trip to take a bath in the Amaime.

Emigdio took off his jacket to replace it with a wire ruana; soche of boots used to put on sandals, fastened a white leather chaps hairy bastard, got a big hat Suaza with white percale cover, and mounted in the sorrel, before taking the precaution of blindfolded with a handkerchief. As Potron became a ball and hid their tails between their legs, the rider shouted: "Now you come with your Tuileries!" Followed by unloading in two strokes of the manatee sound palmirano wielding. Whereupon, after two or three plunges that failed or even move the knight in his chair chocontana, rode and we set off.

As we arrived at the rodeo site, far from the house more than half a league, my partner, then he took advantage of the first llanito apparent for turning and scratch the horse, entered into conversation with me Chuck. Desembuchó he knew about the claims marriage of Charles, who had resumed friendship since they met again in the Cauca.

- What do you say? -Finally ask.

Artfully dodged give answer, and he continued:

- What is deny? Carlos is working boy: then you will be convinced that it can not be allowed unless prior landowner aside the gloves and umbrella, has to do well. Still makes fun of me because I link, I talanquera and barbeo muletos, but he has to do the same or burst. Have not you seen?

-No.

'Well, you'll see. Do I think he will not bathe in the river when the sun is strong, and that if you do not ride the horse saddled, all for no tan and not get your hands dirty? Otherwise it is a gentleman, though: not a week ago I got a hundred patacones trouble lending me I needed to buy some heifers. He knows not check on deaf ears, but that's what time it is called to serve. As for his marriage ... I'll tell you one thing, if you offer me no chamuscarte.

-Say, man, say what you want.

-In your home or living with a long tone, and it seems to me that one of those girls raised between ruffle, such as stories, needs to be treated as a holy thing.

And laughed and continued:

-I say this because that Don Jerome, father of Charles, has more than a sietecueros shells and brave as a sneak pepper. My father can not see it since I have gotten into a fight over boundaries and I do not know what else. The day we find we have to put at night and give yerbamora fomentation of brandy with malambo rubs.

We had reached the place of the rodeo. In the middle of the yard, in the shade of a guasimo and through the dust raised by the moving torada I discovered Don Ignacio, who came to greet me. He rode a roan and cotudo cuartago, harnessed with a tortoise whose luster and deterioration proclaimed their merits. The meager figure of the wealthy owner was decorated with: chaps and ragged lion uppers; silver spurs with slices encascabeladas; gender without aplanchar jacket and white poncho recharged starch, crowning all a huge straw hat, the kind that call when will gallop the wearer: its shade made the nose so large and small blue eyes Don Ignacio, the same game as the head of a key bit stuffed garnets leading by pupils and the long beak.

Ignacio told my father what I had ordered about cattle that were primed in the company.

'All right,' he replied. You see that the herd can not be better, all seem towers. Will not you come to have some fun?

A Emigdio eyes you were watching the slaughter of the cowboys in the corral.

- Ah Tuso! He cried; careful loosen pial8 A tail! A tail!

I apologized to Don Ignacio, while giving thanks, he continued:

'Nothing, nothing, the citizens are afraid of the sun and the bulls, which is why the guys are spoiled in schools there. Do not let me lie the pretty boy son of Don Chomo: at seven o'clock I found aforrado road with a handkerchief, so that was not seen but one eye, and umbrella! ... You, I see, even not using those things.

Then cried the cowboy, who wielded the hot brand in the palette was applying it to several bulls and handcuffed lying in the yard: "Another ... another ... ". Each of those screams still a bellow, and Ignacio did with his penknife one more muesquecilla guasimo wand that served as whip.

As to getting the cattle could be some dangerous hauls, Don Ignacio, after receiving my bachelor, got in except entering a nearby corral.

The site chosen by Emigdio in the river was best suited to enjoy bathing waters Amaime to offer in the summer, especially when we got to the shore. Guabos churimbos, on which thousands of fluttering flowers esmeraldas9, we offer dense shade and padded where extended ruanas litter. In the bottom of the deep pool that was at our feet were even small pebbles and sported silvery sardines. Below, on the stones that covered the current blue herons and white herons fished spying or combed their plumage. On the beach in front ruminating cow lying beautiful; parrots hidden in the foliage of the freshmen chatting in a low voice, and high branches lying asleep in a party of monkeys in lazy neglect. The cicadas made their songs resonate everywhere monotonous. A curious squirrel another protruding from between the reeds and disappeared quickly. Towards the interior of the forest from time to time heard the trill of chilacoas melancholy.

-Hang your chaps away from here-told-Emigdio, because if not, we will leave the bathroom with headache.

Riose him gladly, watching when placed in the fork of a distant tree:

- Would you all smell like roses? A man should smell like goat.

-Certainly, and proof that what you think, everything you carry in your chaps musk of a goatherd.

In our bathroom, is that the night and the banks of a beautiful river to have the courage to confide, whether I trace to give me my friend did them, confesóme that after saving for some time as the memory of relic Micaelina, was madly in love with a beautiful ñapanguita, weakness tried to hide the malice of Don Ignacio, for which he had to pretend desbaratarle all, because the girl was not a lady, and in order to end raciocinó well:

- As if he could suit me to a lady to marry me, so it would be all that I had to serve her instead of being served! And more gentleman I mean, what the hell would I do with a woman that laya? But if you knew Zoila ... Man!, Do not ponder, even you verses ... What verses!, You would salivate: his eyes are able to see a blind man is more sly smile, cutest feet, and a belt ...

-Slowly-I interrupted: ie love you so frantically that You are going to drown if you marry her?

- I'm getting married if it takes the trap!

- With a woman of the people? Without consent of your father? ... It is: you are bearded man, and you know what you do. And Carlos Are you aware of that?

- Not missing anything! God forbid! If you have Buga on the palms of the hands and mouth, do you want. Fortune is that Zoila lives in San Pedro and will not Buga but each yore.

-But I do mostrarías me.

-To you is another matter on which you want to take.

At three in the afternoon I parted from Emigdio, apologizing in a thousand ways not to eat with him, and the four o'clock when I got home.

XX

My mother and Emma came running back to meet me. My father had ridden to visit work.

A little later I was called into the dining room, and soon I go because there expecting to find Maria but I cheated, and as my mother were to ask for it, he replied:

-As these gentlemen come morning, the girls are busily that are very well-made sweets, I think they've done already and to come now.

I was going to leave the table when Joseph, rising from the valley to the mountain herding two mules laden cañabrava, stood in the Altico from which you could see inside, and shouted:

- Good afternoon! I can not be, because I have one and it makes me Chucara night. Here I leave a message with the girls. Depart early morning long, because the thing is safe.

'Well,' I said, go early, say hello to everyone.

- Do not forget the bullets!

And waving his hat continued to rise.

Dirigime to my room to prepare the gun, not because she needed to look for cleaning as an excuse for not staying in the dining room, where the order was not submitted Mary.

I had open in his hand a piston deposit box when I saw Mary coming towards me bringing me coffee, which tried the spoon before me.

The pistons are spread throughout the floor I just came.

Still unresolved at me, gave me good afternoon, with an unsteady hand and placing the saucer and cup on the railing, looked for a moment with my own eyes cowards, that made her blush, and then, kneeling, began to collect pistons.

-That you do not, 'I said, I'll do it later.

-I have very good eyes to look for small things, 'he said, to see the box.

She reached out to receive it, exclaiming to enlarge:

- Oh! If you have watered all!

-Not crowded, helping watched him.

And that they need morning soplándoles said to dust in her pink palm of one hand.

- Why am and why of these?

-For as that hunting is dangerous, I reckon it would be terrible to miss a shot, and I know the box that they are what the doctor gave you the other day saying they were English and very good ...

-You hear it all.

-Something would have heard sometimes not. Perhaps it would be better not to go to that hunt ... Joseph I left a message with us.

- Will you not go?

- And how can I claim that?

- Why not?

Looked at me and said nothing.

'I think there is more said standing up and looking at the ground around him, I'm going. The coffee is already cold.

-Try.

-But not finish loading that shotgun now ...

That's good, said touching the cup.

I'm going to keep the gun and take it, but do not go.

I had entered my room and come out again.

-There is much to do in there.

'Oh yes,' I said, prepare desserts and galas for tomorrow. Are you going then?

He shoulders, while tilting the head to one side, a move that meant: as you want.

'I owe you an explanation, she said, approaching. Want to hear me?

- Do not say that there are things you do not want to hear? Replied by sounding the pistons inside the box.

-I thought you ...

-Is it true that you're gonna say, that you think.

- What?

-That you should hear yes, but, this time, no.

- Too bad you've thought of me these days!

She read, without answering, the signs of the deposit box.

'Nothing you say, then, but tell me what you have supposed.

- What now?

- Do not let me say that not apologize to you?

-What I want to know is why you do that, but I'm afraid to know through what I have given reason at all, and always thought I'd have some that I should not know ... But since you seem to be happy again ... I'm happy too.

-I do not deserve to be as good as you are with me.

-Maybe I who do not deserve ...

'I've been unfair to you, and if you permitieras, knees I'd ask you to forgive me.

Her eyes had long veiled shone with all its beauty, and exclaimed:

- Oh! no, my God! I've forgotten everything ... Do you hear right? Everything!

But on one condition-he added after a short pause.

-The one you want.

The day that I do or say something you dislike, you will tell me, and I will not do or say. Is not that easy?

- And I must not demand of you the same?

No, because I can not advise you, or if you always know what I think is best, well, you know what I have to say before you say it.

- Are you certain, then? Will you live convinced that I love with all my heart? I said softly and moved.

'Yes, yes,' said very quietly, and almost touching my lips with one hand to be silent significarme, took a few steps into the room.

- What will you do? I said.

- Do not hear that John calls me and cries because he does not find me?

Undecided for a moment, her smile was so sweet and so loving languor in her eyes, that she had disappeared and I still looked ecstatic.

XXI

The next day at dawn I took the mountain road, accompanied by Juan Angel, which was laden with some gifts for my mother Luisa and girls. Following May: his loyalty was above all punishment, despite some bad times he had in that kind of expeditions, improper and his years.

After the bridge the river, we find Joseph and his nephew and Braulio coming to get me. He spoke to me about his game project, reduced to strike a single blow to a famous tiger nearby, who had died some lambs. Teníale tracked the animal and discovered one of their hideouts in the source of the river, more than half a league above the possession.

Juan Angel stopped sweating to hear these details, and putting on the litter carrying the basket, we looked with such eyes as if he were listening to discuss a project with murder.

Joseph continued to speak well of his plan of attack:

-I answer with my ears not going. We'll see if the check is so valluno as Lucas says. Tiburcio yes answer. Do you bring the heavy ammunition?

'Yes,' I replied and long shotgun.

-Today is the day of Braulio. He has a great desire to see you do a play, because I have told you and I call the shots missed when referring to the head of a bear and the bullet zampa one eye.

Rio loudly, patting on his nephew's shoulder.

-Well, let's go, 'he continued: but these take the black beans to the lady, because I become;- and fell back to the basket Juan Angel, saying:' Will the child sweets Mary puts for his cousin? ...

'There will come something my mother sends Luisa.

'But what is it that has taken the girl? I saw her last yesterday as fresh and lucid as ever. It looks like a rosebud of Castile.

She's good now.

-And you, what do you not there long, negritico? Said Juan Jose Angel. Charging with the guambía10 and go, to come back soon, because later you should not walk alone here. Do not say anything down there.

- Be careful not to go back! I cried when he was across the river.

Juan Angel disappeared among the reeds like a scared agouti.

Braulio was a strapping young man of my age. For two months he had been in the Provincia11 to accompany his uncle, and was madly in love, for some time, her cousin Transit.

The appearance of the nephew had all the nobility that the old man made it interesting, but the most remarkable thing about her was a pretty mouth without even bozo whose female smile contrasted with masculine energy of the other factions. Manso character, handsome, and indefatigable in the work, was a treasure to Joseph and the most suitable husband for Transit.

Mrs. Luisa and the girls came out to greet me at the door of the cabin, laughing and loving. Our common treatment in recent months had made them less timid girls with me. Joseph himself, in our hunts, is, in the battlefield, had over me a paternal authority, all of which disappeared when they had at home, like a secret our loyal friendship and simple.

- At last, at last! Said Mrs. Luisa taking me by the arm for introducing me to the living room. Seven days! ... one by one we counted.

The girls looked at me grinning.

'But Jesus, how pale exclaimed Luisa is looking more closely. That's not so good, if you come often be big size.

- And how will you look? I said to the girls.

- Hey! Transit-replied: for what is going to look like? If just because they were there in their studies and ...

-We have had so many good things for you Lucy interrupted: we first badea damage the new kills, waiting: Thursday, believing he came, he had a custard so good ...

- And what peje! Luisa huh? -Joseph added, if that was the judgment, we have not known what to do with it. But reason has not come, continued grimly, has been the occasion, and as soon convidarás to pass an entire day with us ... Is not it, Braulio?

'Yes, yes, go and talk about it. When is the big day, ma'am? When's, Transit?

This began as a scarlet, and had not lifted his eyes to see her boyfriend for all the gold in the world.

'That takes Luisa replied: Do not see missing whitening house and put the doors? Will be the day of Our Lady of Guadalupe, as is his devoted Transit.

- And that is when?

- Did not you know? For the December 12. Do not have told these guys that want to do their best man?

-No, and the delay in giving me such good news not forgive is the Transit.

-If I Braulio told me to tell you, because my father thought it was best.

-I am so grateful that choice as you can not figurároslo, but is hoping to make me very soon buddy.

Braulio looked the most tender of his lovely girlfriend, and it embarrassed, hurried out to have lunch, taking with Lucia.

My meals at home and Joseph were not as I described on another occasion I made them part of the family, and no table devices, except the one destined covered that I always received my share of frisoles, porridge, milk and suede hands of Mrs. Luisa sat none other than Joseph and Braulio, a bench of bamboo root. It's easily got used to treat me like.

Traveler years after the country's mountains by Joseph, I have seen sunsets and to get to the cottage tenants happy where I was entertainment: after praising God with the venerable head of the family, household waited around dinner the old woman and loving mother divided: one dish was enough to each married couple, and the little ones were pinicos on knees of their parents. And I diverted my patriarchal gaze of those scenes, I remembered the last happy days of my youth ...

Lunch was delicious as usual, and seasoned with a conversation that left knowing the impatience of Braulio and Joseph to give start to the hunt.

Ten o'clock when ready and all, loaded with the stiff Lucas that Luisa had prepared, and after the inputs and outputs of Joseph to put on your big otter garniel cabuya tacos and other gossip that he had forgotten, we we launched.

We were five hunters: the mulatto Tiburcio, pawn chagra12 Luke, neivano added a neighboring estate, José, Braulio and me. All were armed with shotguns. Trough were the first two, and great, of course, according to them. Joseph and Braulio had also carefully enastadas spears.

In the dog house was not helpful: atramojados13 all in pairs, heading expeditionary swelled howling with pleasure, and even favorite cook Marta Palomo, who were blind rabbits, provided the neck to be counted in the number of the business, but Joseph dismissed him with a "buzz!" followed by some humiliating reproach.

Luisa and the girls were restless, especially transit, you knew it was her boyfriend who was going to take more risks, as their suitability for the case was indisputable.

Taking advantage of a narrow and tangled trail, we began to ascend the north bank of the river. Your biased channel, if such it can be called the bottom of the ravine selvoso, at gunpoint by rocks whose tops were growing, and in roofs, curly ferns and flowering vines entangled by reeds, was blocked in places with huge stones, between which escaped currents in fast waves, gushing white plumage and capricious.

Just over half a league when Joseph had walked, stopping at the mouth of a wide ditch, dry walled by high cliffs, examined some bad gnawed bones scattered in the sand were the lamb that the day before he had put bait the beast. Precediéndonos Braulio, Jose and I got deep the ditch. Traces rose. Braulio, after climbing a hundred yards, stopped, and made a move without looking us to stop. He heard rumors of the jungle; sucked all the air could hold his chest, looked toward the lofty vault cedars, and Yarumos jiguas were upon us, and walked with slow and silent steps. He stopped again after a while, repeated the survey in the first season, and showing the scratches that had the trunk of a tree that rose from the bottom of the ditch, he said, after a review of the tracks: "This way out: it is well known and baquiano eaten." The chamba14 ended twenty yards ahead by a wall from the top of which was known by the hole dug at the foot, which in the rainy days there is despeñaban skirt flows.

Contrary to what I thought appropriate, seek again the river bank, and continue climbing for her. A little footprints found Braulio Tiger on a beach, and this time it came ashore.

It was necessary to make sure if the beast had been there on the other side, or if but was hindered by the currents, and very tegular and impetuous, had continued to rise along the shore where we were, it was most likely.

Braulio, shotgun slung on his back, tying the stream waded waist a rejo the end of which Joseph retained to prevent a misstep did shoot the boy immediately to the waterfall.

Guardábase acallábamos deep silence and the occasional howl of impatience leaked dogs.

-There is no trace here Braulio said after examining the sand and weeds.

At his feet, turned toward us, on top of a rock, he understood by gestures commanded us to be still.

Zafóse shoulder the shotgun, placed it on his chest to shoot on the rocks we had at the back, leaned slightly forward, firm and quiet, and gave fire.

- There! - Shouted pointing to the wooded edges of the rocks which we could not make out, and jumps down to the shore, he added:

- The strong rope, dogs above!

The dogs seemed to be aware of what had happened: While not released, Braulio fulfilling the order, while Joseph helped him pass the river to our right disappeared among the reeds.

- Freeze! - Braulio screamed again, and the banks win and while hastily loaded shotgun, divisándome to me, said:

-You here, boss.

The dogs chased the prey up close, which could not have been easy exit, since the barking coming from the same point of the skirt.

Braulio took a spear in the hands of Joseph, telling the two:

-You lower and higher, to care for this step, because the tiger on his trail again if gets out of where it is. Tiburcio with you, he added.

And to Lucas:

-The two defray the rock above.

Then, with his sweet smile always ended by placing a piston with a steady hand in the fire of the gun:

'It's a kitten, and is already wounded.

In saying the last words we dispersed.

Jose Tiburcio and I went to a rock conveniently located. Tiburcio looked and looked again the prime of his shotgun. Joseph was all eyes. From there we could see what was happening in the rock and could keep pace recommended, because the trees of the skirt, but burly, were rare.

Of the six dogs, two were already out of action: one gutted at the foot of the beast, the other revealing the body for between one of the ribs, torn, had come looking for us and giving expired by the plaintive moans stone we occupied.

With his back against a group of oaks, making the tail wind, ruffling the back, eyes blazing and teeth discovered, tiger snorts grunts throwing, and shaking his huge head, ears made a noise like wooden castanets . When stirring, harassed by dogs, not chastened but not very healthy, looked to his left flank dripping blood, sometimes futilely tried licking, because then I stalked the pack with advantage.

Braulio and Lucas appeared out of the reeds on the rock, but a little further away from the beast we. Lucas was livid, and stains carate of his cheekbones, blue turquoise.

We formed a triangle and the hunters and the piece, both groups can shoot a time on it without offend each other.

- Fire all at once! - Cried Joseph.

- No, no dogs! Braulio replied, and leaving only his companion disappeared.

Generally understood that a shot could end it all, but it was true that some dogs succumb, and not dying tiger, it was easy to make a prank finding us laden unarmed.

Braulio's head, his mouth slightly open and panting, eyes and hair made revolt, looked out among the reeds, a little behind the trees back defending the beast: on the right arm had enristrada the spear, and deviated left with the thickets that she could see well.

We were all silent, the dogs seemed very interested in the end of the game.

Joseph cried at last:

- Hubi! Mataleón! Hubi! Picalo! Truncho!

It would not give respite to the beast, and avoided the risk is high to Braulio.

The dog returned to attack simultaneously. Another of them was dead without a groan.

The tiger gave a horrible meow.

Braulio appeared behind the group of oaks, to our side, holding the spear shaft without the blade.

The beast took on itself around after him, and he shouted:

"Fire! Fire! ', Returning to be a leap in the same spot where the spear had struck.

The tiger was looking. Lucas was gone. Tiburcio was olive color. He aimed and only burned the prime.

Joseph shot the tiger roared again and trying to bite his back, and jumped back on Braulio instantly. This, by re back behind the oaks, rushed toward us to collect the spear he threw Joseph.

Then the beast gave front. Only my gun was available: shot, the tiger sat on the tail, stumbled and fell.

Braulio instinctively looked back to see the effect of the last shot. Jose Tiburcio and I were already close to him, and all at once gave a cry of triumph.

The beast threw sanguaza frothy at the mouth: her eyes were misty and still, and in the last paroxysm of death shaky legs stretched and removed litter the winding and unwinding the beautiful tail.

- Brave shot! ... What shot! Braulio exclaimed putting a foot on the neck of the animal-: In the face! That itself is a steady hand!

Joseph, his voice not quite sure yet (the poor loved his daughter), said wiping the sleeve the brow:

-No, no ... If fuse! Blessed Patriarch! What animal so well bred! Hij ', a demon! If you get no one knows! ...

He looked sadly the bodies of three dogs saying

- Poor Tink!, Is the most sorry ... So beautiful my dog!

Then stroked the other three, that with so great lying tongue out panting and blind eye, as if it had been only a calf cantankerous corner.

Joseph, holding out his poncho in the clean, said:

'Sit down, boy, let's get good leather, because it's you,' and then he cried: Lucas!

Braulio laughed, concluyéndola to say:

'I will put that in the hen house.

- Lucas! - Joseph screamed again, without regard to what his nephew said, but seeing all laughing, asked:

- Hey! Eh! Then what is?

-Dude, if I missed valluno pulled away since the launch.

Joseph looked at us as if it were impossible to understand.

- Timanejo rogue!

And he came to the river, shouted so that the hills echoed his voice.

- Lucas demon!

'Here do I have a good knife for skinning, Tiburcio warned.

No, man, if that's jotico15 caratoso brought the luncheon, and this target will want to eat something and ... me too, because there is no hope of porridge.

But the bag was pointing precisely desired point abandoned by neivano. Joseph, full of joy, brought to where we were and proceeded to open it, after sending coconuts Tiburcio to fill our water from the river.

Provisions were soft and purple masses choclo16, cheese and roast neatly: all this was put on platanillo sheets. He at once took a napkin from a bottle of red wine, bread, plums and figs steps, saying:

-This is a separate account.

The knives came out of the pockets machetonas. José we divided the meat, which together with the masses of corn, was a regional snack. Deplete the red, despise the bread, and figs and plums liked my teammates more than me. No Missed panela, sweet companion of the traveler, hunter and poor. The water was freezing. My cigars humearon olor17 after that rustic banquet.

Joseph was in excellent spirits, and Braulio had dared to call me Godfather.

With skill imponderable, Tiburcio skinned the tiger, knocking the sebum, which supposedly served to whatnot.

Accommodated in backpacks skin, head and legs of the tiger, we set off for the possession of Joseph, who, taking my gun, placed it on one shoulder with it, precediéndonos in progress and calling the dogs. He stopped occasionally to highlight any of the sets of the game or to throw some new curse on Lucas.

Conocíase women counted and recounted to us since we caught sight, and when we approached the house were still undecided between the shock and joy because of our delay and they heard the shots we run risks assumed.

Traffic was who came forward to greet us, noticeably pale.

- Did you kill him? - We cried.

'Yes, dear, replied her father.

All surrounded us, entering the account until the old Marta, who was carrying a capon half-peeled. Lucia came to ask me about my gun, and as I was the shew, added quietly:

'Nothing has happened, right?

'Nothing,' I said gently, wiping his lips a twig.

'I thought I ...

- Has not that fanciful Lucas down here? Asked Joseph.

-The non-Marta said.

Joseph swore.

- But where is what killed? - Said finally making themselves heard, Mrs. Luisa.

'Here,' said Braulio-aunt, and aided by his girlfriend, started desfruncir backpack, telling the girl something that could not hear. She looked at me in a particular way, and the room took a stool for me to sit on the pavement, from which I dominated the scene.

Widespread in the large courtyard, velvety skin, women attempted heave a cry, but the head rolling on the grass, could not contain themselves.

- But how was he killed? Count! -Said Mrs. Luisa: everyone is as sad.

-Tell us, said Lucia.

Then Joseph took the tiger's head between his hands, said:

-The tiger would kill Braulio when Mr. (pointing) gave this bullet.

Foramen showed that the head was facing. Everyone turned to look at me, and each one of those looks had ample reward for an action that merited.

Joseph kept referring to details the history of the expedition, as he injured dogs remedies, lamenting the loss of the other three.

Braulio staking helped by Tiburcio skin.

The women had returned to their chores, and I dozed on one of the benches in the living room where Lucia Transit and I had improvised a ruanas mattress. Servíame cooing sound of the river, the honking of geese, the bleating of sheep that grazed in the nearby hills and ridges of girls washing clothes in the stream. Nature is the most loving of mothers when pain has taken over our soul, and if happiness caresses, she smiles.

XXII

Instances of the Highlanders made me stay with them until four in the afternoon, when, after very long goodbyes, I set off with Braulio, who insisted on accompanying me. Tell me relieved of the weight of the gun and hung from one shoulder one Guambía.

During the march I talked about his upcoming marriage and the happiness that awaited him, loving him as Traffic could be seen. I listened in silence, but he was smiling so do speak for others.

We crossed the river and left the last mountain brow to start descending the bankruptcy of the skirt clean, when Juan Angel, appearing from among some mulberry trees, we stood in the path, saying holding hands in a gesture of supplication :

-I came, my love ... I was ... but I did not do anything sumercé ... I'm not going to be afraid.

- What did you do? What is it? -I interrupted. Do you have sent home?

'Yes, my love, yes, the girl, and as he told me to come back sumercé ...

I could not remember the order he had given.

- 'So fear not you come back? Braulio asked laughing.

-That was, yes, that was ... But as May passed this asustao, then Lord Lucas found me across the river and said that the tiger had killed at Braulio Lord ...

This gave way to a roaring laugh, telling the terrified negrito order to:

- And you were all day stuck between these scrubs like a rabbit!

-As I cried Joseph Lord to return soon, because not only had to walk up there ... Juan Angel replied seeing the fingernails.

- Go! I will mezquino18 'said Braulio, but on condition that you have to go hunt another toe to toe with me.

The black eyes looked suspicious, before resolving to accept and forgiveness.

- Do you agree? I asked absently.

'Yes, master.

'Well, we walk. You, Braulio, trouble not thyself in with me more, turn.

-If I wanted ...

-No, you see that Transit is all scared today. Di beyond a thousand things in my name.

And this Guambía wearing ... Ah you take it, 'he continued, Juan Angel. You're not going to break the shotgun pattern out there? Look who I owe my life to that, 'he said. Be best-watched the recibírsela me.

Say a handshake from the mighty hunter, and we parted. Distant and us, cried:

-What is going on Guambía ore sample that ordered his father to my uncle.

And convinced that he had heard he went into the forest.

Detúveme two rifle shots of the house on the banks of the stream coming down loud to hide in the garden.

By continuing to Juan Angel looked down: was gone, and I figured that, afraid of my anger at his cowardice, would have solved seek protection better than that offered by Braulio with such unacceptable conditions.

I had a special affection for the bold: he told the then twelve years were friendly and could almost be said that beauty. Although intelligent, his reclusive nature was something. The life he had hitherto led was inappropriate to give vent to his character, for reasons to cuddle mediated. Feliciana, his mother, maid who had played roles in the family and enjoyed aya all such considerations, always tried to make his son a good page for me. But outside table service and camera and ability to prepare coffee, otherwise it was awkward and inexperienced.

Very close to the house, I noticed that the family was still in the room, and I inferred that Carlos and his father had been. Desviéme right, jumped the fence of the garden, and went through it to get to my room without being seen.

Hanging the bag shotgun hunting and when I heard a sound of voices unaccustomed. My mother came into my room at the time, and asked the cause of his ears.

-Is-my mother told me that the lords of M. .. are here, and you know that Don Geronimo always speaks as if he were on the bank of a river.

Carlos home! I thought this is the time to prove that my father spoke. Carlos will last a day of love, on occasion to admire his intended. That I can not make him see how much I love him! Unable to tell her I will be her husband! ... This is a torment worse than I had imagined.

My mother, perhaps concerned notándome, said:

-As you become sad.

-No, no, ma'am; tired.

- Hunting has been good?

-Very happy.

- Can I tell your father that you have and the bearskin charge you?

-Not that, but a beautiful tiger.

- What tiger?

'Yes, ma'am, I did the damage here.

'But that must have been horrible.

-The companions were very brave and skilled.

She had already put everything in my power that I could need for bathing and changing clothes, and narrowed the door while after leaving, I warned him not to say that I had returned yet.

He went back inside, and using that voice sweet as that made irresistibly affectionate always advised me, I said:

- Have in mind what we talked the other day about the visit of these gentlemen, no?

Satisfied with the answer, he added:

-Good. I trust that you will be very good.

And cerciorada again that nothing could miss me, left.

What I had said was Braulio mineral, was nothing more than the head of the tiger, and with such cunning had managed to get home that trophy of our achievement.

From the comments of the homemade scene later in the dining room knew this had happened:

I was going to pour his coffee when he arrived Juan Angel saying I came because my father and imposed the contents of the backpack. This, eager to give him Jerónimo your opinion of quartz, sent the sacase negrito, and was doing so when he gave a cry of terror and surprised deer jumped.

Each of those present wanted to find out what had happened. Juan Angel, his back against the wall, eyes pointing sizes and arms outstretched toward the bag, said:

- The Tiger!

- Where? Asked Don Jeronimo spilling coffee taking part, and standing up with more alacrity than expected allowed their spherical abdomen.

Carlos and my father also left their seats.

Emma and Mary approached each other.

- In the Guambía! Replied the challenged.

Everyone returned the soul to the body.

My father shook the bag carefully, and watching film on tile head, stepped back, Don Jerome, another, and resting his hands on his knees, burst:

- Cloverfield!

Carlos, anticipating closely examine the head:

- Horrible!

Philip, who called for the noise came, stood on a stool. Heloise grabbed the arm of my father. John, half crying, tried subírsele on knees to Mary, and this, as pale as Emma, looked anxiously toward the hills, waiting to see me fall.

- Who killed him? Asked Juan Carlos Angel, which had calmed down since.

-The amice shotgun.

- Yea amice single shotgun? Jeronimo-stressed laughing and occupying his seat again.

-No, my love, but Braulio Lord said now on the mound that he owed his life to her ...

- Where is then Ephraim? My father asked uneasily, looking at Mary.

He has remained in the creek.

At that time my mother returned to the dining room. Forgetting that just me, exclaimed:

- Oh my son!

-Comes-and my father watched him.

'Yes, yes, I know,' she said, but how this animal will die?

-Here was the bullet-bending Carlos said to mark the foramen of the forehead.

-But is it possible? Jeronimo asked my father, bringing the bracerillo to light a cigar, is it to be believed that you allow this to Ephraim?

My father smiled to answer with some self-satisfaction:

She ordered now days a bearskin to the foot of my bed, and surely will bring me a tiger preferred.

Mary had seen in the eyes of my mother I could reassure her. He went to the hall leading to John by the hand he, clinging to her skirt and still scared, prevented him from walking. He had to hold him, and told him to leave:

- Crying? Ugly ah! A man with fear?

Don Jerome, who managed to hear, observed, rocking in his chair and throwing a cloud of smoke:

-That one also kill tigers.

-You see Ephraim made a fierce hunter Carlos said Emma, sitting beside him, and at school did not deign to fire a paparote19 bodoquerazo. And no sir ... I remember now that I saw him do asuetos some good shots in the lagoon Fontibón. And these hunts are common?

-Other times, answered my sister died with Joseph and small bears and wolves Braulio very nice.

- I thought we did urge to hunt deer one morning, and getting ready for this shotgun came with my English!

-The lot will be pleased to entertain you: if you had come yesterday, today would have been both to hunting.

- Ah! yes ... if I had known ...

Mayo, who had been shipping some tasty snacks in the kitchen, then went through the dining room. He stopped in view of the head and spine bristling his neck, took a cautious approach the end roundabout way to sniff. Galloping through the house, and returning to the room, began to howl: I was not, and perhaps his instinct warned him that I had run dangers.

My father was impressed howls, was a man who believed in some sort of predictions and omens, concerns race which had been unable to dispense entirely.

-May, May, what's up? Said petting the dog, and with ill-concealed impatience: this child does not arrive ...

At that time I went to the salon in a suit in which I do not really have recognized but closely Transit and Lucia.

Mary was there. No sooner had we changed time for a greeting and a smile. John, who was sitting in the lap of Mary, told me in passing his bad language, pointing to the door of the dining room:

-There's the coconut.

And I entered the room smiling, because I figured that the child was referring to Don Jerónimo.

I took a close embrace Carlos, who came forward to meet me, and by that time forgot almost everything in recent days had been at fault.

Mr. M. ... cordially shook hands in mine, saying:

- Well, well! How could we be if all these old boys have become men?

We the living: Mary was not already there.

The conversation rolled on the last hunt, and I was almost denied by Jerónimo to assure the success of it was due to Braulio, as I stood in front references by Juan Angel.

Emma informed me that Carlos had been prepared for us to do a hunt for deer: he was enthusiastic about the promise I made to give you a nice starting in the vicinity of the house.

After my sister left, he wanted me to see his gun Carlos English, and to that end we went to my room. It was the gun exactly like the one my father had given me on my return from Bogota, but before I see it, I made sure that Carlos had never come to the country such thing.

'Well,' I said, after I examined. With this also would kill animals that class?

-Surely if: a sixty yards away will not drop a line.

- Sixty rods are those shots?

-It is dangerous to have the full range of the weapon in such cases, to forty yards is already a long shot.

- How far were you when you shot the tiger?

-A thirty paces.

-Man, I need to do something good in the hunt we will have, because otherwise I will rust this gun and do not swear or tominejas have hunted all my life.

- Oh! you'll see: I will look, because the deer will enter the Garden.

Carlos gave me a thousand questions about his classmates, neighbors and friends of Bogotá: went for a long memories of student life: Emigdio and spoke to me of their new relationship with him, and laughed heartily remembering the comic denouement of the loves of Micaelina our friend.

Carlos had returned to Cauca eight months before me. During this time his whiskers had improved, and the blackness of them did contrast with rosy cheeks, his mouth kept the freshness that always made her admirable, the curly head of hair and half shadowed his smooth forehead, usually serene like a face porcelain. Definitely was a good boy.

Also spoke to me of their field of heifers fattened now, the good pastures I was doing, and finally founded hope that soon had to be very wealthy owner. I saw him make sure the bad marksmanship event, but tried to avoid me and not interrupt the discomfort of talking about my business.

'But,' said man standing up in front of my desk and after a lengthy dissertation on the advantages of feedlots on guinea-natural grass: here there are many books. You have been carrying around the shelf. I also study, ie, read ... no time for more, and I have a cousin who has endeavored baccalau that engulfs me a flood of novels. You know that no serious studies have been my skinny: why I did not graduate, but I could have.

I can not do without the annoyance it causes me and politics than I litis encocora all that, even though my father grieves day and night that I put in front of their lawsuits, has a mania for litigation, and the most serious issues are about twenty yards square variation swamp or bed of a ditch that has had the good taste to throw off the neighbor a fajilla of our lands.

-Let's see, the label began reading books-Frayssinous, Christ before the Century, The Bible ... Here are many mystical thing. Don Quixote ... Of course: I have never read two chapters.

- Do not, eh?

-Blair-continued; Chateubriand Hortensia ... My cousin has this craze. English Grammar. What language so rebellious! I could not just get.

-But you were talking about something.

-The "how do you do" as the "comment ca vat 'il' in French.

'But you have an excellent pronunciation.

'So I said to stimulate me.

And continuing to consider:

- Shakespeare? Calderon ... Verses, right? Spanish Theatre. Need more verses? Confess, you still do verses? I remember you did some saddened me making me think of the Cauca. Yea you do?

-No.

'I'm glad of it, because you would end by starving yourself.

-Continued-Cortés;? Conquest of Mexico?

-No, it's something else.

-Tocqueville, Democracy in America ... Plague! Ségur ... What Runfla!

On arriving there dining bell rang announcing that the soda was served. Carlos, suspending the enforcement of my books, went to the mirror, combed his whiskers and hair with a pocket comb, folded like a dressmaker a tie, the tie of blue, and left.

XXIII

Carlos and I came into the dining room. The seats were distributed as follows: my father presided over the table to his left my mother had just sat down on his right Mr. Jerome, who unfolded the napkin without interrupting the heavy history of that lawsuit that contended with Don Ignacio boundaries, then the My mother had an empty seat and another beside Mr. M. .., then these, giving front, were Mary and Emma, and then children.

Carlos Cumplíame point out to which of them should fill vacant seats. A time to show it, Mary, not looking at me, put his hand on the chair that was immediate, as he did to tell me, without that they might understand the other, he could be near her. Doubting perhaps be understood, instantly my eyes searched hers, whose language on such occasions was so familiar. However, Carlos offered to the chair she offered me, and I sat next to Emma.

Jeronimo miraculously put an end to his concluding arguments he had presented to the court the day before, and turning to me, said:

-Go to their hard work you interrupt his lectures. From all been there: good memories of the past, we had certain neighborhoods in Bogotá ... plans for the future ... Current. There is no way to see a classmate wanted. I had to forget that you wanted to be. Do not accuse you Carlos for so late, as he was even able to offer me to come alone.

I expressed to Mr. Jerome could not forgive him that I had been deprived for so long the pleasure of seeing him and Carlos, and yet, it would be less resentful if the permanence of them at home was long. To which he replied, his mouth is not as empty as desired outside and looking at sideways while taking a sip of chocolate:

-That's hard, because tomorrow starts the datas of salt.

After a moment's pause, during which my mother smiled imperceptibly, continued:

And there is no remedy: if I'm not there, it should be.

-We have a lot to do, 'said Carlos with some businessman sufficiency, which must have seemed timely to hunt and study knowing were my occupations.

Mary, perhaps resented me, dodged me. She was more beautiful than ever, and slightly pale. She wore a black chiffon uvillas profusely dotted blue, whose skirt, falling into numerous folds, whispered as she walked so softly as the night breezes in the roses from my window. His chest was covered with a transparent scarf of the same color of the suit, which seemed not daring to touch or the base of your throat lily complexion, yet this, in a line of black hair, a little cross diamond shone, the tresses, divided in two braids of abundant locks, hid half the temples and flew on their backs.

The conversation had become general, and my sister asked me why almost secretly had chosen that seat. I replied with a "well be" that did not satisfy her: looked at me with surprise and then looked in vain in the eyes of Mary were tenaciously veiled eyelids satin-pearl.

Raised tablecloths, prayer became usual. We invited my mother to go to the salon: Don Geronimo and my father stayed at the table talking about their business field.

Introduce Carlos's guitar my sister, knowing that he played pretty well this instrument. After some instances agreed to play something. Asked Emma and Mary, while tuning, if they were not fond of dancing, and as would be directed in particular to the last, she told him she had never danced.

He turned to me, then returning to my room, saying:

- Man!, Is it possible?

- What?

-That you have not given some dance lessons to your sister and your cousin. Do not be so selfish thought. Or are you Matilde condition not imposed by generalizaras your knowledge?

She confided in yours to make a paradise of dancers Cauca I replied.

- What's mine? You force me to confess to the ladies who have benefited more if you had not gone to take lessons at the same time I did.

'But that was that she was hoping to meet you in December, since I expected to see in the first dance that prevailed in Gauteng.

The guitar was warm and Carlos played a quadrille he and I had reason to remember.

- What do you remember this part? -He asked putting his guitar on knees perpendicular.

-Many things, but none in particular.

- None?, What jocoserio lance that took place between the two, in home of Mrs. ...?

- Ah, yes, I fall.

-It was he said to avoid a lot of pain for our punctilious teacher: you were going to dance with her, and I ...

-The question was which of our partners should put the quadrille.

-And you must confess that I succeeded because I gave you my post-Carlos replied laughing.

-I had the fortune of not being forced to insist. Make us the favor of singing.

While this dialogue lasted, Mary, who occupied the couch with my sister were headed by Carlos and I, set for a second look at my partner, to notice at what point she was only obvious that I was upset, and then pretended to tie distracted lap curls the tips of her braids.

My mother insisted that Carlos sang. The voice sang a song sound full and who was in vogue in those days, which began:

The grunt is the warrior trunk

Maybe called the bloody fight,

And from the sound of warlike pomp

Run happy to field the champion.

Once Carlos ended his trova, my sister and begged Mary to sing well. This seemed not to have heard what it was.

Will Carlos discovered my love, I told myself, and so to speak complacídose well? I convinced myself after I had misjudged, that if he was capable of a lightweight, never would be a malignancy.

Emma was ready. Approaching Mary, said:

- We sing?

- But what I can I sing? -Answered.

I approached Mary to tell her in a low voice:

- Is there anything you like singing, anything?

Then looked at me as he always did to tell me something in the tone in which he uttered those words a minute and played on his lips a smile like that of a cute girl who wakes caressed by his mother's kisses.

'Yes,' said the Fairy.

The verses of this song were written by me. Emma, who had found my desk, I adapted the music of others that were in fashion.

On one of those summer nights when the winds seem to listen to silence convidarse vague rumors and distant echoes, in which the moon takes or missing, fearing that her light importune, in which the soul, like a lover than a beloved now let us be rid of us slowly and smiling, to render loving more than ever, on a night like this, Mary, Emma and I were on the corridor side of the valley, and after starting last on guitar some melancholy chords, arranged them their voices but virgin and uncultivated nature singing. Sorprendíme, and I found my beautiful and felt bad verses. After the last, Mary rested her forehead on Emma's shoulder, and when he raised, excited murmured in his ear the last verse. Ah! They still seem to retain Mary do not know if a smell, something like the wetness of his tears. Here they are:

I dreamed palm forests roam

Whose flaxen plumage, by plunging

Your hard the sun in the distant mountains,

Criss ruby glow.

The smooth lake was dyed pink

The blue and clear surface,

And its banks herons and doves

Posábanse in the willows and bamboos.

Muda afternoon, before the night moves

Gauze of his garment collected:

Indus in foam sleeping sea

The moon hallóla sun and their feet.

Come with me to wander in the forests

Where the Fairies tune my lute;

They have told me that dream with me,

I will make you immortal if you love me.

My father and Mr. M. .. entered the room in time to the song ended. The first, which only hummed under his breath some air in his country, in the moments when mildness of his mind was full, had love for music and the dance had in his youth.

Don Jerome, after sitting as comfortably as he could on a fluffy couch, followed yawned twice.

-I had not heard that music with those verses-Carlos observed my sister.

She's read a newspaper, 'I said and put the music to sing with others. The bad-I think I added: insulseces published many of this laya in newspapers! Havana Son of a poet, and it is known that Cuba has a nature similar to that of Cauca.

Mary, my mother and my sister looked at each other in amazement, surprised at the coolness with which I cheated to Carlos, but it was because they were unaware of the test that he had done for the afternoon of the books in my shelf exam so bad that standing left my favorite authors, and remembering with some resentment of what he had said about Don Quixote, I added:

'You must have seen those verses in the day, and you do not remember, I think they are signed by a certain Almendarez.

-As she said that, I have such a bad memory for that ... If you are you've heard reciting my cousin ... frankly, I think are best sung by these ladies. Have you please say them, he added to Mary.

This, smiling, asked Emma.

- How to start the first? ... If I forget myself. Dilos you, that you know well.

'But you just sing-Carlos-and watched him recite it easy, for they were ill, those would be good for you.

Mary's repeated, but to get to the last verse his voice was almost tremulous.

Charles thanked him, adding:

'Now I'm pretty sure have heard them before.

Bah, I said to myself: what is certain is that Carlos had seen every day what my bad verses paint, but without realizing it, and looks at his watch.

XXIV

Time to retire, and I feared that I had prepared bed in the same room as Carlos, I went to mine: it came out at that time my mother and Mary.

'I can sleep alone here, is not it? I asked the first, who understanding the reason for the question, replied:

'No, your friend.

- Ah! Yes, I said flowers seeing my vase placed on him in the morning and wearing a scarf Maria. Where do you wear?

-Al oratorio, because there was no time like today to put others there ...

We greatly appreciated the fineness of not allowing the flowers intended for it to me adorn my room that night and were available to another.

But she had left the bouquet of lilies that I had brought from the mountain that afternoon, although it was very visible on my table and introduced them saying:

-Bring also these lilies for the altar: Transit gave them to me for you, to recommend me warn you that you had chosen to sponsor their marriage. And as we all should pray for his happiness ...

'Yes, yes,' he replied, 'So you want me to be her godmother? She added as referring to my mother.

'That's very natural, it said.

- And I so cute I have a suit that works for that day! You need to tell him I have become very happy to learn that we ... I preferred to her godmother.

My brothers, Philip and he was received with surprise and pleasure the news that I would spend the night in the same room with them. Habíanse accommodated in one of the two beds to serve me of Philip, in the curtains of this medallion had caught Mary of Sorrows, who was in my room.

After the children prayed arrodilladitos in bed, I said good night and slept after having laughed at the fears that they got another tiger head.

That night was not only me the image of Mary, the angels of the house slept close to me: at sunrise would come to fetch her to kiss her cheeks and take them to the source, where they bathed their faces with their hands white and perfumed Castilian roses as they gathered for the altar and her.

XXV

Waked at dawn the whispering of the children, who vainly encouraged to respect my dream. Pigeons caught in those days, and forced them to stay alicortadas in trunks empty spying groaned the first rays of light that penetrated into the room through the cracks.

-Do not open 'said Philip not open, that my brother is asleep, and cuncunas dislodge.

'But Mary called us and replied the young.

-There's no such: I'm awake a while, and has not called.

-Yes, I know what you want: I go running first to the creek to say then that only blacks have dropped your hooks.

-As I struggle to put my work well ... Felipe interrupted him.

- See that funny! If Juan Angel which puts you in good puddles.

I insisted on opening.

- Do not open! Felipe replied angrily and-: aguárdate see if Ephraim is asleep.

So saying, he tiptoed to my bed.

Take time by the arm, saying:

- Ah rascal!, So you take away the tiny fish.

Riéronse both put and approached respectfully demand. It was all arranged with the promise I made that afternoon I would go to watch the position of the hooks. I got up and left them in jail busy flapping pigeons looking out at the bottom of the door, crossed the garden.

The blossoms, basil and roses gave the wind its delicate aromas, to receive the caresses of the first rays of sun, and peered over the top of Morrillos, spreading to the zenith blue little clouds of pink and gold.

As he passed by the window of Emma, I heard her and Mary spoke, stopping to laugh. They produced their voices, with the specialty of Mary, by the incomparable whisper their eses, similar to the noise the pigeons and tiles were waking in the foliage of orange and strawberry trees of the garden.

They talked low and Carlos Jeronimo, pacing the hallway of their rooms, when I jumped the fence of the garden to fall to the outside patio.

- Opa! Said Mr M. .. - Madruga you as a good farmer. I thought that was so dormiloncito as his friend when he came to Bogotá, but those who live with me have to get used to mañanear.

Followed by a long list of benefits that provides little sleep, all of which would have been likely responded to what he called poor sleep was nothing bad beginning to sleep early, then confessed that he had the habit of going to bed at seven or eight of the night, to prevent migraine.

Braulio's arrival, whom Juan Angel had gone to call the morning, fulfilling the order I gave at night prevented us from enjoying the end of the speech of Mr. M. ..

Braulio brought a couple of dogs, in which there would have been easy to a less familiar with them than I do, recognize the heroes of our previous day's hunt. May growled at them and came to hide behind me with samples invincible antipathy: he, with his white skin, still beautiful, floppy ears and frown and look severe, dabase before Highlander lajeros imponderable an air of aristocracy.

Braulio humbly greeted and approached the family to ask me while I was holding her hand affectionately. Their dogs made me entertainments in proof that they were more sympathetic to Mayo.

-We will have occasion to test your shotgun told Carlos. I sent order two very good dogs to Santa Elena, and here's a fellow who does not spend with deer jokes, and two puppies very skilled.

- Those? Carlos asked scornfully.

- With such chandosos? -Jeronimo said.

'Yes, sir, the same.

'I see it and I will not believe,' said Mr. M. .. undertaking walks back down the corridor.

They'd just bring us coffee and made myself Braulio to accept the cup intended for me. Carlos and his father did not disguised well the strangeness that caused them my courtesy to the mountain.

Soon after, M. de M. .. and my father rode to visit the farm work. Braulio, Carlos and I, we are dedicated to preparing graduate shotguns and load that my friend wanted to try.

Doing it when my mother informed me that he wanted to talk secretly. She waited in her sewing. Maria and my sister were in the bathroom. Making me sit near her, she said:

-Your father insists that Mary realizes the claim of Carlos. Do you think it should also be well?

'I must do what my father has.

-It seems to me that you think that way by obeying, not because impress stop which take such a decision.

-I offered to observe the behavior. Moreover, Mary is not even my fiancee and is free to decide what he likes. I offered to say nothing of the agreement with you, and I complied.

-I am afraid that the emotion will cause Mary to imagine that your father and I are far from approving what happens between you, you do much harm. Not your father wanted to talk to Mr. M. .. Mary's illness, fearing deemed that as a pretext for rejection, and as he and his son know that she has a dowry ... Otherwise I do not want to say it, but you understand. What should we do, say thou that Mary did not even remotely think that we are opposed to is your wife while I simultaneously comply with recently warned by your father?

-We only need half.

- What?

'I'll tell you, and I promise I approve, I beg you now to approve it. Mary Revelémosle secret that my father has imposed on the consent has given me to see her as the one to be my wife. I offer to you that I will be cautious and leave nothing to my father noticed that can make him understand this disloyalty necessary. Will I still keep that behavior he demands, without causing Mary penalties that will make you more harm than confess everything? Trust you me: Is not it true that there inability to do what my father like? You see: Do not you think so?

My mother was silent a moment, and then, smiling in the most affectionate, said:

'Well, but do not forget that you should not promise what it can accomplish. And how do you talk about the proposal Carlos?

- Do you? He asked, amazed.

'I'll tell you, and I promise I approve, I beg you now to approve it. Mary Revelémosle secret that my father has imposed on the consent has given me to see her as the one to be my wife. I offer to you that I will be cautious and leave nothing to my father noticed that can make him understand this disloyalty necessary. Will I still keep that behavior he demands, without causing Mary penalties that will make you more harm than confess everything? Trust you me: Is not it true that there inability to do what my father like? You see: Do not you think so?

My mother was silent a moment, and then, smiling in the most affectionate, said:

'Well, but do not forget that you should not promise what it can accomplish. And how do you talk about the proposal Carlos?

-As talk to Emma in the same case, and saying after what he has promised me to express. If I'm not mistaken, the first words you will experience a painful impression, because they give you a reason to fear you and my father strongly oppose our link. She heard what had once talked about his illness, and only affable giving you followed yesterday and having conversation between her and me, have calmed. Forget me indispensable to give reflections on the proposal Carlos. I will be listening to what you speak, the racks behind that door.

This was the oratory of my mother.

- Do you? He asked, amazed.

'Yes, ma'am, I do.

- And what avail yourself of this deception?

-Mary is happy to have done so, in view of the results.

- What results you promise, then?

-Know all she can do for me.

'But is not it better if you want to hear what is going to tell me that she always ignore what you hear and I consented?

-It will, if you wish.

Do you have a face-to fulfill that.

'I beg you not object.

'But you're not seeing what you intend to do, if she comes to know, it's like I promise one thing unfortunately not know if I can keep our promise, as if the disease reappear, your father will oppose your marriage , and I would do the same?

She knows, she never consent to be my wife, if the wrong reappears. But what you have forgotten what the doctor said?

-Do therefore what you want.

-Look here his voice already here. Ensure that Emma will not come up to enter the chapel.

Mary became rosy and laughing even than he had been talking with Emma. Crossed with mild and almost childlike way the room of my mother, who did not discover it when he went to get his.

- Ah! He exclaimed; Right here were you? And coming to her: But how pale you are! Feeling sick in the head, right?. If you had taken a bath ... improvement that both ...

-No, no, I'm good. I hoped to talk to you alone, and as this is a very serious thing, I fear that this could produce you a bad impression.

- What is it? What is it? ...

'Sit here,' said my mother fixing a taburetico to her feet.

He sat down, and, trying futilely to smile, his face took an expression of gravity lovely.

-Say you already said as trying to control the emotion, running both hands over his forehead, and then assuring them the tortoiseshell comb her hair holding gold as a gleaming thick cord that encircled the temples.

I'm going to tell you about how it would speak to Emma in the same circumstance.

'Yes, Madam, I hear.

-Your dad has asked me to tell you ... that M. de M. .. asked your hand to his son Charles ...

- Yo! Exclaimed astonished and doing an involuntary movement to stand up, but fell back in his chair, covered his face with his hands, and I heard sobbing.

- What should I say, Mary?

- He has commanded you to tell me? He asked in a choked voice.

-Yes, daughter, and has done his duty haciéndotelo know.

'But why did you tell me? - What did you want me to do?

- Ah! Tell me no ... I can not ... not.

After a moment, looking up to look at my mother, who could not help crying with her, said:

-All I know, is not it?, All you wanted to tell me.

-Yes, everyone knows that, unless Emma.

-Only she ... My God! My God! -Added hiding his head in the arms resting on the knees of my mother, and remained so for a moment.

Then lifting his face pale and sprayed by a shower of tears:

'Well,' he said: and you turned, all I know already.

But Mary-le-gently interrupted my mother is it, then, so unfortunately that Carlos wants to be your husband? Is not that ...?

-I pray ... I do not want, I do not need to know more. Yea, you have let me propose? ... All, all have agreed! Well, I say-added voice strong despite her sobs say to you that I will die consent. Ah! Does that not lord knows I have the same disease that killed my mother, still very young she? ... Oh! What will I do now without it?

- And I'm not here? Do not love you with all my heart? ...

My mother was less strong than what she thought.

As tears rolled down my cheeks felt hot dripping on my hands, resting on one of the buttons on the door that hid me.

Mary said to my mother:

-But then why did you propose this?

-Because it was necessary that this 'no' out of your mouth, but I'd give it supusiera me.

And you just assumed that I would give, is not it?

'Maybe someone else also assumed. If you knew how much pain, how many sleepless nights this matter has caused the more guilty you judge! ...

- Dad? Less pale and said.

'No, to Ephraim.

Mary uttered a faint cry, and dropping her head on my mother's lap, she froze.

This opened her lips to call, when Mary returned to straighten slowly stood in almost smiling up and said, returning to ensure hair with trembling hands.

-I was wrong mourn, does not it? I thought ...

-Calm down and wipe those tears: I want to see you as happy as you were. You estimate the chivalry of his conduct ...

-Yes, ma'am. I do not know him that I cried right? -Handkerchief wiping said my mother.

- Has not done well in consent Ephraim me to tell you everything?

-Maybe ... of course.

-But you say it in a way ... Your dad called his condition, although not necessary, to let you freely decide in this case.

- Condition? ? Condition for?

She demanded that I not tell you never knew and consentíamos what happens between you.

Mary's cheeks were stained, hearing this, the softer flesh. His eyes were fixed on the ground.

- Why demanded that? He said at last in a voice I could barely hear. Do I have myself to blame? ... Am I wrong, then? ...

-No, daughter, but your dad thought you needed precautions disease ...

- Precautions? ... Am I not good anymore? Do not think that I will not suffer anything? How can Efraín cause my bad?

-It would be impossible ... love you so much, and perhaps more than you do to it.

Mary shook her head from side to side as respondiéndose herself, and then shaking it with the way he used to as a child to ward off a memory funky, asked:

- What should I do? I want to do and all that.

-Carlos would have occasion to speak today of its claims.

- Me?

-Yes, hears him say, keeping of course all the serenity that you can, you can not accept your offer, although much honor you because you are very young, leaving him to know that because you give that negative real shame ...

'But that will be when we all gathered.

'Yes,' replied my mother, pleased revealing candor of her voice and her looks. I think I deserve to be very condescending to me.

To which I replied no. Bringing his right arm my mother's head to his, remained so briefly showing the expression of his face the most unblemished tenderness. Hastily crossed the room and disappeared behind the curtains of the door leading to his room.

XXVI

My mother imposed hunting our project, we made earlier served lunch to Carlos, Braulio and me.

With difficulty I managed to resolved the mountain to come to the table, which occupied the opposite end we were Carlos and me.

Quite naturally, we talk about the game we had in hand. Carlos said:

-Braulio responds to load my gun is perfectly graded, but continues ranchado that is not as good as yours, although they are the same factory, and have shot himself with mine on a citron, achieving introduce four posts. Not so, my friend? Ended up going to the mountain.

-I answer he replied that the pattern-kill seventy steps one Pellar with that shotgun.

'Well, we'll see if I kill a deer. How to hold the hunt? He added, turning to me.

-It is known, as long as you have wants to finish the job close to home: Braulio rises to walk her dogs collapsed Lift: Juan Angel is stationed inside the Broken Honda with two of the four I sent dogs bring Santa Elena; your page with the other two wait in the river to prevent the escape us Novillera venison, you and I will be ready to go to the appropriate point.

The plan seemed good to Braulio, who after ensillarnos horses helped by Juan Angel, was launched with it to play the part he played in the raid.

The horse I rode retinto, hit the pavement when we were going out and, eager to show off their skills, arched neck fine and glossy as satin black, shaking his curly mane sneezing. Charles Knight was a brown coral Quito General Flores had sent gifts in those months my father.

Recommended to M. de M. .. the most attention, for if the deer came into the garden as we promised, we left the courtyard to undertake the ascent of the skirt, which ended incline to thirty blocks to the east, at the foot of the mountains.

Passing turning the house facing balconies Emma department, Maria was leaning against the railing of one of them seemed to be in one of those moments of complete distraction that often abandoned. Heloise, who was at her side, playing with loops destrenzados and thick hair of her cousin.

The noise of our horses and dogs barking Mary pulled its distress at the time I greeted? Sign Carlos and imitated me. I noticed that she remained in the same position and place until we get into the canyon of the Honda.

May walked us to the first stream to wade; stopping there as to reflect, to gallop back toward the house.

'Hey,' I said to Carlos, after half an hour passed, during which he referred without resting the most important episodes of the deer hunts the mountain and I had done-; hears the shouts and the barking of Braulio of dogs that have raised test.

The mountains are repeated, and if he silenced at times, began again with greater force and less distance.

Shortly after the bank declined by Braulio clean Forest Glen. No sooner was next to Juan Angel, let the two dogs that he wore halter and stopped for a few moments grasping the pestorejo, until it was persuaded that the dam near the pass where we were: animólos with repeated cries, and disappeared fast.

Carlos, Juan Angel and I were deployed in the skirt. Soon he began to saw through it, followed closely by one of the dogs of Joseph, the deer, down the ravine less than we had supposed.

A Juan Angel eyes whitened her laugh and let see how far the wheels of his fine teeth. However, having been ordered to remain in Canada, if the deer came back to her, crossed with Braulio, and almost a couple of our horses, grasslands and streams of the river that separated us. In falling to the valley of this deer, the dogs lost the trail, and he went down instead.

Carlos and I started to dismount Braulio help at the bottom of the valley.

Lost more than an hour back and forth, finally heard the barking of a dog, which gave us hope that he had found the track again. But Carlos swore to leave a Bejucal they had gotten without knowing how or when the brute had left his black piece go downstream.

Braulio, who had lost sight of for some time, a voice shouted such that despite the distance we could hear:

- There he goes, there it goes! Let each allííí shotgun; Get out to liiimpio because the deer becomes the Hooonda.

Charles was the pageboy at his post, and he and I went to take our horses.

The piece came to that time of the plain, far ahead of the dogs, and went down to the house.

-Get down I shouted to Carlos-wait for it over the fence.

He did so, and when the deer was struggling, tired and, by jumping the fence of the garden, shot him followed the deer; Carlos was stunned.

Braulio arrived at that moment, and I jumped off the horse, flanges botándole Juan Angel.

In the house were all that was happening. Don Jerome saved, shotgun in hand, the rail corridor, and going to shoot the animal, blissfully feet became entangled in an era plants, which was causing him to time my father said:

- Beware, beware! You see it all come around.

Braulio monitored to venadito, thus preventing it despedazasen dogs.

The animal entered the corridor desatentado and trembling, and lay almost drowned beneath a sofa, where he drew Braulio when Carlos and I arrived as a good step. The game had been fun for me, but he tried in vain to hide the impatience that had caused him to miss such a beautiful shot.

Emma and Mary timidly approached to play the fawn, begging matásemos not: he seemed to understand that they defended, as the moist eyes and looked astonished, roaring softly, as he had done anything to call his mother. He was acquitted, and Braulio atramojarlo handled and put in place appropriate.

After all, May the prisoner came, sniffed the distance that prudence required, and re-laid in the living room, put her head on her hands as calmly, without so exotic behavior sufficed to deprive him of my love .

Soon after, at parting Braulio me to return to the mountain, he said:

Her friend is furious, and I've put so to get back at the derision of my dogs did this morning.

I asked him to explain to me what he said.

-Continued-I figured you Braulio-cede him the best shot, so I left the shotgun ammo Carlos when I gave it to load.

-You did very badly, he observed.

-Do not do it again, not with him, because I do not hunt puts us more ... Ah! Miss Mary has given me a thousand errands for Transit: thank you so much you are willingly to be our sponsor ... I do not know what to do so you know: you should tell him.

-I will do so, loses care.

'Goodbye,' said holding out his hand frankly, without ceasing to touching his hat with the other-; until Sunday.

He left the yard calling his dogs with acute wheezing occurred in such cases, pressing with the thumb and forefinger lip.

XXVII

Until then I had gotten that Carlos did not make me any confidence about the claims in an evil hour for him had taken him home.

But then we are alone in my room, where I was pretending desire to rest and that us to read something, I knew I was going to put me in a difficult situation which had escaped there by dint of skill. He lay down on my bed complaining of heat, and as I said I was going to send some fruit to be delivered, I noticed that he caused injury he had suffered from intermittent. I approached the stand asking him what he wanted us to read.

'Do me a favor and do not read anything,' he answered.

- Want to take a dip in the river?

-The sun has me headache.

I offered to absorb alkali.

-No, no, this happens rehusándolo replied.

Then knocking boots with whip in her hand:

I swear never to hunt any species. Caramba! Nah, you look at that shot that err ...

-That happens to us all-we watched remembering Braulio's revenge.

- How everyone? Mistaken to him a deer at that range, only happens to me.

After a moment's silence, said to look for something in the room:

- What have been the flowers that were here yesterday?

Today not been replenished.

'If I'd known you pleased to see them there, the place would have done. In Bogotá were not fond of flowers.

And I began to leaf through a book lying open on the table.

I've never been, 'said Carlos-but ... Not read, man! Look, do me the favor of sitting around here, because I have to refer very interesting things. Close the door.

I saw no way out, I made an effort to prepare my face as best as I could in that set, resolved in all cases to hide the enormity Carlos was making me folly who committed their trusts.

His father, who came at that time to the threshold of the door, delivered me from the torment that would hold me.

Carlos Jeronimo said externally-: you need here.

There was in the tone of his voice seemed to mean something to me, "That is well under way."

Carlos figured that gloriously marched affairs. He jumped to his feet answering:

I'm going at this time;-and left.

I pretended to not be read as calmly at that moment, he probably would have approached me to tell me smile: "In view of the surprise that you prepare, you will forgive me that I have not said anything so far about this issue» ... But I should have seemed so indifferent to what was happening as I tried to fake it, which was getting long.

From the sound of the footsteps of the couple, who entered the room met my father.

Not wanting to see me again in danger of Carlos I speak of your affairs, I went to my mother's quarters. Mary was in the sewing room: I was sitting in a chair cenchas, which fell frothy, arregazada at intervals with bands of blue ribbon, her white muslin skirt, her hair without braids yet, rodábale in loops on the shoulders. On the carpet at his feet had fallen asleep Juan, surrounded by his toys. She, with her head slightly tilted back, seemed to be watching the child, having been dropped from the hands that sewed the lawn, lay on the carpet.

Just heard footsteps looked up at me, was passed through the hands to clear them temples of hair that covered them, and bowed with shameful alacrity to pick the seam.

- Where is my mother? I asked, looking at her for leaving behold the beauty of the sleeping child.

-In Dad's room.

And finding in my face that looked timidly saying this, his lips tried to smile.

I half kneeling, wiping his forehead with my handkerchief 'wee.

- Oh! Exclaimed Mary Did saw he was asleep? I'm going to bed.

And went to take John. I was lifting and Mary in my arms and waited in theirs: I kissed her lips parted and purplish Juan, and his face closer to Mary, she spent hers on that mouth to receive our caresses smiled and hugged him tenderly against his chest.

He left to return moments later to take his seat, near which I had placed mine.

She was arranging her utensils sewing box that had cluttered Juan, when I said:

- Have you talked to my mom today about some proposal Carlos?

'Yes,' he replied without looking at extending the arrangement of the box.

- What did he say? Stop that now and talk formally.

He looked even something on the ground, and finally taking affected an air of seriousness, which did not exclude the vivid flush of her cheeks and veiled evil gleam in his eyes, said:

58

-Many things.

- What?

-Those that you passed her to tell me.

- Me? Why do you treat me now?

- Do not see it is because sometimes I forget ...?

-Tell it that you spoke my mother.

-If she sent me that says ... But what I said, yes you can tell.

Well, to see.

-I told him ... Also, do not say those.

-You tell me the other time, is not it?

-Yes, not today.

'My mother has told me that you are encouraged to talk back to him what you owe, so that you understand what it estimates to honor that makes you.

Then looked at me intently, without answering.

-It must be so I continued.

He looked down and kept silent, apparently distracted in order to nail the needles on your pillow.

-Mary, do not you hear me? I added.

-Yes.

And get my eyes again, I was not separate from her face. Then I saw tears glistened on her eyelashes.

'But why are you crying? I asked.

No, if you do not cry ... Did I cry?

He took my handkerchief wiped his eyes hastily.

'I have made you suffer with it, right? If you have to be sad, no more about it.

-No, no, let's talk.

- Work out Is much sacrifice to hear what you say today Carlos?

-I have to give mom and taste, but she promised to accompany me. Be there, is not it?

- And why so? How will the opportunity to talk to him?

'But you're so close as possible.

And getting to hear:

-Is-coming mom continued, putting his hand in mine, to let her touch my lips, as he did when he wanted to complete, when we parted, my happiness a few minutes.

My mother came, and Mary, already standing, I said:

- Bathroom?

'Yes,' I replied.

And oranges when you're there.

-Yes.

My eyes must have completed as tenderly as my heart because she wanted these responses, satisfied with my disguise, smiled upon hearing.

I was just finishing getting dressed in the shade of the orange bathroom in time that Don Geronimo and my father, who wanted to show the best adornment of your garden, came to him. The water was level with the stream, and looked at her, wandering supernatant or transparent background, roses estefana had spilled into the pond.

It was a black estefana twelve year old daughter of our slaves: their nature and beauty made her sympathetic to everyone. He had an affection for his lady fan Mary, who took pains to make her dress gracefully.

Estefana arrived shortly after my father and Mr. M. .., and convinced that he could come and I presented a cup containing orange prepared with wine and sugar.

-Man, your child you live here like a king, 'said my father Jeronimo.

This he said, giving time back to the orange group to take the road from home:

-Six years has lived as a student, and you have yet to live and another five at least.

XXVIII

That evening, before the ladies were lifted to make coffee, like they always had strangers at home, I brought the conversation catches referred children and the cause for which they had offered that day to witness the placement of hooks in the creek. He accepted my proposal to elect such a site to walk. Only Mary looked at me as if to say "Yea no remedy?".

We crossed and the garden. It was not until Mary and also my sister, who had gone to find out the cause of his delay. I gave my mother's arm. Emma politely refused to rely on the Charles, on the pretext of bringing the hand to one of the children: Mary accepted almost shaking, and putting his hand on him, he stopped to wait for me, just was it necessary meaning you can not hesitate .

We had reached the point where the banks in the basin of the valley, carpeted with fine grass, stand at intervals stained black stones white moss.

Carlos's voice took on a confidential tone had hitherto been definitely become confident and began to make a detour to take good wind. Mary tried to stop again, in their eyes at my mother and I had almost a plea, and I had no recourse but to try not to find them. He saw something in my face showed the torment to which I was subjected, for in his face pale and I noticed a strange resolution frown on it. On the continent of Carlos persuaded me that it was high time that I wanted to hear. She started to answer, and as his voice, though shaky, was clearer than he seemed to want, came to my ears these broken phrases.

It would have been better that you speak only with them ... Be estimating the honor you ... This negative ...

Carlos was puzzled: Maria was released from his arm, and an end of speaking playing with the hair of John, seizing her by the skirt showed him a bunch of tree pendant adorotes immediately.

I doubt that the scene I just described with accuracy as I can, which was estimated to be worth by Jerónimo, which hands into the pockets of his blue sucks, approached at that time with my father to This all happened as if he had heard.

Maria cleverly added to our group on the pretext of helping John to pick some berries he could not. As I had already taken the fruit to give it to the child, she told me to recibírmelas:

- How do I return not with this man?

Inevitably, I replied.

And I approached Carlos inviting him down a bit more for the plain for us to see a beautiful haven, and urged him as naturally as I could pretend, we came to bathe in the morning. Site was quaint but decidedly Carlos saw it, less than in any other, the beauty of the trees and the vines flowered bathing in the foam, like garlands unleashed by the wind.

The Sun at the end of dyed hide hills, forests and streams with topaz color glows, with gentle light and mysterious callers farmers 'Sun of the deer', probably because at that hour leave these people in the thickets to find pasture in the grasslands of the high blade or the bottom of the cactus growing between the cracks of the rocks.

By joining Carlos and I were the other group, they were about to take the road to the house, and my father, with an opportunity perfectly understandable, said Don Jeronimo:

-We should not spend from now infirm; return accompanied.

That said took Mary's hand to put it on his arm, leaving M. de M. .. take my mother and Emma.

They have been more gallant-we-told Carlos pointing to my father and to his.

And still, carrying me in her arms to John, who opened his own saying I had submitted:

-Let me moose, because there are thorns and I'm tired.

Mary Refirióme after my father had asked, they began to beat the cuestecillas of Vega, who had told Carlos, and as graciously insisted on to tell him, because she kept silent, resolved at last, well animated, tell what had responded to Carlos.

- You mean, my father asked almost laughing, heard the labored relationship she had just done-that is, that you will not marry ever?

Answered, shaking his head in denial, afraid to see it.

-Daughter, will you have already seen a boyfriend? Said my father said: Do not you say no?

-Yes I say Mary answered her very scared.

- Is it better that you've neglected handsome? And to tell you this, my father ran his right hand over his forehead to get face him. You think you're really pretty?

- Me?, No sir.

-Yes and you have said some many times. Tell me how is that lucky.

Mary trembled without daring to answer a word, when my father continued saying:

-The end of you deserve, you want it to be a useful man ... Come on, Confess, do not you have said that I have told you everything?

'But do not count.

- So you have secrets for your dad? 'He said looking at her affectionately and plaintively, which encouraged Mary to answer:

- Why, do not say you have to be told everything?

My father was silent for a while. It seemed that some memory apesaraba. They climbed the steps of the garden corridor when she heard him say:

- Poor Solomon!

And while passing one hand by the hair of his friend's daughter.

That night at dinner, the eyes of Mary to find me, began to reveal what between my father and she had passed. He would sometimes thoughtful, and I thought I noticed that her lips silently uttered some words, like you used to distracted with the verses that he liked.

My father tried, as he could, to make less difficult the situation of M. de M. .. and his son, who, so you could tell, had talked with Don Geronimo about what happened in the afternoon: every effort was useless. Having said since morning Mr M. .. that madrugaría next day, insisted that he must be very early in his estate, and retired with Carlos at nine in the evening, after having said goodbye to the family in the living room.

I accompanied my friend to his room. All my affection for him had been revived in the last few hours of his stay at home: the nobility of his character, that nobility that gave me so much evidence in our lives of students, magnified back to me. I could almost reprehensible the reservation I had been forced to use for him. If when I learned of his claims, I told myself, I had trusted my love for Mary, and in those three months it had become for me, him, unable to face the dire predictions made by the physician, had given up of its intent: and I, less loyal and more inconsequential, nothing would reproach me. Very soon, if not already understand them, you have to know the causes of my reservation, the reservation time that could have done so much harm. These reflections distressing me. The information received from my father to handle that case were such that it could open up to them. But no: what actually happened, what had to happen and it happened, was that love, taken possession of my soul forever, had made insensitive to any other feeling, blind as not to come to Mary.

As soon as we were alone in my room, I said, taking all the air of frankness student in his face without completely disappeared denouncing disgruntled:

-I have to apologize to you about a lack of confidence in your loyalty.

I wanted to hear and confidence, so scary for me the day before.

- What is missing? 'I replied: I have not noticed.

- What have not you noticed?

-No.

- Do not know the subject with my father and I came?

-Yes.

- Are you aware of the result of my proposal?

-Not good, but ...

-But you can guess.

-It's true.

-Good. So why not talk to you about what he intended, before contacting any other, before consulting with my father?

-An exaggerated delicacy of you ...

-There's no such delicacy, what occurred was clumsiness, lack of foresight, forgot … whatever you want, but that is not called as you call.

He paced the room, and then stopping in front of the chair which I occupied:

'Listen,' he said and admírate of my naivete. Caspita! I do not know what the hell good is it having lived twenty-four. A little over a year since I left you for ringing the Cauca, and wish you would have expected as much as you wanted. Since my arrival home I was subjected to the most obsequious attentions of your father and your family all: they saw me as a friend of yours, perhaps because they had done to know the kind of friendship that united us. Before you came, I saw two or three times to Miss Mary and your sister, and home visiting, and here. A month ago I talked my father would give me pleasure to wife taking one of the two. Your cousin had died in me, unbeknownst to her, all those memories of Bogotá tormented me so much, like I said my first cards. I agreed with my father to ask him for me the hand of Miss Mary. Why not see you tried before? It is true that the prolonged illness of my mother kept me in the city, but why do not you write? Do you know why? … I thought to make you the confidence to push yourself my pretensions was like something in my favor, and pride prevented me. I forgot you were my friend, you would have the right, you have to forget it too. But if your cousin had loved me, if it was not anything but the considerations your friendship I was right, it would have been love, what you would have consented to be my wife without her …? Go! I'm a fool to ask you, and you do not answer me very sane.

'Look,' he said after a moment he was leaning on the window: you know I'm not a man of those who are cast to die for these things: always remember that I laughed at the thought that faith in the great passions French dramas of those that made me sleep when you were reading me in the winter nights. What there is another thing: I have to marry, and flattered me the idea to go to your house, if your brother almost. It has not happened that way, but instead look for a woman who loves me without making me worthy of your hate, and …

- From my hatred! I exclaimed, interrupting him.

-Yes, dispenses my frankness. How childish … no … what would have been unwise to put myself in that situation! Bello result afflictions for your family, regret to me, and lost your friendship.

-Much to love you-continued after a pause; much, since few hours I have enough to know, despite what you've tried to hide it. Is not it true that you love and come to love when you thought you were eighteen?

'Yes,' I replied seduced by his noble frankness.

- What about your father ignores him?

-No.

- No? Asked admiringly.

Then he referred to the conference had days earlier with my father.

- Yea, everything, everything arrostras? -Questioned me amazed, I had just completed my relationship. And the disease is probably his mother? … So maybe you are spending half your life sitting on a grave? …

These last words made me shiver with pain: these, spoken by the mouth of a man who does nothing but affection for me could dictárselas, for Carlos, whom no hallucination deceived, had a solemnity terrible, more terrible than the yes with which I had to answer.

Púseme standing, and to offer my arms to Carlos, almost tenderly clasped me in his. I left him overwhelmed with sadness, but free of remorse and humiliated when I began our conference.

I returned to the living room. While my sister was rehearsing in a waltz guitar again, Mary told me that the conversation had taken the ride back to my father. He had never been so expansive with me remembering that dialogue, modesty often watched him eyes and pleasure playing him on the lips.

XXIX

The arrival of the post and the visit of Messrs. M. .. chores had gathered at my father's desk. We work all the next day, almost without interruption, but at times we meet with the family in the dining room, the smiles of Mary made me sweet promises to break time: they have me was possible mild to most drudgery .

At eight p.m. accompanied my father to his bedroom, and responding to my usual farewell, said:

'We've done something but we need much. So until early morning.

On days like this, Mary was waiting forever for the night in the hall, talking to Emma and my mother reading to a chapter of this *Imitation of the Virgin* or teaching prayers to children.

It seemed so natural that I needed to spend a few moments beside him in that hour, that's granted me as something that was not allowed to refuse. In the living room or dining room always reserved a seat me immediately to his, and a checkerboard or the cards served us an excuse to talk alone, less with words than with looks and smiles. Then his eyes in rapturous languor, fleeing not mine.

- Did you see your friend this morning? He asked, trying to find answers on my face.

-Yes, why are you asking me now?

'Because I could not do before.

- What interest you to know?

- Have you urged him to pay him a visit?

-Yes.

You're going to pay it,, right?

-Certainly.

-He loves you a lot, does not it?

-So I've always believed.

- And believe it yet?

- Why not?

- Do you want it like when you were both in school?

-Yes, but why talk about this now?

'It's because I want you you were always his friend, and that he continue to be so yours ... But you will have not said anything.

- Nothing to do?

-Well that.

- But of what?

-If you know what they say ... Do not you say no?

I delighted in the difficulty was to ask if she had talked about our love for Charles, and he replied:

It's the first time I do not understand you.

- Hail Mary! How do you not understand? What if you told about what ...

And as I was staying at her at the same time that your child smile I desire, continued:

'Well, do not tell me;-and began to make turrets with checkers that we played.

-If you do not look at me, I said no I confess what I said to Carlos.

-Yeah, well ... to see, di-answered me trying to do what I demanded.

-I have told everything.

- Ah, no, everything?

- Was I wrong?

Yes it must be so ... But then, why did not you tell before I came?

-My father opposed it.

-Yes, but he would not come, would not it have been better? -No doubt, but I should not, and today he is pleased with me.

- Will it be your friend?

-There is no reason to stop being so.

Yes, because I do not want for this ...

-Carlos will thank you as well as I that desire.

- So you separate from him as usual?. And he is gone? Happy?

-As happy as it was possible to get.

'But I have no guilt, right?

-No, Mary, not unless he believes you before you have done so.

-If you want to see, so it should be. And you know what happened all so with that sir?

- Why?

- But watch out laughing!

-I will not laugh.

-But if you're laughing.

It's not what you say but what you've said; di Maria.

'It was because I've prayed a lot to the Virgin to make everything happen so, since my mom told me yesterday.

- What if the Virgin not been granted what you asked?

-That was impossible always gives me what I ask, and as this time I prayed so much, I was sure I would hear. Mom is going, he added, and Emma is sleeping. You do not?

- You wanna go?

- What will I do? ... A lot will write tomorrow too?

-Apparently so.

- And when transit comes?

- What time comes?

-Sent word that at noon.

-At that time we will have completed. Tomorrow. Answered my farewell with the same words, but admiring me to stay with the handkerchief she was holding gave me closer. Mary did not understand that this was a treasure perfumed handkerchief to one of my nights. After nearly always refused to grant such a right, until the days came mingled our tears many times.

XXX

The next morning, my father dictated and I wrote while he was shaving operation that interrupted the work never started, however the care that she spent forever. His curly hair, still abundant in the back of the head, and leaving would infer how beautiful hair he wore in his youth, it seemed a little long. Falling half opening the door to the corridor, called my sister.

She's in the garden, Mary replied from my mother's sewing kit. Do you need something?

'Come you, Mary answered in time that I had some letters to the sign it concluded. Would you go down tomorrow? -I asked the first signing.

-Sure.

-It will be good, because there is much to do: going both desocuparemos us soon. Maybe Mr. A. .. write about his journey in this email: already late to tell you when to be ready. Enter, daughter added, turning to Mary, who waited outside to have found the door ajar.

She came giving us good morning. Whether you had heard the last words of my father on my trip, it could not do without their great shyness in front of it, the more so since he had spoken of our love, got a little pale. While he had just signed, the gaze of Mary blades paced the room, after having met secretly with mine.

'Look,' said my father smiling to show the hair-do not you think that I have a lot of hair?

She smiled at the answer:

-Yes, sir.

'Well, cut it out a bit. And took scissors to give them a case that was on one of the tables. I'll sit so you can do better.

That said, curl up in the middle of the room with his back to the window and us.

-Watch out, my daughter, when she said trasquilarme would begin. Are principiada the other letter? -She said to me.

-Yes, sir.

Began dictating talking to Mary while I was writing.

- So funny to you to ask you if I have a lot of hair?

'No, sir,' answered consultándome if the operation went well.

-For as you see, continued my father was so black and thick as others I know.

Maria released which had at that time in the hand.

- What is it? He asked, turning his head to see it.

-I'm gonna comb to cut better.

- Do you know why they fell and encanecieron so soon? He asked after dictating a sentence.

'No, sir.

-Care, child, wrong.

Mary blushed, looking at me with all the pretense that it was necessary for my father not noticing in the mirror of the bathroom table that was in front.

'Well, when I was twenty-continued-that is, when I got married, I used to bathe the head every day with cologne. What nonsense, right?

And yet she observed.

My father laughed that laugh that used sound harmonious.

I read the end of the sentence written, and he delivered another, continued its dialogue with Mary.

- Are you now?

'I think so, right? Consultándome he added.

When Mary was inclined to shake hair cuts that had fallen on the neck of my father, wearing a pink braids fell to him to toe. I was going to lift it, but my father had already taken. Mary returned to his place behind the chair, and he said after looking in the mirror carefully:

-Now I'll put you where he was, to reward you how well you did;-and approaching her, she said, placing the flower as gracefully as he could have done Emma: I can still be envious.

He stopped her who showed willing to withdraw for fear of what he might add, kissed him forehead and whispered:

-Today is not like yesterday, will end early.

XXXI

Eleven o'clock. After work, I was leaning on the window of my room.

Those moments of self-forgetfulness, that hovered in my mind that I almost regions were unknown, a time when the pigeons were in the shade on orange trees burdened by their gold clusters, loving cooed, in which voice Mary, yet sweet lullaby, reached my ears, had ineffable charm.

Childhood, in his insatiable curiosity is amazed that nature, divine enseñadora offers back to their looks, adolescence, guessing that all castes involuntarily delights visions of love ... feeling of a happiness so often expected in vain they know only those hours not bring in measures that the soul seems to strive to return to the delights of an Eden-dream or reality-who has not forgotten.

There were branches of roses, which took away the stream of lymphs petals mild to spruce fugitive was not the majestic flight of the black eagles on nearby peaks, that was not what my eyes, it was no longer 'll see, what my spirit broken by sad realities not only looking or admiring his dreams: the world watched entranced in the dawn of life.

I saw the black and winding road to the hills to Transit and father, who came in fulfillment of what Mary had promised. I crossed the garden and up the first hill to await them on the bridge of the waterfall, visible from the living room of the house.

As we were in the open, yet the Highlanders were short for me, told me all the things they used in passing a few days without seeing each other.

Braulio asked to Transit.

He was enjoying the lovely sunshine for revuelta.2l And the Madonna of the Chair?

Traffic and ask for Mary used since noticed the striking resemblance between the face of the future and godmother of a beautiful Madonna of the oratory of my mother.

-The living is good and waiting-I replied, graffiti, full of flowers and lighted to make you very happy.

So we approached the house, Mary and Emma went out to meet Transit, which said, among other entertainments, he was very good-looking, and it was true, as the embellished happiness.

Joseph received, hat in hand, the affectionate greetings of his ladies, and by breaking out the backpack that brought back full of beans for gift, came with us, urged by me, to my mother's room. On their way through the hall, Mayo, sleeping under a table, he snarled, and the mountain he said laughing:

- Hi, Grandpa! Still not love me? Is it because I'm as old as you.

- And Lucia? Asked Mary to Transit-why would not accompany you?

If so loose-no, and so montuna.

-But Ephraim says that he is not well-Emma watched him. Transit laughed before responding.

With Mr. is less shameful, because as is so often there has been losing fear.

We try to know the day that marriage had to be made. Joseph, to bail her daughter, said:

-We want to make today in eight days. If properly designed, will do so: at home much up early and not stopping, arrive at the village when the sun rears, leaving you out of here at five, we reach coming, and as the priest will have everything ready, we will dispatch early . Luisa is hostile parties, and girls do not dance we will, therefore, like every Sunday, with the difference that you will visit us, and Monday each in his office: do not you think? He concluded, turning to me.

-Yes, but how will the people walk Transit?

- Hey! Cried Jose.

- Then how? She asked admiringly.

-A horse, are not mine there?

-If I prefer to go on foot, and Lucia is not only that, but they are afraid of bestias22.

- But why? Emma asked.

-If in the province only whites go to horse father is not it?

-Yes, and those who are not white, when they are old.

- Who told you that you are not white-asked-Transit, and white as few.

The girl blushed like a cherry, to answer:

-Those are the people I say rich ladies.

Joseph, then he went to greet my father took leave promising to return in the evening, despite our request for him to stay and eat with us.

At five, as the family come out to accompany Transit to foot of the mountain, Mary, who was next to me, I said:

-If you had seen my goddaughter with the wedding dress that you've done, and the earrings and necklace that you have given Emma and Mommy, I'm sure you would have looked very pretty.

- Why do not you call me?

-Because Transit opposed. We have to ask Mom what they say and do the godparents at the ceremony.

-Really, godchildren and teach us what to respond to marry, if we will END to offer.

Neither the eyes nor lips of Mary responded to this reference to our future happiness, and remained pensive as we walked the short distance we needed to get to the edge of the mountain.

Braulio was there waiting for his girlfriend, and stepped forward to greet smiling and friendly.

-They are going to do at night to lower-Transit said.

They took leave of us affectionately Highlanders. He had admitted some space in the jungle when we hear good singing voice Braulio vueltas23 Antioquia.

After our conversation, Mary had not come to be cheerful. I vainly tried to hide the cause, well known for my bad: she thought to see the happiness of Traffic and Braulio, that soon we were going to separate, they may not see each other again ... perhaps the disease that had killed his mother. And I did not dare to disturb the silence.

Coming down the last hill, John, whom she held his hand, I said:

-Mary wants me to be nice to walk, and she is tired.

Ofrecíle then my arm to lean, which he could not do for attention to Emma and my mother.

We were now within walking distance of the house. The afterglow were going out that when the sun had left on the mountains of the West, the moon, rising over the mountains behind us that we walked away, the restless cast shadows of the willows and garden creepers dimly lit walls.

I spied the face of Mary, without her noticing, looking for symptoms of evil, which always preceded suddenly melancholy that had seized her.

- Why are you sad? I asked at last.

- I have not been for as long? He replied as if waking from a slumber. Do you?

'It's because you've been well.

-But how could I not be content?

-Back to be as cheerful.

- Alegre? Asked as-admired, what will you be as well?

'Yes, yes.

-Look, I'm like you, 'she said, smiling; Nothing more you demand? ...

-Just ... Ah! Yes: that which I have promised and have not given me.

- What is it? Would you believe that I do not remember?

- No? What about the hair?

- And if you notice the comb?

-You may say I was cutting a ribbon.

- Is this? She said after searching under the shawl, showing something that negreaba in hand and I hid it shut.

-Yes, that, give it to me now.

-If a tape resaving answered what I was shown.

Well, not the will demand more.

- So good! And then I have to do I cut? Is missing compose well, and am just ...

'Tonight.

-Also, tonight.

My arm gently pressed his naked of muslin and lace sleeve, his hand slowly rolled up to meet mine, the left likewise lift up my lips and leaning harder on me to climb the ladder corridor, told me in a slow voice silenced and vibration:

- Now if you're happy? Let's not be sad.

He wanted my father to read him that night something desktop the latest issue of The Day After the reading, he retired, and I went to the room.

John approached me and put his head on one of my knees.

- Do not sleep tonight? I asked stroking.

-I want you to make me sleep, 'he answered in that language that few could understand.

- And why not Mary?

'I am very angry with her, said settling better.

- With her? What have you done?

-If it is what I want tonight.

-Tell me why.

-I told him to tell me the story of the cap, and did not want, you've asked me kisses and not ignored.

Juan complaints made me fear that the sadness of Mary had continued.

And if tonight you fearful dreams I said to the boy she will not rise to accompany you, as you have mentioned that it does.

-So, tomorrow I will not help to get flowers for your room or take him to the bathroom combs.

'Do not say that, she loves you: go and tell him to give you kisses and you asked me to make you sleep hearing the story.

'No,' he said, standing up and as excited about a good idea: I'll scold traértela for that.

- Me?

I'm going to bring it.

So saying they went after him. Soon appeared in the role of the driving force of the hand. She smiled and asked:

- Where are you taking me?

'Here,' said John, forcing her to sit beside me.

Referee Mary everything he had talked his consent. She, taking John's head in his hands and touched his forehead, and said,

- Ah ungrateful! Go to sleep with him since.

Juan began to mourn holding out arms to take it.

-No, my love, no, my lord, she told him: your jokes are Mimiya;-and caressed.

But the child insisted that I received.

- So why do it with me, John? -Continued Mary quejándosele. Well, the Lord is man tonight I will take you to the room the bed of his brother and he does not need me, I'll stay alone and crying because I want more.?

He covered his eyes with one hand to make him believe that cried: Juan waited a moment, but as she persisted in pretend crying, slowly slipped from my knees, and approached her face trying to discover him. Finding Mary's lips smiling, and loving eyes, laughed too abrazándosele the waist and rested his head on her lap, saying:

-I love you like the eyes, I love you like the heart. I'm not brave or foolish. Tonight I will pray the very formal blessed that I do other pants.

-Show me pants that make you, 'I said.

John stood on the couch, between Mary and me, to make me admire his early shorts.

- How beautiful! I said hugging him. If you love me and are quite formal, you do get a lot, and I'll buy saddle, chaps, spurs ...

And a black horse he interrupted.

-Yes.

Abrazóme giving me a long kiss, and grabbed the neck of Mary, who turned his face to dodge the lips, forcing her to receive the same treat. He knelt where he had been standing with folded hands and prayed devoutly blessed sleepy rested in her lap she gave him.

I noticed that the left hand of Mary playing with something on the hair of the child, whereas a mischievous smile to her lips stuck out. With a quick glance showed me in the hair of John the loop that I had promised, and I hurried me to take them, when she, holding them, he said:

- And for me? ... exigírtelo may be bad.

- Mine? I asked.

Significóme yes, adding:

- Do not remain either in the same locket that I have of my mother?

XXXII

The next morning I had to make an effort for my father did not understand how painful it was to accompany me on a visit to the farms below. He, as it did every time I went to take a trip, however short it was, was involved in arranging everything, but it was not necessary, and repeated his orders more than usual. As it was necessary to take some delicate provisions for the week we were going to stay out of the house, provisions to which my father was very fond, laughing him to see that Emma and Mary accommodated in the dining room within cuchugos John Angel should be worn round the head of the chair, said:

- Good God, daughters! Does all that will fit there?

'Yes, sir,' said Mary.

'But this will do for a bishop. Aha! You're the most committed to spend not bad.

Mary, who was kneeling accommodating provisions, and gave him back to my father turned to say timidly time I got:

-For as many days are in to stay ...

-Not many, child replied laughing. For me it say I appreciate everything, but this guy gets so listless there ... Look, he added to me.

- What?

'Well, all I get. With such accoutrement can happen until I resolved to estarme fortnight.

-But if mom who has commanded 'observed Mary.

-Never mind, Jewish-and sometimes used to call when joking with her, everything is good, but I see here the last red wine, and there's not, it is necessary to carry.

-If it does not fit-Mary replied smiling.

'We'll see.

And personally went to the cellar for wine stating: returning with Juan Angel, also reloaded with some cans of salmon, repeated:

-Now we'll see.

- Does that also? She cried watching cans.

As my father was out of a can and wealthy cuchugo, Mary, alarmed, he observed:

-Is that it can not stay.

- Why, my daughter?

-Why is pasta that you love and ... because I did.

- And also for me? My father asked softly.

- Why, are not as wealthy?

-I say that ...

-She interrupted right back standing up. Here missing some tissues.

He disappeared to return a moment later.

My father, who was tenacious when joking, he said again in the same tone as before, bending to put something close to it:

-There will change for wine pasta.

She hardly dared to look at him, and noticing that lunch was served, he said, rising:

'It's the table set, sir-and turning to Emma: let a lack estefana what, she'll do well.

When I walked into the dining room, Mary left my mother's apartment, and stopped there.

-Short-now told the hair you want.

- Ah, no, I do not.

-Say from whence then.

-Where undetected. And I handed scissors.

He had opened the locket she wore hung around his neck. The box empty introducing myself, I said:

Put it here.

- What about your mother?

I'm going to put it up so you do not see yours.

Did so, saying:

'I think you're happy now.

-No, no, it is not to displease my father is so fair that I desire to help you manifest in your work and help you.

'True: it should be, and I will seek to show that I am also sad for Mom and Emma not suffer me.

Piénsame much-I said kissing his mother's hair and the hand with which he settled.

- Oh, a lot, a lot! Replied looking at me with that tenderness and innocence that twin knew so well in his eyes.

We split up to the dining room for different inputs.

XXXIII

The soles of seven days had gone over us, and late at night we were surprised their work. In the past, my father lying on a cot, dictated and I wrote. The clock struck ten classroom: I repeated the last word of the sentence he had written, he gave no more: then turned me believing that I had heard, and was fast asleep. He was a man relentless, but this time the work was excessive. Lowered the light in the room, I rolled the windows and doors, and waited until she woke up, pacing in the spacious hallway to the end of which was the desktop.

The night was calm and quiet: the vault of heaven, blue and clear, looked all the brilliance of your summer clothes, in black foliage ceibas rows that starting from the sides of the building closed the patio, in the branches of the orange that lingered in the background candelillas24 countless fluttering, and only occasionally perceived the cracking of the branches attached, the flutter of a frightened bird or wind sighs.

The white portico fronting the building that opened into the courtyard, stood out in the darkness of the plain projecting their capitals on the formless mass of distant mountain ranges whose peaks appeared at times illuminated by flashes of Pacific storms.

Mary told me, listening to the whispers remained quiet, breaths of that nature in his dream-Mary will sleep smiling at the thought that tomorrow I will be back to your side ... But then! That was terrible after was my trip.

I seemed to hear the gallop of a horse person to cross the plain, I assumed it would be a servant who had been sent to the city for four days, which looked forward to, because I had to bring important correspondence. A little closer to home.

- Camilo? I asked.

'Yes, master,' said handing me a pack of cards after praising God.

The noise woke the spurs of the page to my father.

- What is this, man? Inquired the newcomer.

-I dispatched twelve, my master, and as the spill reaches the Guayabo Cauca had to linger much in step.

-Well: Feliciana tell you to eat right place, and takes great care that horse.

My father had reviewed the signatures of some of the letters containing the package, and finally finding he wanted, he said:

-Start with this.

I read aloud some lines, and at a certain point I stopped involuntarily.

He took the letter, and with pursed lips, as he devoured the contents with eyes, finished reading the paper and threw it on the table saying:

- That man has killed me!, Read that letter: what happened after your mother feared.

I picked up the letter to convince me that it was true what I imagined.

High-added-Leela my father pacing the room and wiping the sweat dampened his forehead.

-That has no remedy said just concluded. What amount and in what circumstances? ... I am the only culprit.

I interrupted to express the means by which we could avail ourselves believed to make less severe loss.

'That's true with any observed hearing me and calmly, and will. But who would have feared! I will die without having learned to distrust men.

And telling the truth many times in your business life had received the same lessons. One night, while he was in the city without the family, came to his room a dependent who had commanded the Chocoes considerable change effects for gold, sending urging foreign creditors. The agent said:

-I come to you to give me money to pay the freight of a mule, and a bullet: I played and lost everything you gave me.

- All, all is lost? -He asked my father.

-Yes, sir.

-Take that drawer you the money you need.

He called one of his pages added:

-The Lord just in: notifies inside to be served.

But those were different times. Windfalls have to suffer in youth with indifference, without uttering a complaint: then trust the future. Those received in old age seem cowardly struck by an enemy: it's just the distance remaining to the grave ... And, how rare are the friends who can be dying for his widow and his children! The many breath spying last of one whose hand, frost and are shaking, only to become the executioners of orphans! ...

Three hours had passed since the end of the scene I have just described as the memories I have left of that fatal night, which had to be like so many years later.

My father, a bed-time, he said from his bed, a few steps distant from mine:

-It should hide your mother as possible what has happened, and will also be necessary to delay our return another day.

Although he had always heard that his peaceful sleep relief served in all the misfortunes of life, when a bit of me talking and I was convinced that he was sleeping, I saw in his sleep as intrepid resignation, had such courage in his calm , I could not stay for much less contemplating space.

Dawn had not yet, and I had to go in search of better air to calm the kind of fever that had tormented me for the sleepless night. Only the song of Titiribi and the neighboring forest guacharacas heralded the dawn: nature seemed to stretch on waking from sleep. At the first light of day began to flutter in the banana groves and poke and tiles; pairs of pigeons undertook trip to neighboring fields, the outcry of flocks of parrots mimicked the sound of a bustling creek, and the blooming of We tread the cocoa, herons stood with mild and slow flight.

Not admire those songs again, to breathe those aromas, to contemplate those landscapes full of light, as in the happy days of my childhood and the beautiful of my adolescence: strangers live today with my parents!

Apagábase afternoon the next day, when my father and I climbed the green skirt stretched to reach the house of the saw. The mares grazing on the sidewalk and then lead us chugging along frightened, and pellares stood on the banks of the streams to threaten us with their singing and gyrations.

And we could see closely the western corridor, where the family was waiting for us, and my father went there to take care conceal the cause of our delay and to seek to appear calm.

XXXIV

Not all the people who were waiting in the corridor: not found among them Mary. Some blocks before reaching the patio door on our left and on one of the large stones which overlooks the valley better, she was standing, and Emma encouraged her to come down. We approached them. Mary's hair, long, loose curls shining, negreaba on muslin green suit mortiño: sat down to prevent the wind stir the skirt, saying to my sister, who laughed at their eagerness:

- Can not you see I can not?

-Girl-my father told surprised and smiling-how have been jump there?

She, ashamed of mischief, just correspond to our greetings and answered

As we were alone ...

-That is my father interrupted him-we should go so you can get off. And how Emma got?

-That's funny, if I helped.

It was that I was not scared.

-Come, then, my father concluded addressing me but watch ...

I knew he'd stay. Mary had just told me with his eyes: "Do not go." My father remounted and headed for the house: my horse slowly followed suit.

-Over here was where we went-I told Mary and dimples showing some cracks in the rock.

When I finish my climbing maneuver, I reached out, too shaky to help, but really want to keep me hasten to clasp in mine. I sat down at her feet and she said:

- Do not you see what work? What will be the dad?. He'll think we're crazy.

I looked at her without answering: the light in her eyes, cowardly before mine, and the soft pallor of her cheeks, I said, as at other times, that this was her as happy as I am.

'I'm single repeated Emma, who had misheard her first threat, and walked a few steps to make us believe that he would comply.

-No, no, wait for us a moment-no more Mary pleaded rising.

Seeing that I did not move, he said:

- What is it?

-It is good that we are here.

-Yes, but Emma wants to leave and mom will be waiting for: help me down, now I have no fear. To see your handkerchief.

I squirmed adding:

-You got to this point, and when I reach to shake hands, I'll get it from him.

Convinced that lower risk could not be seen, he did as he had planned, and telling the foot of the cliff:

- And you now?

Seeking the least high stone Gramal jumped to, and offered his arm to dirigiésemos us home.

-If I had not come, what would you have done to lose?, Loquilla.

'Well, have fallen one: going down when you arrived, but I feared falling because it was very windy. Yesterday we went there too, and I got well.

- Why have taken so long?

-For letting concluded some business that could not be arranged from here. What did you do these days?

-Want to pass.

- Is that all?

Sewing-brainer.

- What?

-In many things you think and do not say.

- Not to me?

-To you less.

'All right.

-Because you know them.

- Did not you read?

No, because it makes me sad to read alone, and I do not like stories of *the Fifth evenings or afternoons Farm*. Was going to re-read *Atala*, but as you said you have a ticket somehow. ..

And to my sister who preceded us a few steps:

-Hey, Emma ... What eagerness to go so fast?

75

Emma paused, smiled and kept walking.

- What were you doing at ten night before?

- Last night? Ah! 'Said stopping-why do you ask?

-At that time I was very sad thinking about those things you think and do not say.

-No, no, you do.

- Yes what?

-Yes you can say them.

'Tell me what you did, and I will tell you.

'I'm afraid.

- Fear?

-Maybe it's a nonsense. She was sitting on the porch with Mom on this side, keeping him company, because I was not sleepy said: heard that sounded like the leaves of your bedroom window, and fearful that I had left open, the room took a light to go see what had ... Nonsense: scare me again when I remember what happened!

-Just because.

-Open the door, and saw perched on a leaf of the window, waving in the wind, a black bird and size like a large pigeon: I squealed had never heard before, seemed dazzled a moment with the light I had in hand, and turned it off passing overhead at run time we were frightened. That night I dreamed ... But why have you been so?

- How? I replied, hiding the impression that this story caused me.

What she told me had happened at the very hour when my father and I read the letter unfortunate, and the black bird was the same that I had hit the temples during the storm of the night that Mary was repeated access; the same as in awe, and heard buzzing over my head sometimes at sunset.

- How? Mary replied to me I see I was wrong to refer that.

- And you figure that?

-Not that I suppose.

- What do you dream?

-I must not tell you.

- Not later?

- Ah, maybe never.

Emma was opening the patio door.

-Wait for us-Mary said hey, that now it is really.

We meet her, and walked the two hold hands as we needed to get the runner. Sentíame dominated by an indefinable dread, was afraid of something, but I could not guess why, but fulfilling my father's warning, I tried to control myself, and I was as calm as I was possible, until I retired to my room under the pretext of changing my costume way.

XXXV

The next day, December 12, was verified Transit marriage. After arrival they sent word to

Joseph that would be between seven and eight in the parish. Habíase purposed that my mother, Mary, Philip and I would be the ride, because my sister had to stay fixing not know what gifts to be sent early in the morning to the mountain, so that there encontrasen grooms on their return.

That night, after the dinner, my sister played guitar sitting on a sofa in the corridor to my room, and Mary and I were talking reclining on the railing.

Have-I-say-something bothering you, and I can not guess.

-But what can it be? Do not you see me happy? I have not been as you expected it would be to return to your side?

-No, you have made efforts to show well, and yet I have never figured out what you, that pretended.

- But you?

-Yes.

You're right, I am pretending to live clarified.

'No, sir, I do not say always, but tonight.

-Always.

-No, it was today.

-Going for four months living cheating ...

- Me too? ... Me? You fool me!

And see my eyes was to confirm for them what they feared, but as I was laughing at his eagerness, as if ashamed of it said:

-Explain that.

-If you have no explanation.

-For God, for ... for God's sake, tell me.

'Everything is true.

- Not!

'But let me conclude: to get back what you just think, I will not tell if you beg me so you know that I love most.

-I do not know what will.

'Then convince yourself that you have deceived.

-No, no, and I'll tell you, but how I can tell?

-Think.

'I thought,' said Mary after a moment's pause.

-Say it.

-So you want more after God and your ... I want it to be me.

'No, not so.

- And what then? Ah! Is that what you say is true.

-Di otherwise.

I'm going to see, but if you want this time ...

- What?

-Nothing, hey: do not look.

'Do not look.

Then he decided to say very softly.

-By Mary you ...

-I Love Therefore I concluded, taking my hands in hers that his gesture confirming his innocent plea.

Tell me and insisted.

'I've been cheating, because I have not dared to confess how much I love you really.

- More yet! And why did not you tell me? 'Because I've been afraid ...

- Fear of what?

-That you love me less, less than I do.

- Is that why? Then you are deceived.

-If you would have told me ...

- What the eyes do not say these things without one want?

- Do you think so?

-Because yours have taught me. Now tell me the reason why you've been so tonight. Did you see the doctor these days?

-Yes.

- What did he say about me?

-The same as before: you'll never have novelty, not talk about it.

-One word and no more: what else did he say? The thought that my illness is the same as my mother ... and perhaps he is right.

- Oh, no: I never said. And you're not, then, good now?

-Yes, and yet many times ... I have often thought with horror of this evil. But I have faith that God heard me: I've asked so fervently that I give back ...

'Maybe not as much as me.

-Ask him forever.

-Always, Mary. Look, it is true that there is a cause for you like I have tried to be calm tonight, but you see I've done a long time ago forgotten.

I told him that we had received the news two days ago.

- And that black bird! I concluded then said, and returned with horror gaze to my room.

- How can you worry so much with a chance?

'I dreamed that night that is what worries me.

- Do you remain not tell me?

Not today, someday. Conversemos time with Emma before you go: it's so good to us ...

Within half an hour we broke up very early promising to start our trip to the parish.

Before the five named Juan Angel at my door. Felipe and he made such a noise in the corridor preventing mounting and securing harness horses, which they had expected before I came to his aid.

Prepared all, Mary opened the classroom door: introducing myself a cup of coffee, wearing two estefana, I said good morning, and then Philip called for him to receive the other.

-Today itself it said grinning. What is fear, and the Retinto is furious.

She was as bewitching as my eyes had to tell him: a graceful black velvet hat trimmed with ribbons and buckled under Scottish beard with other peers, which could be seen on the wing, half hidden by the veil blue dotted still a rose dew lay on the thick, shining braids whose limbs hid: arrezagaba the hands with a black skirt, belting under a bodice of the same color, a blue belt diamond brooch, and a broad layer is apparent from the shoulders in many folds.

- In which horse you want to go? I asked.

-In Retinto.

- But that can not be! I replied surprised.

- Why? Are you afraid that I boat?

-Of course

-If I've ridden in it again. Am I as before? Ask Emma if it is not true that I'm prettier than her. You see what is the Retinto tame me.

-But if not allowed to be touched, and doing so while not ride, can be frightened with the skirt.

-I promise not to show even the whip.

Philip Knight and the Goat, which was the name of the horse chestnut, suffocating him with his new spurs, crossing the yard.

My mother was also apperceived to go: put it on your favorite roan, unique, according to her, it was a beast. No I was very quiet when I ride the Retinto to Mary: she, before jumping to the rack to tortoise, patted the horse's neck, restless until then: it froze waiting for loading, and bit the brake, attentive even the slightest sound of clothing.

- See? -Mary and told me about the animal, and he knows me: when Dad bought it for you, this hand was sick, and I did that Juan Angel cure him well all afternoon.

The restless horse sneezed again, because surely knew that voice caressing.

We left, and Juan Angel drove us over the head of the chair containing the mess they needed dresses ladies in town.

The beast of Mary, smug with their weight, seemed to look softer step and graceful: her mane of raven shaking on arched neck, and falling through the ears short and restless, importunate watched her bright eyes. Mary went into it with the same air of abandonment naturally when resting on a soft armchair.

Having walked several blocks, seemed completely lost him fear the horse, and I was feeling uneasy about the spirit of the animal, so I told my mother not come on hear:

I'm going to give it a fuetazo, one.

-Watch it.

-It is one only, so you see that nothing does. You are ungrateful to Retinto because you want more that you're going gray.

- Now that you know that much, it will not!

-On this night you were going to call the doctor.

- Oh, yes, it is an excellent animal.

And after all, not estimates as it deserves.

-You less because you mortify unnecessarily.

-You will see that it does nothing.

- Beware, beware, Mary! Me a favor and give me the whip.

'I'll leave it for later, when we get to the plains.

And he laughed at the anxiety that I wore with such a threat.

- What is it? Asked my mother, who was already on our side, because I had shortened the step to that end.

'Nothing,' said Lady Mary: Ephraim is convinced that the horse is going to bounce.

'But if you ... I started to answer, and she surreptitiously putting fuetecito handle on the lips as though to be quiet, then handed it to me.

- And why are you so brave today! Asked my mother. The other time I rode a horse that you were afraid.

And had to change it for you, said Philip.

-You are making me very badly, 'said Mary be flushed-looking: the man was already convinced that I was beautiful.

- So you're not afraid now? My mother insisted.

-I have answered 'Yes' but not both, because the horse has been tamed, and as some people scold if heaves ...

When we got to the Pampas, the sun, and the mists torn entoldaban mountains behind us, wrapped in metallic glow strips forests in tortuous or remote isolated groups interrupted the plain of the creeks lymphs vadeábamos, polished ran by that light lost in the shadows, and seemed distant Zabaletas riots liquid silver and blue fringed by forests.

Mary left then drop the veil on his face, and through the restless sky-colored gauze, sometimes my eyes sought hers, to which all the splendor of nature around us I was almost indifferent.

As we set out in the big woods, crossed the plain, long time ago that Mary and I we kept silence, only Philip had not interrupted his talk with a thousand questions about how much my mother saw.

In a time when Mary was close to me, I said:

- What do you think so? You are again like last night, and just now it was not. Is it so big that misfortune has happened?

-No thought of her, you make me forget.

- Is it as inevitable that loss?

'Perhaps not. In what I've been thinking about is the happiness of Braulio.

- In his only?

-I is easier to imagine the Braulio. He will be quite happy today, and I'm going to be away, I'll leave you for many years.

She had heard me without looking at me, and finally lifting eyes, which had not been off the glow of happiness that shone on that morning, said lifting the veil:

- That loss is not as great?

- Why do you insist on talking about it?

- Can not you guess? Only I have thought so, and this convinces me that I should not trust you with my thoughts. I'd rather not have seen me're happy cheerful today after what you told me last night.

- And that news caused you joy?

-Sadness when I gave it to him but later ...

-Then what?

I thought otherwise.

-What made you move from sadness to joy.

-Not so much, but ...

-Be as you are today.

- Do not tell? I knew you could not like me so, and I do not think I can be foolish.

- Did you? And you would think that can happen?

- Why not? I am a girl capable as anyone else, to see things not as they should be serious.

-No, you're not well.

'Yes, sir, yes, at least until I apologize. But let's talk a while with mom, lest much surprised that converses with me and meanwhile I will resolve to tell you everything.

So we did, but after a quarter of an hour, my horse and Maria again mate. We went back to the campaign and watched the turret whitewash parish and color the rooftops amid the foliage of orchards.

-Say, Mary, 'I said then.

'You see that you are willing to excuse yourself. What if the reason I'm going to say is not enough? Would have been better not to be happy, but as you refused to teach me to pretend ...

- How to teach what you do not know?

- What a great memory! I forgot what you said last night? I will take advantage of that lesson.

- Since today?

-From now replied smiling as seriously trying to pretend. Hey, since I have not been able to do without being happy today, because after we parted last night, I thought of the loss suffered by dad, can be ... And what would he think of me if you knew this?

-Explain yourself, and I'll tell you what to think.

-If that amount is lost is much-resolved to tell me then, combing the mane of the horse with the whip handle, he had already returned, Dad ... you need more, he will consent to you to help him from Now ...

-Yes, yes, I answered his gaze dominated shy and anhelosa to confess what could show both the guilty suspicious.

- So is not it?

My father-relieve you of the promise I have made to send to Europe to finish my studies, I will promise to fight by his side until the end to save his credit, and he will consent, must consent ... So we split up you and I never ... not separate us. And then suddenly ...

Without looking up I meant yes, and through her veil, which was playing with the breeze, her modesty was the modesty of an angel.

When we reached the village, came to greet us and tell us Braulio that the priest was waiting. My mother and Mary had changed clothes, and went out.

The old priest, seeing us approach his house next to the church, met us, inviting us to lunch with him, for which we apologize when we finely.

At the ceremony empezarse, Braulio's face, though somewhat pale, denounced his happiness. Transit doggedly looked down, and said in an agitated voice to reach out the turn, Jose, placed beside the priest, shaky hand wielded with one of the candles, and his eyes, which were constantly passing the priest's face to that of her daughter, if you could not tell they were watery, yes they had cried.

While the minister blessed the bride and groom holding hands, Transit dare look at her husband: in that look was love, humility and innocence, was the only one that could promise the man she loved, after he had just pronounce before God.

We hear all the mass, and to leave the church Braulio told us that while they rode the people would come, but that's not very far would reach.

Within half an hour we gave scope to the cute couple and Joseph, who carried forward the old mule that had led Rucia with gifts for the priest, vegetables for the market and the clothing of the boys gala. Traffic was only because her Sunday dress, and the wedding did not suit her best: panama hat, which fell below the braids on black shawl of purple attic: pink gingham skirt with many boleros and slightly gathered for rid of the dew of Gramal, revealed sometimes their beautiful feet, and her veil, upon discovery, white shirt and black silk embroidered red.

We shorten the step to go with them for a while and wait for my mother. Traffic was with Mary, taking the skirt fluff that had collected in the grassland: spoke little, and in his bearing and countenance discovered a set of such modesty, appreciation and pleasure, it is hard to imagine.

As we parted from them promising to go to the mountain that afternoon, Transit Mary smiled with a sweetness almost hermanal: it retained between his hand timidly offered her goddaughter, saying:

-I am very sorry to think that you're going to go all the way on foot.

- Why, Miss?

- Miss?

-Godmother, right?

'Yes, yes.

-Good. We'll go slowly, right? -He said to the Highlanders.

Braulio answered 'Yes' and if you are not ashamed today also lean on me to climb the steep slopes, you will not get so tired.

My mother, who with Philip overtook us at the time, called Joseph to carry next day the family to eat with us, and he was committed to strive for it that way.

The conversation became general during the return, what Mary and I will try to distract my mother, who complained of fatigue, as always rode horses. Just as we approached the house I told Mary in voice only I could hear:

- Are you going to say that today Dad?

-Yes.

-Do not tell today.

- Why?

'Because.

- When do you want me to tell?

-If after these eight days do not speak any trip, find occasion to tell. And you know what is the best? One day after you have worked a lot together: then it is known that he is grateful for what you help.

-But in the meantime I can not stand the impatience that I will not knowing whether to accept.

- What if he does not agree?

- Do you fear?

-Yes.

- What do we do then?

-You, obey.

- Do you?

- Ah, who knows.

-You must think I agree, Mary.

-No, no, because if I cheated, I know that this deception would a great evil. But do as I say and may be that everything goes well.

XXXVI

We had arrived. I missed seeing the windows of the room closed my mother. He had helped her to alight and was doing the same with Mary while Heloise came out to greet, sign insinuándonos noise we did not.

'Dad,' he said has become a lie, because he is sick.

Mary and I could only assume the cause, and our eyes met to tell him. She and my mother immediately went to see my father, and I followed them. As he knew that we had worried, stammering voice told us the chills:

'It's nothing, maybe I got up without caution, and I have a cold.

His hands and feet stiff and feverish forehead.

Within half an hour, and my mother Mary were already in costume house. Lunch was served, but they did not go to the dining room. As I rose from the table, Emma came to tell me that my father called me.

Fever was taken increase. Mary was standing and leaning against one of the columns of the bed beside Emma and my mother at the bedside.

-Turn off some of those lights, 'said my father while I walked.

Only one had, and was on the table that hid the curtains.

-Here is Ephraim and told my mother-.

We thought he had not heard. After a moment, he said to himself:

-It has but one remedy. Why not come to dispatch of Ephraim after all?

I pointed out that was present.

'Well,' continued bring them to sign them.

My mother leaned his forehead on one hand. Mary and Emma tried to find out, looking at me, if there were really such letters.

-So you are more rested and despatched everything better.

- What a man, what a man! Murmured, and then lethargic stayed.

Llamóme my mother to the living room and said:

'I think we should call the doctor, what do you say?

I think it should be called, because, although the fever passes, nothing is lost to make her come, and if ...

-No, she interrupted: whenever he starts like illness is serious.

After I sent a page for the doctor, I went back to my father, who called me again.

- What time again? He asked.

-More than one hour.

- Where is your mother?

I'm going to call her.

-Who knows nothing.

'Yes, sir, are you peaceful.

- Did you put the postscript to the letter?

-Yes, sir.

- Did you get the cabinet that correspondence and receipts?

We dominated, insurance, the idea of remedying the loss he had suffered. I had heard my mother this last dialogue, and as he seemed to fall asleep, I asked:

- Have you had your father some trouble these days? Have you received any bad news? What you do not want me to know?

'Nothing has happened, nothing is hidden from you I replied pretending as naturally as I could.

-So, what does this delirium? Who is the man who seems to complain? ... What letters talk so much?

I can not guess, ma'am.

She was not satisfied with my answers, but I should not give others.

At four in the afternoon came the doctor. The fever had subsided, and the patient remained delirious in some times, sluggish at others. All home remedies for cold course were applied until then had been ineffective.

Having the doctor willing to prepare a bath and you need to apply suction cups to my father, went with me to my room. While confeccionaba a potion, I tried to tell her about the disease concept.

'It's probably a brain fever,' he said.

- And that pain complains that in the region of the liver?

-It has to do with the other, but not negligible.

- Does it seem to you very grave evil?

-So these fevers usually start, but if you attack time is achieved often overcome. Is his father fatigued much these days?

'Yes, sir, we were up yesterday in the estates below and had a lot to do.

- Have you had a setback, a serious dislike?

-I think I should talk to you with the frankness that the circumstances require. Three days ago I received the news that his with a business whose success needed to have, had miserable.

- And he did that much impression? Excuse me if I speak to you this way, I think it essential. Sometimes you will have during their studies, and more frequently in practice, to be convinced that there are diseases coming from suffering mood disguised with other symptoms, or complicated with the most known to science.

-You can be pretty sure that misfortune that I have spoken to has been the main cause of the disease. Yes it is necessary to warn you that my mother does not know what happened, because my father so wanted to avoid the regret was accordingly.

-All right: you have done well in talk that way: is true that I know prudently take advantage of secrecy. Feel all that much! Now we will go by way more known. Come said standing up and taking the cup that had mixed drugs-: I think this will do very good effect.

It was now two o'clock. The fever had not surrendered a point.

The doctor, after watching until that time, I hail retired pleading if there was any symptom.

The room, sparsely lit, was in deep silence.

My mother sat in a chair near the head: the movement of his lips and the direction of their gaze, fixed on a *eccehomo,* hung over the door leading into the lounge room, could know who prayed. Already, by the words of my father rave had tied, anything that happened was hiding. At the foot of the bed, kneeling on a sofa, and half hidden by the curtains, Mary tried to return the heat to the feet of the patient, who had complained of cold again. I approached her to say very softly:

-Retire to rest awhile.

- Why? He replied, raising his head, which was resting on one arm: head disheveled as beautiful in the evening when it was decorated beautifully as the previous morning walk.

-Because you will do wrong to spend all night awake.

-Do not believe it, what time is it?

-It's going on three.

'I'm not tired: soon to dawn: while you sleep, and if necessary I will call.

- How are your feet?

- Ah, very cold.

-Let me replace there a while, and then I'll retire.

'All right,' said getting up gingerly to not make a sound.

He handed me the brush, smiling to show me how I should take it to scrub plants. After I had taken his place, he said:

-It is but for a moment, while I see what has John and back.

The little boy had awakened and called her, missing not see it close. There was then the quiet voice of Mary, saying sweet nothings to John, to get not get up, and the sound of kisses stroking it. Soon the clock to give the three: Mary turned to claim me his seat.

- Is it time to drink? I asked.

'I think so.

-Ask my mother.

Taking this potion and I light, we approached the bed. Our calls my father opened his eyes, markedly injected, and tried to shade them with one hand, bothered by light. He was urged to take the drink. Sat up again complaining of pain on the right side: and after examining with uncertain look about him, said a few words in which there was "thirst".

-This is the calm-my mother watched him presenting the cup.

He sank into the pillows, saying to take both hands to the brain:

- Here!

Met again to make an effort to get up, but to no avail.

My mother's face left prostration know what that's unnerving.

Mary sitting on the edge of the bed and propped on pillows, said the sick with loving voice:

-Dad, try to take this up, I'll help.

'Now, daughter replied weakly.

She managed to lay him down on his chest, as he held the back with his left arm. Mary Black braids shaded gray head and venerable that they so lovingly offered her womb by her pillow.

After taking the potion, my mother handed me the cup and Mary returned to my father gently placed on the pillows.

- Oh! Jesus! How has prostrated! -I said it very quietly, then we were near the table where she placed light.

'That drink is narcotic-I pointed to reassure.

-But the delirium is not as constant as. What has the doctor said?

-It is necessary to wait a little more energetic remedies.

'Go to bed, that we are now, hey, are the three thirty. I wake up to Emma to accompany me, and you also get Mom rest awhile.

'You've gone pale, this is going to make a lot of damage.

She was in front of the vanity mirror of my mother, and looked at him running his hands through the temples for medium hair grooming to answer:

-Not so: see how nothing I note.

-If you rest for a while now, it may be, I will call when it is day.

Get all three leave me alone, and I sat at the bedside.

The patient continued restless sleep, and is sometimes perceived delirium slurred words.

For an hour paraded in my imagination all the horrific pictures that would come after a disaster, in which I could not stop thinking without my heart contracted painfully.

It began to dawn, some bright lines coming through the cracks in the doors and windows of the lamp light was becoming more and more pale and could hear the chants of coclíes and domestic birds.

He entered the doctor.

- Have they called you? I asked.

-No, it is I need to be here now. How has it continued?

I pointed out what I had observed, his pulse, while looking at his watch.

Absolutely nothing, as he said to himself. Does the drink? She added.

-La has taken again.

-Give him another shot, and not to bother him again, I will now caustics.

Hicímoslo all helped by Emma.

The doctor was visibly worried.

XXXVII

After three days, the fever still resisting all efforts to combat health care: the symptoms were so alarming, that he or she could hide at times the anxiety that dominated him.

It was twelve o'clock. The doctor called me disimu-ladamente the hall to tell me:

-You do not know the danger he is her father and I have no other hope that I have in the effects of copious bleeding that I will give, for which it is prepared properly.

If she and the medications taken this afternoon here at dawn produced an excitement and a growing frenzy, hard to get as a crisis. It's time to show you he continued after a pause if coming the day has not appeared this crisis, nothing remains for me to do. For now, do you remove the lady, because what happens or does not want, she should not be in the room's past midnight, and that's a good excuse to take some rest beg. If you it sees fit, the ladies also pray to be left alone.

I noticed that he was sure that they would resist and that since they got, what more could desconsolar my mother.

I see that you are in charge of what is happening, without losing the value that the case requires, 'he said carefully examined in the light of the plug immediately, lancets from its holster pocket. Do not despair yet.

We left the room to go to put into practice what he considered as a last resort.

My father was dominated by the same torpor: during the day and the night so far had not stopped delirium. His immobility was something that produced recent depletion forces: almost deaf to every call, only the eyes, which opened with difficulty sometimes let know he heard, and his breathing was anhelosa.

My mother wept sitting at the head of the bed, resting his forehead against the pillows and taking the hands of my father's. Emma and Mary, helped by Luisa, that night had come to replace their daughters, preparing supplies for the bathroom that is going to give the bleeding.

Mayn called light; Mary approached the bed rolled down his face as he reluctantly few tears as the doctor was doing the exam he wanted.

At the time, finished and all that the doctor estimated as end resort, said:

-When the clock strikes half past two, I should be here, but if I miss the dream, call me.

Noting the patient then he added:

-You must stop completely calm.

He retired after saying some joke almost smiling girls on the need for the old-time sleeping: cheerfulness worthy thanked for because he had no other object than to reassure them.

My mother went back to see if what I had for an hour been doing dildo had any effect, but we managed to convince her that the doctor was full of hope for the next day, and overwhelmed by fatigue, fell asleep in the department of Emma, where Luisa was keeping him company.

The clock struck two.

Mary and Emma knew because the doctor wanted the manifestation of certain symptoms, and peered curiously anhelosa long with my father's dream.

The patient seemed quiet, and had asked once water, but with a weak voice, quite intelligible, which made them conceive hope that the indentation produced good results.

Emma, after futile efforts to prevent it, he fell asleep in the chair that was at the head of the bed. Mary, reclining at first in one arm of the small sofa we occupied, had dropped on it, surrendered at last, head, whose profile highlighted in the color purple damask cushions, having been unmasked the wearing silk shawl , negreaba rolled on the snowy lawn of the skirt, which seemed faded with boleros, in favor of the shade, made of foam. In the silence that surrounded us was perceived her breathing, soft as a child who has fallen asleep in our arms.

The clock struck three. The clock noise did make a slight movement to join Mary, but was again the most powerful dream I will. Sunk in the garment waist that she fell to the carpet, a foot was visible almost childlike, footwear with a dotted red sequin slipper.

I gazed with inexpressible tenderness, and my eyes, turned sometimes into the bed of my father, tornaban get it, because my soul was there, stroking the face, listening to the beating of the heart, every moment expecting to hear some word I reveal any of your dreams, because his lips as trying balbucirla.

A sick painful groan that broke my spirit reliever alienation, and reappeared as frightening reality was.

I approached the bed, my father, who was leaning on one arm, looked at me with tenacious force, after saying:

-Bring me the clothes, it's too late now.

-It is night, sir, 'I replied.

- How the night? I want to get up.

'It's impossible, he observed quietly. Do not you see that would cause a lot of damage?

He dropped his head back on the cushions, and quietly uttered words I did not understand, shaking hands pale and emaciated, as if he were making an account. Seeing find something to him, I presented my handkerchief.

'Thanks,' he said, as if talking to a stranger, and after wiping his lips with him, looked on the bedspread that covered him, a pocket for storage.

He fell asleep several times. I approached the table to tell the time in that delirium had begun, when he sat on the bed and pulling back the curtains that hid the light, revealed head look pale and astonished, saying:

- Who's there? ... Hello! Hello!

Overcome fear of certain invincible, despite what promised that delirium so like madness, tried to reduce it to go to bed. Nailing me a look almost terrible, asked:

- Was not he here? At this time has risen from that chair.

- Who?

Said the name that I feared.

A quarter of an hour, she sat up again stronger voice telling ya:

-Do not allow to enter, I wait. To see the clothes.

I begged him not to insist on getting up, but imperative tone replied:

Oh! What nonsense! ... The clothes!

It occurred to me that Mary, who had exerted on him in such moments as powerful influence, could help, but I decided to separate myself from the bed, afraid that my father get up. The state of real weakness was that prevented him from prolonged sitting, and leaned back seemingly quiet. Then I went to Mary, taking her hand and hung it on the side, I called very softly. She, without taking his hand from mine, joined without opening his eyes, but then he saw me quickly cover their shoulders with the shawl, and standing said:

- What does it take, huh?

-It-I replied that delirium has begun, and I want you to accompany me if the access is very strong.

- How long?

-Go for an hour.

He went to bed almost happy for the good news that I gave her, and tiptoed away from him, came to me:

'But he's asleep again.

-You will see that it is short.

- Why I'd woken before?

-You slept so deeply that I was sorry to.

- And also Emma? It's her fault that I have slept myself.

Emma approached me and said:

'Look how pretty it is. Poor! Does the call?

'You see,' I said to awaken pity who sleeps well.

It took her lower lip to my sister, and after taking his head with both hands, bowing called until their foreheads touched. Emma woke almost scared but smiling to the point, took on theirs hands caressed Mary temples.

My father had just sat down with more ease than had hitherto had. He remained silent for a moment as spying dark angles of the room. The girls looked terrified.

- I'm there! -He at last broke, I at this moment!

He looked for something on the bed, and going back to who he believed was waiting, he added:

-Excuse me do it wait a moment.

And turning to me:

- My clothes! ... What's this? The clothes!

Mary and Emma were motionless.

'It is not here-I answered gone to get her.

- What has been taken away?

-The change will have gone to the other.

'But what is this delay? Said wiping the sweat from his forehead. Are the horses ready? -Continued.

-Yes, sir.

-Go and tell that I hope to Ephraim we ride before it gets too late. Move, man! Juan Angel, coffee. No, no ... This is intolerable!

And he approached the edge of the bed to jump to the ground. Mary aproximóse telling him:

-No, Dad, do not do that.

- What does not? -Replied tartly.

-What if the doctor lifts are impatient, because you will do evil.

- What doctor?

'Well, the doctor who has come to see, because you are sick.

'I'm good, you hear? Well!, And I want to get up. Is this child where he is, that is not listed?

-I need to call Mayn, I whispered to Mary.

'No,' he answered, pausing for a hand and hiding her body that gesture with my father.

'But if it is essential.

-Is that you should not leave us alone. Tell that to wake Emma Luisa to call you.

I did so, and Emma went.

My father insisted, and irritated, to rise. I had to catch the clothes and asked me to help you dress resolved, before closing the curtains. He jumped out of bed immediately thought that dress. He was livid, his brow contracted; agitábale constant tremor lips as if he were possessed with anger, and his eyes had a sinister glow in orbits round everywhere looking for something. The bleeding foot prevented him from walking well despite that it had accepted my arm for support. Mary, standing, hands folded in her lap and letting know the eagerness in his face and the pain that tormented, did not dare to take a step towards us.

-Open the door, 'said my father approaching leading to the chapel.

I obeyed. The oratorio was no light. Mary hastened to precede us with, and placing it near that beautiful image of the Virgin that much resembled him, spoke words that I heard, and pleading eyes brimming with tears were fixed on the face of the image. My father stood in the doorway. His eyes became less uneasy, and leaned more strength in my arm.

- Would you like to sit? I asked.

-Yes ... well ... We replied in a voice almost gentle.

I was back to accommodate me in bed when the doctor came: they told him what had happened and was happy, after pressing.

Within half an hour, came Mayn again examine the patient, who was fast asleep: prepared a potion and handing it to Mary, said:

-You going to give you this, urging him to take it that we dulzurita.

She took the cup with some trepidation, and approached the bed taking me light. The doctor hid behind the curtains to see the sick without being seen.

Mary called my father and softer accent. He, he awoke, put her hand to the side, while complaining, was fixed on Mary, who urged him to take the potion, and said:

-By spoonfuls, I can not get up.

She began to give the drink well.

- Is it sweet? He asked.

'Yes, but is that enough already.

- Do you have a lot of sleep?

-Yes. What time is it?

It's going to dawn.

- Your mom?

-Taking a break. Take a few spoonfuls over this and then sleep easy.

The head meant no. Mary sought the doctor's eyes for advice, and he made a sign to give him more of the drink. The patient refused and she said, making as if to prove the contents of the cup:

-If it is very nice. Another spoonful, another, and no more.

My father's lips fell trying to smile, and received the liquid. Mary wiped them with his handkerchief, saying with the same tenderness with which John used to say goodbye after leaving bed.

'Well, then: now sleep much.

He closed the curtains.

-With a nurse like you, the doctor looked at him as she put the light on the table is not none of my patients die ...

- Does this mean that now? ... She interrupted.

-All answer.

XXXVIII

After ten days, my father was recovering, and the joy was back to our house. When a disease has made us fear the loss of a loved one, fear that stirs our sweetest affections toward her, and is in the care they lavish him away and the danger, capable of disarming tenderness death itself.

The doctor had recommended that efforts be made to the spirit of the patient as peacefully as possible. He carefully avoided talk business. Then he could get up, we urge you to choose a book to read in some times and chose the Journal of Napoleon on St. Helena, reading always moved him deeply.

Gathered in the sewing of my mother, took turns reading Emma, Mary and I, and if we noticed once dominated by sadness, Emma played guitar to distract. Sometimes he used to talk about the days of his childhood, his parents and siblings, or enthusiastically referred us travel I had done in his youth. Sometimes joking with my mother criticizing the customs of Chocó, on hearing her laugh make the defense of their homeland.

- How old was I when we got married? Once asked, after speaking of the early days of her marriage and a fire that was completely ruined after two months of that verified.

Twenty-she said.

-No, daughter, was twenty. I cheated on Mrs (as she called her mother in law) afraid that I believed very young. As women, when their husbands start to age, never remember well the years that they have, I was easy then rectify the account.

- Twenty years more? Emma asked admired.

'I hear,' said my mother.

-And you, what, Mom? Asked Mary.

-I was sixteen: a year more than you do.

-But tell me tell my father said the importance given to me since I was fifteen, that's when I decided to marry her and become a Christian.

-Come on, Mom, 'said Mary.

'Ask him first,' said my mother, what was settled for what he calls the importance for him gave me.

We all turned to my father and he said:

-A married.

Interrupted the conversation the arrival of Juan Angel, bringing people coming from correspondence. He delivered newspapers and two letters, both signed by Mr. A. .., and one fairly late date.

Then I saw the signatures, they went to my father.

- Oh, yes, 'said devolviéndomelas-; expecting letters from him.

The first came down to announce that he could not take his trip to Europe, but after four months, which warned that preparations precipitasen not mine. I dared not run a single gaze to Mary, fearful of provoking so thrilled that I dominated but came to my aid that I instantly reflection that if my trip is not frustrated, I had still more than three months happiness. Mary was pale, and pretextaba find something in your sewing box, which was on his knees. My father, completely calm, waited for me to conclude the reading of the first letter to say:

-What is to be done: see the other.

I read the first lines, and understanding that would hide my embarrassment Serme impossible, I went to the window to see better, and thus able to give back to those who hear. The letter said that literally, in substantial part:

"A fortnight ago I wrote to you telling you that I saw pointed to four months delay my journey, but having paved when and how I did not expect the problems that I had made, I hasten to write you this letter in order to announce that I will be 30 next January in Cali, where I hope to find Ephraim us to march to the port on February 2.

"Although I was despite knowing that he had a serious illness had you in bed, shortly after I received the pleasant news that was already out of danger. I give you and your family's congratulations for the speedy recovery of his health.

"So I hope that there will be no problem whatsoever for you to give me the pleasure of taking the pleasant company of Ephraim, by whom, as you know, I have always so special affection. Please show this part of my letter. "

When I find my seat, I found my father's eyes fixed on me. Mary and my sister went to the hall at the time, and I held the first chair that had just left, this seat to be more in the shade.

- How many have today? My father asked.

-Twenty-replied.

-It is only one month, it is necessary not to fall asleep.

There was the accent with which he spoke those words, and in his face, all the tranquility that reveals an unchangeable resolution.

A page came to tell me that the horse was ready an hour before preparing commanded him.

-When you return from your walk, my father said to me, answer this letter, and the people will carry yourself, because tomorrow anyway you should give back to the farms.

-I said I will not dwell out.

I needed to hide what he suffered; calling in solitude sweet hope that I was flattered to me then just before the reality of the dreaded trip, needed mourn alone, that Mary did not see my tears ... Ah, if she had been told how much flowed from my heart at that moment, and would not have expected.

I went down to the broad plains of the river, where the plains approaching less impetuous: forming majestic curves, initially passed through the midst of hills neatly carpeted, rolling the sparkling streams to join him, and then continues stroking the leaves of the coal and guava from the shore hides under the latest tapes after mountain which seems to give in whispers his last farewells to solitude, and one loses so far, far away in the blue pampa, where at that time the sun to hide tornasolaba purple and gold of his stream.

When I came up through the winding paths of the bank, and the night was adorned with all the splendor of summer. The river passed dawns glowing foam and waves rocking the reeds as telling secrets to auras coming to peinarles plumages. The backwaters unshaded reflected on your trembling the stars, and where the branches of the jungle of both banks were linked pavilions forming mysterious, shining the light of the fireflies wandering phosphate. Only the grilling of night insects disturbed the silence of the woods, but from time to time the Bujío, guardian of the black thickets, fluttered around me making me hear his sinister hiss.

The house, though lit and was silent when in the stands gave the horse to Juan Angel.

I expected my father pacing in the hall: the family was gathered in the oratory.

-You took my father said to me: 'Do you want us to write these letters?

-I want something we talked before about my trip.

-Let's see-he said sitting on a sofa.

I remained standing near a table with his back to the candle lighted us.

-After the mishap occurred, 'I said after that loss, I can appraise the value of which I consider essential to convey to you that I do not have to make the sacrifice that requires the completion of my studies. Before that the interests of the house suffered this embezzlement indicated to you that I would be very satisfying hereinafter help in their work, and to his refusal then nothing could replicate. Today the circumstances are very different: all makes me hope that you will accept my offer, and I gladly waive the right to send me you want me to end my career, because it is my duty to relieve you of that kind of commitment to me has contracted.

'All this,' he replied to some extent is thought judiciously. Although today there is reason to be more fearful than before that trip you, I can not know, despite everything, you dominate the talk and noble sentiments. But I must warn you that my decision is irrevocable. The costs that the rest of your education cause me nothing worse in my situation, and upon completion of your career, the family will reap abundant fruit of the seeds that I sow. Otherwise he added after a short pause, during which he turned to pace around the room-I think you have the noble pride necessary to pretend not cut so well unfortunately what you have started.

-I will do my best, 'I said, and completely hopeless, do all I can to match what you expect of me.

-It must be. Go quiet. I'm sure you come back I will have succeeded in carrying out projects with fortune I have to pay what I owe. Your position will therefore be very good in four years, and Mary will then be your wife.

He was silent again for a few moments, and finally stopping in front of me, said:

-Let us therefore write; brings needed here, I do not leave the desk bad.

I had just dictate a long and affectionate letter to Mr. A. .., and my mother wanted, which was presented at that time in the room, heard her read. This was basically what I was reading at the time Mary came bringing the tea for my father, helped by estefana:

"Ephraim is ready to go to Cali on January 30, will find you there and may continue to Buenaventura on February 2, as you wish."

Followed the style formulas.

Mary, who gave me back, put on the table and within reach of my father wearing plate and cup. He was doing fully illuminated by the light of the table was almost livid: to get the kettle that had estefana, leaned with his left hand on the back of the chair I occupied, and had to sit on the couch immediately while my father served sugar. He presented the cup and she stood up to fill it, but his hand shook so that watching my father poured the tea, looked to Mary saying:

-Just ... enough, child.

He was aware of him the cause of this disturbance. Following Mary with her eyes as she walked into the dining room hurriedly, and then fixing it in my mother, I asked this question to his lips did not need to utter:

- See this?

All were silent, and I just went with the pretext of bringing desktop supplies he had brought.

XXXIX

At eight o'clock the bell rang in the dining room, but I thought with the serenity needed to be close to Maria after what happened.

My mother knocked on the door of my room.

- Is it possible, 'he said when he had entered, they dominate so let this weigh? Do not you therefore make you as strong as other times could you? So it must be, not only because your father will be upset, but because you are called to give encouragement to Mary.

In his voice, to speak well, a sweet accent counterclaim twinned with the most musical of tenderness.

He continued making me the list of all the benefits that this trip was going to report me without disimularme pains for which would have to pass, and ended by saying:

-I, in four years you will not be at my side, I see in Mary not only a beloved daughter but the woman destined to make you happy and who has known both deserve the love you have: you constantly talk about you and will try make you wait for your return as a reward of your obedience and yours.

Then lifted his head, who held my hand on the table, and our eyes filled with tears were sought and promised what lips can not say.

-Go, then, to the dining room, 'he said before leaving, and hides as possible. Your father and I have been talking a lot about you, and is very likely to be resolved to do what they can serve and more comfort.

Only Emma and Mary were in the dining room. Whenever my father stopped going to the table, I sat at the head. Seated on either side of it, I expected the two. He spent some space without us to talk. Their faces, both so beautiful, denouncing greater penalty that might have been expressed, but was less pale that of my sister, and their eyes were not that bright languid beautiful eyes have cried. This said,

- Will you finally hacienda tomorrow?

-Yes, but I'll be there but two days.

-You will carry Juan Angel to see your mother, maybe it is worse.

-I will take. Higinio writes Feliciana is worse and the doctor Mayn, who had been prescribing, has stopped doing so since yesterday, have followed Cali, where it was called urgently.

-Tell Feliciana many things on our behalf affectionate-Mary told me: if you still sick, I plead my mom to take us to see it.

Emma again interrupted the silence that had followed the previous dialog to say:

-Transit, Lucia and Braulio were here this afternoon and felt much not find: I left many salute. We thought we'd go see them next Sunday: are handled as finely during Dad's illness.

-We will be on Monday, which I will be here, 'I said.

-If you had seen what was sad when I told them about your trip to Europe ...

Mary hid her face turned me as you find something on the table immediately, but I had already seen shining tears she tried to hide.

Estefana came at that time to say that my mother called.

Paseábame in the dining room, hoping to talk to Mary before they retire. Emma ran me sometimes the word as to distract from the painful thoughts that were tormenting me know.

The night continued serene: the roses were still, in the nearby treetops not perceived a whisper, and only sobs disturbed the calm river and impressive silence. About the clothes laundered turquíes mountain torn some clouds as snowy chiffon shawls did the wind wave over blue skirt of an odalisque, and the transparent dome of the sky arched over those unnamed peaks, like an urn convex blue crystal encrusted diamonds.

Mary took longer. My mother came to tell me what will happen to the hall: I figured he wanted to relieve their sweet promises.

My father sitting on a couch beside him Mary, whose eyes rose to me. The pointed to a vacant place near it. My mother was placed in a chair occupied immediately to my father.

'Well, my daughter said this to Mary, who, with downcast eyes still, playing with one of her hair peinetitas; Would you repeat the question I asked when your mom came to me the answer Ephraim before?

My father smiled and slowly shook her head in denial.

And then, how do? He insisted.

Mary dared to look at me for a moment, and I look revealed that all had not yet all our days of happiness!

- Not true, again asked my father to promise to Ephraim to be his wife when he returns from Europe?

She returned after a few moments of silence, to get my eyes with his, and hiding their eyes black again and prudish, said

-If he wants it ...

- Do not know if I want to? -Replied my father almost laughing.

Mary stopped blushing, and live on her cheeks inks showed that blush, did not disappear from them that night. Mirábala my mother eyes more tender than a mother can look. I thought for a moment I was enjoying one of those dreams in which Mary spoke to me with that accent he had heard, and that their eyes had the bright humidity that I was spying on them.

- You know I love you so?, Is not it? I said.

-Yes, I know, replied dully.

Ephraim-Di-now my father said no smile-and the conditions that you and I will make that promise.

-Provided Mary said you leave happy ... as possible.

- What other daughter?

-The other is to study hard to go back soon ... Is not it?

'Yes,' replied my father, kissing his forehead and to deserve. Other conditions you shall put them. 'So you like? He added, turning to me and stood up.

I had no words what to say, and strongly shook his hand in mine he tended to tell me:

-As of Monday, because, in my mind you instructions and often reads the statement.

My mother came up to us and embraced our heads involuntarily joining them so that my lips touched Mary's cheek, and left leaving us alone in the room.

Long time since I had to run my hand on the couch grabbed Mary's and our eyes met for not stop looking until his lips uttered these words:

- How good dad! Is not it true?

It means that yes, without my lips could lisp a syllable.

- Why do not you speak? Do you look good laying conditions?

-Yes, Mary. And what are yours in payment of so much good?

-A single.

-Dila.

-You know it.

'Yes, yes, but today you say it.

-You love me and always said, and his hand was linked more closely with mine.

XL

When I got to the farms in the next morning, I found room in the house that replaced the physician in Mayn Feliciana assistance. He, by his bearing and countenance, looked more like a retired captain who claimed it to be. I did know that he had lost all hope of saving the patient, as he was attacked from hepatitis in the last period and to resist all kinds of applications, and manifesting being of opinion concluded that a priest was called.

I entered the room where Rachel was. Juan Angel was already there, and was surprised that his mother did not answer the praise to God. The find in such a desperate state Feliciana was bound to move me.

I gave orders for an increase in the number of slaves who served him, I put it in a more comfortable piece, to which she had opposed humbly, and was sent by the village priest.

That woman was going to die far from home, the woman who was so sweet affection I had since I was at our house, in whose arms she fell asleep many times Mary as a child ... But here's his story, reported by Feliciana with rustic and pathetic language, entertained some evenings of my childhood.

Magmahú since adolescence had been one of the most distinguished leaders of the armies of Achanti25, powerful West African nation. The courage and skill he had shown in the frequent wars that King Say Tuto Kuamina held until the death Achimis Orsué, leader of the offense; complete victory over the tribes that reached the coast revolted against the king by Carlos Macharty, to Magmahú who killed himself on the battlefield, made the monarch with glory and wealth, at the same time entrusting the command of all troops, despite the likes of the fortunate warrior, who never forgave him for not having Please deserved size.

After the peace achieved with short maturity Macharty, for the English, with its own army and, threatening the Achantis, all the forces of the kingdom came to campaign.

Empeñóse battle, and few hours were enough to convince the British of the failure of his deadly weapons against the value of the Africans. Still indecisive victory, Magmahú, shimmering gold, and terrible in his anger, the hosts ran encouraging them with his fearlessness, his voice dominating the sound of the enemy batteries. But in vain repeated orders sent to the heads of the reserves to come into battle attacking the weaker side of the invaders. The night stopped the fight, and when the first light of the next day Magmahú mustered his troops, decimated by death and desertion and cowed by the chiefs that prevented the victory, he realized that he would be defeated, and prepared to fight and die. The king, who came in such terrible moments of his troops to the field, saw them, and sued for peace. The British held the granted and treated with Tuto Say Kuamina. From that day Magmahú lost the favor of his king.

Irritated the courageous leader with the unjust behavior of the monarch, and not wanting to give his rivals the pleasure of seeing him humiliated, decided to emigrate. Before leaving the currents determined to shed the blood of Tando and the heads of their most beautiful slaves, as an offering to their God. Including Sinar was younger and handsome. Son of Orsué it, the unfortunate leader of the Achimis, was taken prisoner in the bloody brave dealing day when his father was defeated and killed, but fearing his fellow slaves Sinar and the relentless fury of Achantis, they had hidden the noble lineage of prisoner they had.

Only Nay, Magmahú only daughter, knew the secret. As a child when Sinar still came as a house servant Orsué winner, captivated at first meekness worthy of the young warrior, and later her wit and beauty. He taught the dances of their homeland, the songs of love and country senses Bambuk26, he meant the wonderful legends that his mother had entertained in childhood, and if some tears rolled then the complexion of the uvea of the cheeks slave, Nay used to say:

'I ask your freedom my father to go back to your country, because you are so unhappy here.

And Sinar not answer, but her big eyes and looked left to mourn his young lady so she looked at the time the slave.

Nay One day, accompanied by his servants, had gone to pace near Cumasia, Sinar, who led the beautiful ostrich that his wife was sitting on soft cushions as Bornu, the bird was walking so abruptly, that found little far away from the party. Sinar, pausing, with flaming eyes and a smile of triumph on his lips, Nay said pointing to the valley at their feet.

Nay, behold the path that leads to my country: I will run from my enemies, but you will go with me, you will be queen of the Achimis, and the only woman mine: I will love you more than the hapless mother crying my death, and our descendants will be invincible in his veins carrying my blood and yours. Look and see: who dares to stand in my way?

Saying these last words lifted the width panther skin cloak that fell to his shoulders, and he shone under the butts of two pistols and a saber Turkish garrison girded with a red shawl Zerbi.

Sinar knees, covered with kisses the feet on the soft slopes Nay ostrich feathers, and loving it with the peak pulled the colorful robes of her mistress.

Muda and absorbed her to hear the words of love and tremendous slave finally rested on her lap the beautiful head of Sinar saying

-You do not want to be ungrateful to me, and say you love me and take me to be queen of your country, I should not be ungrateful to my father, who loved me before you, and whom my flight cause despair and death. Wait and depart together with your consent; expected, Sinar, that I love you ...

And Sinar shivered as her forehead Nay the burning lips.

Days and days ran, and Sinar expected, because in their slavery was happy.

Magmahú came to campaign against the tribes by Macharty insurreccionadas and Sinar not accompany his master to war as the other slaves. He had told Nay:

'I prefer to die rather than fight against people who were allies of my father.

She, on the eve of marching troops, gave his lover, without him seeing Oceans, a drink in which a plant had dezumado soporific, and the son was well Orsué unable to march because they remained for several days dominated by a dream invincible, which interrupted Nay at will, and to pour oil on the lips aromatic and invigorating.

But after the war declared by the British to Say Tuto Kuamina, Sinar was presented to Magmahú to say:

-Take me to the battles: I will fight by your side against whites, I promise you will deserve their hearts eat roasted by the priests, and they bring in neck tooth necklaces blond men.

Nay gave precious balms to heal wounds: sacred feathers and putting in the plume of her lover, sprinkled with tears of ebony chest that she had just anointed with fragrant oil and gold dust.

In the bloody day in which Chief achantis, envious of the glory of Magmahú prevented him from achieving victory over the English, a bullet broke the left arm of Sinar.

After the war and made peace, the intrepid captain Achantis returned home humiliated, and Nay for a few days just stopped weeping wipe that anger tore his father, to go secretly to give relief to Shinar, healing lovingly the wound.

Magmahú resolution taken by leaving the country and offer sacrifice to the river that bloody Tando, spoke thus to his daughter:

-Come on, Nay, seek less ungrateful soil it for my grandchildren. The most beautiful and famous leaders of the Gambia, which I visited in my youth, I knew puffed asylum in their homes, and their most beautiful preferirte women. These arms are still strong to fight, and I have to be powerful enough wealth wherever a roof cover us ... But before leaving aplaquemos need to anger the Tando, wroth with me for my love of glory, and to sacrifice the cream of our slaves; Sinar including the first ...

Nay fell senseless to hear that terrible judgment, leaking from his lips the name of Shinar. The picked up their slaves, and Magmahú, beside himself, Sinar summoned to his presence. Unsheathing his sword, he stammered with anger:

- Slave!, You put your eyes on my daughter as punishment will be closed forever.

-You can do, 'said the youth-serene: mine is not the first blood of the kings of Achimis with your sword turns red.

Magmahú aback on hearing these words, and the tremor in his right hand on the floor resounded the curved scimitar wielding.

Nay, disposing of his slaves, who terrified the stop, entered the room where Magmahú Shinar, and it abrazándosele to the knees, with tears bañábale feet exclaiming:

- Forgive, sir, or fall upon us both!

The old warrior, throwing him the fearsome weapon, slumped on a couch and muttered to hide his face with his hands:

- And she loves it! ... Orsué, Orsué!, And you have avenged.

Nay sitting on the lap of his father, clasped in his arms, covering him with kisses and cana hair, told him sobbing:

-You will have two children instead of one: aliviaremos your old age, and his arm will defend you in battle.

Magmahú lifted his head, and making as if to Sinar to come over, he said, his voice and face terrible, extending his right hand toward him:

-This hand killed your father tore her breast the heart ... my eyes and enjoyed in agony ...

Nay sealed with Magmahú his lips, and turning abruptly to Shinar, tended her beautiful hands to him, telling him with loving accent:

-These healed your wounds, and these eyes have cried for you.

Sinar fell on his knees before his mistress and his master, and he, after a moment, he said hugging her daughter:

-Here's what I will give proof of my friendship the day you are sure yours.

I swear by my gods and yours, 'said the son-Orsué than mine will eternal.

After two days, Nay, Sinar and Magmahú Cumasia left for the dead of night, carrying thirty slaves of both sexes, to ride camels and ostriches, and others charged with the most precious jewels and dishes possessed; lot of tíbar27 and cauris28, food and water to a long journey.

Many days spent in that perilous pilgrimage. The caravan was fortunate to take good, long and not tripping over sereres29. During the trip, Sinar and Nay sadness dissipated Magmahú heart joyful singing duet songs, and clear nights the moonlight and the shop side of the caravan, rehearsing the happy lovers funny dances to the sound of the trumpets of ivory and slaves lire.

Finally they reached the country of Kombu-Manez, on the banks of the Gambia, and that tribe celebrated with sumptuous feasts and sacrifices the arrival of such illustrious guests.

From time immemorial became the Kombu-Cambez Manez and a cruel war, fueled war in both countries not only that professed hatred but by criminal greed. Both sides changed to European slave traders, who were prisoners in the fighting, weapons, gunpowder, salt, iron and other spirits, and failing to sell enemies, bosses sold their subjects, and often those and these their children.

The courage and military skill Magmahú and Sinar were for a time of great benefit to the Kombu-Manez at war with its neighbors, as repeated battles waged against them, in which were a success hitherto achieved. Magmahú pointed to a choice between that or kill prisoners who were sold to Europeans, had to agree to the latter, at the same time getting the advantage that the chief of the penalties imposed Kombu-Manez feared those of his subjects enajenasen that your dependents or children.

One afternoon that Nay had gone with some of his slaves to bathe on the banks of the Gambia and Sinar, under the shade of a giant baobab, were isolated spot where always a few hours in the days of peace, love waiting with impatience, two fishermen moored their canoe in the same bank where Sinar was, and in it were two Europeans: one was laboriously ground, kneeling on the beach and prayed for a few moments: the pale rays of the dying sun, through the foliage, you illuminated the face tanned by the suns and fringed by thick beard, almost white. How to get on his knees on the sands had placed the rods wide hat wearing, Gambia breezes played with his long, tangled hair.

He had a black cassock, muddy and tattered, and shone on his breast a crucifix of copper.

So he approached Nay found in search of her lover. The two fishermen were up to that time the body of another European, who was dressed in the same manner as his partner.

Fishermen Sinar referred to how they had found the two white under a shed of palm leaves, two leagues above the Gambia, expiring the young and the old anointing to pronounce sentences in a foreign language.

The old priest remained for a while oblivious of his surroundings. Then they stood up, Sinar, leading by the hand to Nay, frightened by this weird alien figure suit and asked him where he came from, what was the purpose of your trip and what country was, and was surprised to hear him respond , although with some difficulty, in the language of Achimis:

-I come to your country: I see your chest painted red snake Achimis of nobles, and speak your language. My mission is peace and love: I was born in France. Do the laws of this country do not allow funeral of the deceased from abroad? Your fellow wept over those of other two brothers, put crosses on their graves, and many carry gold earrings the neck. Will you let me, then bury abroad?

Sinar answered

-Looks like you're telling the truth, and you should not be bad as whites, although you seem, but there are those who send more than me among Kombu-Manez. Come with us, I'll introduce you to your boss and take the corpse to see if your friend can bury it in their domains.

As they walked the short distance that separated them from the city, Sinar spoke with the missionary, and esforzábase Nay to understand what they were saying; seguíanle driving the two fishermen in a blanket the body of the young priest.

During the dialogue, Sinar became convinced that the alien was true, by the way he answered the questions put to him about the country of Achimis: he reigned in his brother, Sinar and thought he was dead. Explícóle missionary means that he used to captured the affection of some tribes of Achimis; affection was to source the wisdom with which he had cured some patients, and the fact they have been one of the King's favorite slave. The Achimis had given a caravan and supplies to the coast would be directed to the sole of his comrades who survived, but caught on the trip by a party enemy, one of his guards abandoned them and were slain, the victors contented with leave without desert guides to priests, perhaps fearful that the vanquished volviesen to fight. Many days they traveled with no other guide than the sun without food and fruits that were in the oasis, and so had come to the banks of the Gambia, where, consumed by fever, the young man had just expired when the fishermen found.

Sinar Magmahú and led the presence of the head priest of Kombu-Manez, and the latter said:

-Here's a foreigner who begs you let him in your domains bury the body of his brother, and take break to continue their journey to their country: however, promises you heal your son.

That night, his slaves Shinar and two missionary helped bury the corpse. The old man kneeling on the edge of the pit that slaves were filling, sang a song deeply sad, and the moon shone in the white beard minister to wet tears rolling foreign land that hid the valiant friend.

XLI

Just under two weeks had passed since the arrival of the French priest of the country-Manez Kombu. Sinar is because only could understand him, or because he liked the treatment of European gave daily long walks together, which noted that her lover returned Nay worried and sad. Supúsose her that news Sinar facing their country abroad, must have been sad, but later thought better ascertain the cause of this melancholy, imagining that memories of the homeland, fueled by the relationship of the priest, did wish Orsué son back to the look on his native soil. But as the loving tenderness towards her Sinar increased rather than decreased, sought to take advantage of a timely opportunity to confide their anxieties.

Apagábase a hot afternoon, and sat on the bank Sinar, seemed dominated by sadness in the last days of slavery had so tenderly to Nay. This spotted him and approached him with silent steps. With neat short crimson skirt dotted with silver stars, the sky color wide shawl that after hiding within, crossing, hung from the waist, red turban pinned with needles of gold and agate necklace and bracelet, should be more seductive than ever. He sat next to his beloved, but he continued thoughtfully. At last she said:

-I never thought when approached as desired by you before that my father should make me your wife, you would be as you see. Do you love him and less than before? Am I less tender with you, or do not look as beautiful as the day that I deserved to confess your love?

Sinar, eyes fixed on the fugitive Gambia waves, seemed not to hear. Nay stared silently for a few moments with tears in his eyes, and his chest heaved a sob at last. On hearing Sinar turned hastily towards her, and seeing her tears, she kiss tenderly, saying:

- Do you cry? So get the happiness that we have waited and finally arrives?

- Alas! 'd Never been deaf to my voice I had never searched my eyes without flattering yours show themselves, which is why they cry.

- When, say, the slightest accent troubled yours not the deepest of my dreams when, but do not wait or you saw, I stopped feeling if you approached me?

He takes a moment, and your innocence, Sinar, confirms your disdain and my misfortune.

-Sorry, Nay, forgive me, because I thought of you.

- What did he say this foreigner?-Nay asked him, and wiped away her tears, and playing with corals and teeth necklaces warrior, why seek solitude with him so many times I told myself I was not hateful ? Did he tell you that women in his country are white as ivory, and his eyes are deep blue waves Tando? My mother told me me and forgot tell you ... She spoke much of the country of a foreign whites like you love, as she loved him, but since he left Cumasia this man, my mother became odious to Magmahú: she worshiped other gods, and my father .. . My father gave him death.

Nay silent for a long time, and showed Sinar again dominated by sad thoughts. Waking suddenly embebecimiento that sort of takes the hand of his beloved, she climbs to the top of the rock, from which they could see the shimmering desert without limits and here and there the mighty river, and says:

-The Gambia, like Tando, born from the womb of the mountains. The mother is never making of his son. Do you know who made the mountains?

-No.

-A god made them. Have you seen the Tando back in your career?

-No.

-The Tando like a tear going to get lost in a vast sea, to the roar of which the sound of a river is like your voice compared to that during hurricane storms gigantic shakes these forests as if they were weak reeds. Do you know who made the sea?

-No.

-Ray ripping clouds and falling on the glass it shatters baobab, as your plant undoes one of dried flowers, the stars like gold and pearl embroider your robes Calin, studded sky, the moon, which place you contemplate in solitude imprison leaving my arms, the sun Bruno jet your complexion and gives light to your eyes, the sun before which the fire of our sacrifices is less than the brightness of a firefly: all are works of one god. He does not want another woman who loves you and he sends me love you as myself, he wants me to laugh if you laugh, I cry when you cry, and instead of your touch as you defend my own life , that if you die I cry on your grave until ready to hang out with you beyond the stars, where I'll wait.

Nay, both hands clasped on the shoulder of Shinar, and absorbed in love watching him, because he had never seen so beautiful. Clasping him to her heart, kissed him with burning lips and continued:

'That tells me abroad to teach I will: your God must be our God.

'Yes, yes,' said Nay surrounding it with arms, and after him, I only love you.

XLII

At dawn on the day that the chief had ordered Kombu-Manez be given first to the pompous festivities which were held in celebration of the marriage of Shinar it, Nay and mission creep down the banks of the Gambia, and finding there the innermost site, the missionary stopped and said to them:

The god who brought you love, the god that your children will love not disdain for palm temple halls hide us, and right now you are viewing. Let us bless you.

Ahead of them to the bank, said in a solemn voice slowly and a prayer repeated lovers kneeling on either side of the priest. Then they poured water on his head pronouncing the words of baptism.

The minister stood praying just some space, and coming back to Sinar Nay and made them bind his hands, and before bendecírselas told either words Nay never forgot.

And last night Was that the nobles of the tribe went home in dances and feasts Magmahú. Beautiful women around them, and they and they sported their finest jewelry and dresses. Magmahú, by his gigantic stature and wearing fancy costume, stood out among the warriors, and Nay had humiliated for six days and galas and charms the most beautiful wives and slaves of Kombu-Manez. Aromatic resin torches, held by Cambez perforated skulls, dead in the fighting for Magmahú, illuminating the spacious rooms. If at times the martial music ceased, were replaced by the soft and voluptuous lyres. The guests hurried with expensive excess liquor and narcotics, and all had been slowly surrendering to sleep. Sinar, fleeing from the din of the party, rested on a bed of their rooms while Nay cooled her forehead with a feather fan scented.

Suddenly he heard in the neighboring forest some detonations followed by other rifles and other who came to the house of Magmahú. The stentorian voice called to Shinar, who rushed out wielding a saber in his looks. Nay was hugging her husband when Magmahú said this:

- The Cambez! ... Them! ... They will die beheaded! He added unnecessarily removing the brave lying inert on the couches and floors.

Some efforts were made to get up, but the more it was impossible.

The thunder of guns and war cries were coming. Burned the houses of the people closest to the shore, a red glow lit the match, and he flashed wounded by the swords of the fighters.

Magmahú and Sinar, deaf to the cries of women, deaf to the cries of Nay, ran to the spot where the fighting was fiercest in time that a compact mass and disorderly soldiers went to the house of the chief Ashanti, Sinar him and calling them with hoarse voices. They tried to hide in rooms Magmahú, but to no avail, and late and the courage with which foreign leaders and encouraged fighting Kombu-Manez warriors.

Heart pierced by a bullet, fell Magmahú. Few of his companions stopped running the same fate.

Sinar fought to the end to defend melee Nay and his life, until a Cambez captain, whose right hand hung bloody French missionary head, shouted:

-Surrender and I will give you life.

Nay hands then presented to the man atase. She knew the fate that awaited him, and fell down before him said:

-Sinar not kill, I am your slave.

Sinar had fallen wounded by a saber cut on the head, and bound him, and like her.

The ferocious winners toured the rooms quenching their thirst for blood at first, and then tying saqueándolos and prisoners.

The brave Kombu-Manez had slept in and woke up a feast ... or slaves awoke.

When masters and servants and, no winners and losers, reached the banks of the Gambia, whose waves reddened the latest flare-fire, made Cambez hastily embark in canoes than expected, leading many prisoners, but no sooner had unleashed to indulge these currents, a large discharge of rifles, made by some Kombu-Manez that afternoon and returned to combat, sailors surprised last had left the bank, and the bodies of many of them floated little about water.

Dawn when the victors canoes docked to the right bank of the river, and leaving some of his soldiers in them, the others continued to march overland convoy guarding the prisoners, and finding here and there masses of fighters who had undertaken withdrawal in the middle of the woods.

During the long hours of travel to reach the vicinity of the coast, Nay did not allow drivers who approached Shinar, and he saw tears rolling endlessly down her cheeks.

Two days, one morning before the sun frightening away the last shadows of the night, leading to Nay and other prisoners to the seashore. Since the day before had been separated from her husband. Some prisoners were waiting canoes beached on the sands, and a long way on the sea wind ruffled the smooth, whitened the sails of a brig.

- Where's Sinar, not coming with us? Nay asked one of the chiefs fellow prisoners to jump into the canoe.

-Since yesterday I sailed, 'he replied, will be on the ship.

Already in him, Nay searches among prisoners crammed into the hold to Shinar. Call him and nobody responds. Their eyes look lost it again in the bilge. A sob and the name of his mistress came at a time of his chest, and fell as dead.

When he awoke from that dream disruptive and frightening, was found on deck, and saw only around the hazy horizon of the sea. Nay did not say goodbye to the mountains of his country.

The cries of despair that gave convinced of the reality of his misfortune were interrupted by the threats of a white crew, and as she threatening me put words that perhaps understood his gestures, raised on Nay wielding the whip, and ... again make it insensitive to their plight.

One morning, after many days at sea, with other slaves Nay was on deck.

Due to the epidemic which had attacked the prisoners were left breathing air, fearing no doubt the captain of the ship died some. He heard the cry of "Land!" Given by the sailors.

She lifted her head to the knees, and saw a darker blue line that constantly surrounding the horizon. Some hours later the brigantine entered a port in Cuba, where they had landed some blacks. Women between them, they would be separated from the daughter of Magmahú, embraced his knees sobbing, and the men said goodbye, doubling theirs before it and without trying to hide the tears they shed. Almost considered fortunate few who remained beside Nay.

The ship, after receiving new charge, departed the next day, and navigation that followed was more painful by bad weather. Eight days have passed, and one night when visiting the cellar master, slaves found dead two of the six who were chosen among the most handsome and robust reserved. The one death was given, and was bathed in the blood of a wide wound in his chest, and which looked stabbed the unfortunate sailor probably had collected on the cover: the other had succumbed to fever. The two were stripped of crickets in a single sweep imprisoned them both, and soon saw the bodies out Nay to be thrown overboard.

One of the slaves of Nay and three heads Manez Kombu-mates were the last that remained, and they succumbed another the same morning that the ship was approaching a coastline understood Nay called Darien. In favor of a strong north wind and storm surge, the brig went into the Gulf and cautiously placed within walking distance of Pisisí.

Late at night, the captain did put in a boat with three slaves Nay remaining, and embarking he also ordered the sailors to handle it should should be aimed at certain blip that indicated on the coast. Soon they were on land. The slaves were tied with ropes before landing, and leading one of the sailors, followed by short time a hilly path. At a certain point, the captain gave a particular signal with a whistle, and continued to advance. Repeated the sign, was answered by a similar one when I could see, half hidden among the lush foliage of trees, a house, in which he was then running to a white man with a light in his hand, he made eye shadow with the other trying to make the newcomers approaching. But some dogs barking threatening prevented travelers huge advance. Those voices stilled by his master and some servants, the captain was able to climb the stairs of the house, built on estantillos, and after cuddling with the owner, engaged dialogue, during which the captain spoke definitely of slaves, since frequently noted. Gave orders to go up with them, and went out into the corridor that time a young, white and quite beautiful, who cordially greeted the sailor. The homeowner did not seem satisfied after examination made of the three co-Nay, but to look at it, he stopped talking to white women in a language sweeter than he had used until then, and it seemed more musical to answer it, leaving Nay see in their eyes that thanked compassion.

The homeowner was an Irishman named William Sardick, established two years ago in the Gulf of Urabá, not far from Turbo, and his wife, who heard Nay name Gabriela, a mestiza, cartagenera birth.

XLIII

Explotábanse at that time many gold mines in the Chocó, and if you consider the rudimental system used to make them, well worth considerable qualified products. Owners slave gangs dealing in such work. Atrato Introducíanse by most foreign goods consumed in the Cauca, and naturally dispensed to those for the Chocó. Markets in Kingston and Cartagena were most frequented by traders importers. Turbo was in a cellar.

This indicated, it is easy to estimate how tactically Sardick had taken up residence: the committees of many traders, buying gold and the frequent changes to the coastal Cribs made of tortoiseshell, ivory palm, leather, cocoa and rubber, salt, brandy, gunpowder weapons and trinkets, were, not counting their profits as a farmer, speculations have it quite lucrative to the smiling avivarle satisfied and hoping to return to their country rich, for he had come miserable. Servíale powerful aid of his brother Thomas, established in Cuba and slave ship captain who've followed in their journey. Downloaded the brig of the effects brought on that occasion and that on arrival at the port of Havana had received, and occupied with indigenous productions, held by William for some months, all of which were executed in two nights and as quietly by the servants of the smugglers, the captain prepared to depart.

The man who had treated so ruthlessly co-Nay, from the day when lifting a whip on her inert collapse saw his feet, he dispensed all the consideration that his strong nature was capable. Nay Understanding the captain was to embark, could not stifle her sobs and wails, assuming that this man would soon see the coast of Africa, from where he had taken. He approached him, asked him to his knees and not to leave her gestures, feet kissed him, and imagining their pain could understand, he said,

-Take me with you. I will be your slave; seek to Shinar, and you'll have two slaves instead of one ... You who are black and you cross the seas, and we know where to find it ... We worship the same God as you, and you will be true, provided that we do not ever detach.

It must be beautiful in its painful frenzy. The sailor stared silently smiling lips plególe stranger than blond beard caressing failed to ensure, pasóle by a shadow red forehead and left eyes see the meekness of the Jackal when he caresses the female . Finally, taking her hand and leading her to his chest, he hinted that if he promised to love be leaving together. Nay, haughty as a queen, stood up, turned her back to Ireland and entered the room immediately. Hence the received Gabriela, who after telling fearful be silent, he meant that he had done well and promised to love her very much. And after pointing out the sky showed him a crucifix, was astonished to see Nay knees before him, sobbing and praying to God that if asking what the men refused.

After six months, Nay and made himself understood in Castilian, thanks to the consistency with which Gabriela insisted on showing his tongue. This wise and how he became the African, and understand him what he had achieved in its history, the more and more interested in his favor. But almost no time were no tears in the eyes of the daughter of Magmahú: the song of any American bird that reminded him of his country, or the sight of flowers resembling those of Gambian forests fanned her pain and made her moan . As for the Irish short trips Gabriela allowed to sleep in his room he had presented Eibon often heard in dreams call her father and her husband.

The farewells of fellow sufferers had been breaking the heart of a slave, and finally came the day when the last goodbye. She had not been sold, and was treated with less cruelty, not so much because amparase affection of his mistress, but because the mother would be unhappy, and his master expected do it better once the manumiso born. That greedy contraband trading with the blood of kings.

Nay had decided that the son of Sinar not slave.

On one occasion when he talked about the sky Gabriela, use all their wild frank to ask:

-The children of slaves, if they die baptized, can they be angels?

The Creole guessed criminal thinking Nay caressed, and resolved to let you know that in the country where he was, his son would be free when he turned eighteen.

Nay replied in a tone of regret only:

- Eighteen years!

Two months later she gave birth to a child, and insisted that he immediately cristianara. So the first kiss stroked his son, realized that God had sent him a comfort, and proud to be mother of the son of Shinar, returned to their lips smiles that seemed to have escaped them forever.

A young Englishman who was returning from the West Indies into New Granada rested by chance in months in the house of Sardick before undertaking the laborious navigation of the Atrato. He brought with him a beautiful three year old girl who seemed to love tenderly.

They were my father and Esther, which was just beginning to get used to respond to its new name of Mary.

Nay assumed that the girl was motherless, and he became particularly dear. My father was afraid to entrust it, even though Mary was not happy but in the arms of the slave or playing with your child, but Gabriela reassured him telling him what she knew of the story of the daughter of Magmahú, relationship moved abroad. Understood this imprudence committed by the wife knowing Sardick to give the date when the African had been brought ashore grenadine, because the country's laws from 1821 banning the importation of slaves, and by virtue, and his son Nay were free. But saved himself well to make known to Gabriela's error, and waited a favorable opportunity for William to propose to sell him to Nay.

An American who was returning home after performing in Citará a cargo of flour, stopped Sardick house, hoping to continue their journey to Pisisí arrival of the boats coming from Cartagena imported goods driving my father. The Yankee saw Nay, and paid his gentleness, William spoke of the desire for the food I had to wear a beautiful slave conditions, for which the requested order to give it to his wife. Nay was offered, and the U.S., after haggling the price one hour, weighed one hundred and fifty to Irish gold castellanos payment of the slave.

Nay knew immediately by Gabriela, to refer it was sold, that small portion of gold, white heavy by his view, was that the estimated price, and smiled bitterly at the thought that changed by a handful of Tibar . Gabriela did not hide it in the country where the son had Sinar would slave.

Nay was indifferent to everything, but in the afternoon, when at sunset my father was walking by the sea shore holding the hand of Mary, approached him with his son in his arms: in the face of the slave appeared as a mixture of pain and anger wild, which surprised my father. Fell down at his feet, told him in bad Castilian:

-I know that in this country where I have my son be slave: if you want it to drown tonight, buy me, I consecrate to serve me and love your daughter.

My father paved everything with money. Signed by the new U.S. sales document with all the formalities palatable, then my father wrote a note on it, and spent the statement Nay Gabriela to hear her read. In these lines renounced the right of ownership may have on her and her son.

Tax Yankee what the English had done, he said admired:

I can not explain the behavior you. What black wins this be free?

-Is-my father replied that I did not need a slave but a lot aya want this child.

And Mary sitting on the table he had just written, she did betray him to the role Nay, he at the same time saying the wife of Shinar these words:

-Save this well. You are free to stay or go live with my wife and my children in the beautiful country in which they live.

She received a letter of release from the hands of Mary, and taking the child in her arms, covered her with kisses.

Grasping after my father's hand, tocóla her lips, and the tears came to his son.

So they went to dwell in the house of my parents Feliciana and Juan Angel.

At three months, Feliciana, and as beautiful again in his misfortune that was possible, we lived with my beloved mother, who always distinguished with special affection and regard.

In recent times, by his illness, and more, for it to be apparent, looked in Santa R. .. the garden and dairy, but the main focus of his tenure there was greet my father and me when we went to the mountains.

Children Mary and I, at times it was more accommodating Feliciana us, we used to caress calling Nay, but soon noticed that sad if we gave that name. Ever, who sat at the head of my bed, early evening, entertained me with one of his fantastic tales, remained silent after it was over, and I thought I noticed that she was crying.

- Why are you crying? I asked.

-So you're a man, 'he said with his most affectionate accent do you take us to travel and Juan Angel and me, is not it?

'Yes, yes,' I said excitedly: go to the land of those beautiful princesses of your stories ... shew me the ... What's his name?

-Africa-answered.

I dreamed that night with golden palaces and delicious music listening.

XLIV

The priest had administered the sacraments to the sick. Leaving the doctor at the head and rode to the village to make arrangements for the funeral and to mail that letter fatal to Mr. A. ..

When I returned, Feliciana seemed less broken, and the doctor had conceived some hope. She asked each family, and the mention of Mary, said:

- Who could see before you die! I would have much preferred my son!

And then, as to satisfy the stated preference to her, said:

-If it were not for the child, what would become of him and me?

The night was very bad for the patient. The next day, Saturday, at three in the afternoon, the doctor came into my room saying:

-He will die today. What was the husband of Rachel?

I replied-Sinar.

- Sinar! What has been done? In the delirium pronounce that name.

I had the condescension of the doctor trying to soften recounting the adventures of Nay, and I went to her room.

The doctor told the truth: he was dying and his lips uttered only that name whose eloquence could not measure the slaves around her, not even his own son.

I went to tell him so that he could hear me:

- Nay! Nay! ...

She opened her eyes and blotchy.

- Do not you know me?

He made a sign with his head yes.

- You want me to read a few sentences?

He made the same signal.

It was five o'clock when did you move away to Juan Angel of her mother's bed. Those eyes were so beautiful, and no longer turned yellow light in Recessed orbits: the nose had sharpened: lips, funny if slightly thick, retostados fever now, let see teeth no longer moist: with clenched hands holding a crucifix on his chest, and tried in vain to pronounce the name of Jesus, I would repeat, the only name I could give back to her husband.

Night had fallen when it expired.

After the slave was dressed and placed in a coffin, covered from the throat to the feet of a white linen was placed on a table in mourning, whose four corners were lighted candles. Juan Angel to the head of the table shed tears on the front of his mother and his chest went hoarse with sobs plaintive cries.

Mandé order the captain of the slave gang to bring that night to pray at home. They were getting quieter, and men and children occupying the entire length of the western corridor, the women knelt in a circle around the coffin, and as the mortuary room windows fell into the corridor, both groups were praying at the same time.

After the rosary, a slave sang the first verse of one of those painful salves full of melancholy and heart wrenching cries of a slave who prayed. The crew repeated in each verse sung chorus, harmonizing the serious voices of men with the pure, sweet women and children. These are the verses of that song I have kept in mind:

In dark dungeon

whose sun mask grating

Blacks and high embankments

That surround prisons;

In chains only

I drag, silence turban

This eternal solitude

Where the Wind or listen ...

I die without seeing your mountains

Oh fatherland, where my crib

She rocked under forests

That will not cover my grave.

While the song sounded, lights were shining coffin tears streaming down their faces masked half of the slaves, and I tried vainly hide mine.

The crew was removed, and were only a few women were taking turns to pray all night, and two men to prepare the bier on which the dead had to be taken to the people.

It was late at night when I managed to fall asleep Juan Angel surrendered by their pain. I then retired to my room, but the sound of the voices of women who prayed and hit the machetes of the slaves who prepared the stretcher guaduas woke me every time I had sleep onset.

At four, Juan Angel was still asleep. The eight slaves who led the body, and I, we set off. Had ordered the butler Higinio to make the bold wait at home, avoid the terrible lance goodbye to his mother.

None of which we accompanied Feliciana uttered a single word during the trip. The farmers market leading food overtook us missed the silence, being belief among villagers of the country delivered to a disgusting orgy in night vigil they call, nights where relatives and neighbors who has died meet at the home of the bereaved, the pretext of praying for the dead.

Once the funeral prayers and Masses were finished, we went with the corpse to the cemetery. Since the pit was finished. Passing with him under the cover of the cemetery, Juan Angel, who had eluded the vigilance of Hyginus to run for his mother, overtook us.

Placed the coffin on the edge of the pit, hugged him and prevent him ocultasen. It was necessary to approach him and tell him, as she stroked the tears enjugándole:

-It's not your mother that you see there, she is in heaven and God can not forgive that desperation.

- He left me alone! He left me alone! Repeated the unhappy.

-No, no, I answered: Here I am, I've always loved and love you much: you are Mary, my mother, Emma ... and all mothers give thee.

The coffin was already at the bottom of the pit, one of the slaves threw up the first shovelful of dirt. Juan Angel, almost angrily rushing towards him, took her two-handed blade movement that filled us with amazement at all painful.

At three in the afternoon of the same day, leaving a cross on the grave of Nay, we headed your son and I to the sierra30 hacienda.

XLV

After a few days, began to subside grief Feliciana's death had caused in the minds of my mother, Emma and Mary, without thereby ceases to be it the frequent subject of our conversations. All we tried to relieve Juan Angel with our care and affection, this being the best we could do for his mother. My father told him that was completely free, although the law put an under his care for a few years, and would henceforth be considered only as a servant of our house. The black, already knew of my next trip, said that all he wanted was to be allowed to accompany me, and my father gave some hope to please.

Despite what happened the night eve of my departure to Santa R. .. Mary remained for me only what had been until then: chaste mystery that had watched our love, watched it yet. Just we took the liberty of walking sometimes alone in the garden and in the garden. Forgotten time of my trip, she frolicked around, picking flowers to put on your apron mostrármelas come later, leaving me to choose the most beautiful for my room, pretending disputándome some want to save for the oratory. Ayudábale me to water their favorite eras, which was collected for the sleeves revealing his arms, not noticing how beautiful I looked. We sat on the edge of the collapsed, crowned with honeysuckle, where we saw boil and meandering river currents in the deep bottom of the valley and hilly. Afanábase distinguish myself sometimes by sudden flashes of gold on the Sun left to hide, sleeping lions, giant horses, castle ruins jasper and lapis lazuli, and the forge was pleased with childlike enthusiasm.

But if the slightest circumstance made us think about the dreaded trip, his arm is not mine desenlazaba and stopping at certain sites, I sought his eyes moist, after spying on them something invisible to me.

One afternoon, beautiful evening that will live forever in my memory, the dying light of sunset afterglow blended color under a lilac sky with rays of the rising moon, bleached like a lamp across a globe of alabaster . Winds frolicking down the mountains to the plains: birds nest in hurrying sought the foliage of the groves. The loops of the hair of Mary, who ran the garden slowly grabbed my arm with both hands, I had toyed with the front more than once, and she had tried the temple lay on my shoulder, nothing we said ... Suddenly he stopped at the end of a street of rosebushes, looked for a few moments at the window of my room, and his eyes turned to me to say:

'Here was, so I was wearing ... Do you remember?

- Always, Mary, ever! ... I answered her hands covering her with kisses.

-Look, that night I woke up trembling, because I dreamed that you did that you do now ... See the newly planted rose bush? If you forget me not flower, but if you remain as you are, give the most beautiful roses, and I have promised to the Virgin so let me know if you're good for him always.

I smiled so innocently touched by.

- Do not you think this is so? He asked seriously.

I believe that the Virgin will not need so many roses. He made us to come to the window of my room. Once there, his arm unlink mine: he went to the creek, distant about steps, knotted at the waist the shawl, and fetching water in the hollow of their hands together, knelt at my feet to drop to drop on an onion retoñada, saying:

-It is a clump of lilies of the mountain.

- What have you planted there?

Because here ...

'I know, but I was hoping that you had forgotten.

- Forget? Because it is so easy to forget! He said without getting up and looking at me.

Her hair unbraided rolled to the ground, and the wind made some of their loops touch the white musk rose immediately a.

- But do not know why you find here the bouquet of lilies?

- Why did not I know? Because that day was who assumed that I never wanted to put flowers on his desk.

Look at me, Mary.

- What for? Replied without looking up from matita that seemed examine carefully.

-Each lily is born here is a cruel punishment for a moment of doubt. Did I know if it was worth anything? ... We will plant your lilies away from this site.

Bend one knee in front of her.

- No, sir! He replied matita alarmed and covering with both hands.

I went back on its feet, and idly waiting for her to finish what he was doing or pretending to do. She tried to see me without my noticing, and laughed at last lifting his face full of rewards for a moment supposed severity, saying:

'So very brave, right? I'll tell you, sir, why are all the lilies of the mat.

In trying to get up, grabbed the hand that I offered, fell again kneeling, stopped because some hair tangled in the branches of the rose: the split, and shaking her head to fix her hair, her eyes were a fascination almost new. Leaning on my arm, observed:

-Come on, it will darken.

- What are the lilies? I insisted as we rode slowly into the hall of the mountain.

-You know what will kill the new roses I showed you, right?

-Yes.

'Well, the lilies will for a similar thing.

-A watch.

- Would you like to find in every letter of mine to receive a piece of the lilies to give?

- Ah, yes.

'That will tell you many things and sometimes not be written and other work would be hard pressed to express well, because I've finished teaching ensure that my letters are going well placed ... also true ...

- What is it?

-They both are to blame.

After being distracted by breaking underfoot, precious shoes, dry leaves of mamey mandules and watered by the wind in the lane we followed, said:

I do not want to go to the mountain tomorrow.

- But you will not feel Transit? A month ago she got married and we have not made the first visit. Why do not you want to go?

-Because ... for nothing. We say we are busy with travel ... Anything. It comes with Lucia on Sunday.

'All right. I'll be back early.

-Yes-and no hunting.

-But that condition is new, and Carlos would laugh at me you know that tax.

- And who is going to tell him?

-Maybe it myself.

-And that why?

To console the one-shot that missed so pitifully to fawn.

'Really. A tiger would have been otherwise, because of course it must be scary.

-I do not know is that Carlos had no shotgun ammunition when fired: Braulio had taken.

-And why did Braulio that?

-To take revenge. Carlos and Mr M. .. had mocked that morning of the thinness of the dogs of Joseph.

-Braulio did wrong, right? But if he had not done so, the fawn would not be alive. You have not seen how happy it makes if I approached him: May has got to want it, and often sleep together. It's so cute! As you may have cried her mother!

-Drop it to go away, then.

- Does she still look the mountains?

'Perhaps not.

- Why?

-Because Braulio assures me that the deer he killed soon after in the same ravine where it came Shorty was the mother.

- Oh! What a man! ... Do not ever kill doe.

We had reached the corridor, and John, with open arms, went to meet Mary, she got up and disappeared with him, having made him lay his head on one of those sleepy shoulders of pearl pink shawl that neither her nor her hair is dared at times to hide.

XLVI

At noon the next day I came down from the mountain. The Sun, from the zenith, no clouds that prevented him, throwing bright light all that trying scorch the foliage of the trees did not defend its rays of fire. The woods were silent: the breeze moved the branches and not a bird flapped them cicadas tireless celebrating that day of summer is adorned with December: the crystal waters of the fountains were rolling through the streets hasty to go under secretearse tamarind and hobos, and then hide in the leafy yerbabuenales: the valley and mountains seemed illuminated by the glow of a giant mirror.

Seguíanme Juan Angel and Mayo. I spotted Mary, who came to the bathroom accompanied by John and estefana. The dog ran toward them, and began to spin around the beautiful group, sneezing and giving aulliditos as he did to express happy. Mary came to me with anhelosa look everywhere, and I saw at last time I jumped the fence of the garden. Dirigime to where she was. Her hair, keeping braids ripples had them printed, fell in bunches and disorderly on the shawl of white skirt, which reflected in his left hand, while her right was fanning herself with a branch of basil.

She sat under the branches of orange bath, on a carpet that had just issued estefana, when I went to greet her.

- What sun! -He said, for not coming sooner ...

-It was not possible.

Almost never possible. Would you like to swim and I wait?

-Oh, no.

-If it is because something is missing in the bathroom, I can wear it now.

- Roses?

-Yes, but when you come and you will.

John, who had been doing wobble bunches of oranges that were within reach and almost on the grass, knelt before Mary for her to unbutton her blouse.

That day I had a plentiful supply of lilies, as well as I had saved Transit and Lucia, found many along the way: I chose the most beautiful to give to Mary, and Juan Angel getting from all others, threw them to the bathroom . She said:

- Oh! What a pity! So cute!

-The mermaids' I said do the same with them while they were bathing in the backwaters.

- Who are the mermaids?

-Some women who want to look like you.

- Me? Where you've seen?

-In the river saw them.

Mary laughed, and when I walked away, I said:

-But I will not dwell for a while.

Half an hour later he entered the room where I was waiting. Their eyes had the brightness and the soft pink cheeks both embellished to leave the bathroom.

Seeing me, he stopped crying,

- Ah! Why here?

Because I assumed that you would enter-.

'And I, I expect.

He sat down on the couch prompted, and then something broke in his mind, to say:

- Why is it, huh?

- What?

-This always happens.

-You have not said why.

-What if I imagine that you do something, you do it.

- Why me know also something that you come, if you've taken? That unexplained.

-I wanted to know, for days, if this happening to me now, when you're here already, you can guess what I do and I know you're thinking ...

-In you, right?

-Will. Come to Mama's sewing, which I have not done anything wait today and she wants me to what I'm sewing later.

- We'll be alone?

- And what is this new endeavor that we are always alone?

-Everything that hinders me ...

- Chit! ... Said putting his finger to his lips. You see? They are added in pastry-sitting. Yea, these women are very beautiful? She asked, smiling and fixing the seam. What are their names?

- Ah! ... are very cute.

- And living in the mountains?

-On the banks of the river.

- The sun and water? There should be very white.

-In the shadows of the great forests.

- What do they do there?

I do not know what to do, what I do know is that I can not find them.

- How much does this misfortune happens to you? Why did not you wait? Being so beautiful, you'll be sorry.

-Are ... but you do not know what it is to be well.

'Well, I'll explain you. How are you? ... No, sir! -Added hiding in the folds of the Ireland that was on her lap, the right hand that I had tried to take.

'All right.

-Because I can not sew, and do not say what are the ... What are their names?

-I will confesártelo.

-Let's see, then.

'They're jealous of you.

- Angry with me?

-Yes.

- Me!

-Before I only thought in them, and then ...

- Afterwards?

-The forgot you.

'Then I'm going to get very proud.

His right hand was already playing on one arm of the chair, and that was how I used to tell me I could take it. She went on to say:

- In Europe there are mermaids? ... Listen, my friend, are in Europe?

-Yes.

-So ... Who knows!

-Surely those cheeks are painted with red flowers juice, and put corset and boots.

Mary was sewing, but her right hand was not steady. While unraveling the thread, I noted:

-I know one that is completely devoted to see beautifully shod feet and ... The flowers of the bath is going to go down the drain.

- Does that mean I should go?

-Is that I feel sorry for you loss.

-Anything else is.

'Really, that gives me grief ... and another thing that we see so often alone ... and Emma and Mommy will come.

XLVII

My father had decided to go into town before my departure, both because business required it urgently, to take time to fix my trip there.

On January 14, the eve of the day he was to leave us, at seven in the evening and after working together a few hours, I take his fourth part of my luggage that should continue with his. My mother settled trunks kneeling on a rug, and Emma and Mary helped him. There were no longer to accommodate my dresses but Mary took some pieces of them that were in the immediate seats, and to recognize them asked:

- Does this also?

My mother received them unanswered, and sometimes took his handkerchief to his eyes as he was placing the.

I left, and returned with some papers that were put into the trunks, I found Mary lying on the rail corridor.

- What is it? 'I said. Why are you crying?

-If you do not cry ...

-Remember what you promised me.

-Yes, I know: have value for all this. If it were possible to give me part of yours ... But I have promised my mom or not you mourn. If your face is saying no more than these tears say, I hide them ... but then, who shall know ...?

I wiped my handkerchief with which rolled down his cheeks, saying:

-Wait, I'm back.

- Here?

-Yes.

I was in the same place. I sat next to her on the railing.

'Look,' he said, showing me the dark valley: look how they have grieved the evenings, when the August return, and where will you be?

After a few moments of silence, he added:

-If you had not come, if as dad thought, you had not returned before going to Europe ...

- Would it have been better?

- Is it better? ... Better? ... Have you ever thought?

-You know that I could not believe it.

-I do, when Dad said that he heard of the disease I had, are you ever?

-Never.

- And in those ten days?

-I loved as now: but what the doctor and my father ...

'Yes, mom told me. How can I pay you?

'I've done what I could push yourself a reward.

- Anything worth this much?

-Love me like I loved you then as I love you today, love me a lot.

- Oh, yes. But even ingratitude, that has not been for pay you what you did.

And briefly leaned his forehead on his hand linked with mine.

-Before he continued, raising his head slowly I would have died of shame to talk so ... Maybe I do not either ...

- Wrong, Mary? Are not you, then, almost my wife?

-Is that I can not get used to that idea, so long seemed an impossible ...

- But today? Still today?

I can not imagine what it will be you and how it will be me then ...

- What do you seek? -Asked me feeling my hands searched his.

'This,' I replied, sticking out of the ring finger of the left hand a ring on which were engraved the initials of the names of their parents.

- To use it you? As you do not use rings, had not offered.

-'ll Give it back the day of our wedding: meanwhile replace it with this, is that my mother gave me when I left for college: inside the ring are your name and mine. I do not come, yes you, right?

Well, but it will not ever give it back. I remember in the days of leave you dropped in the stream of the garden: I mismatch for buscártela and I got wet as much, mom got mad.

Something dark like the hair of Mary and swift as the thought crossed before our eyes. Mary gasped and covered her face with her hands, exclaimed in horror:

- The black bird!

Trembling took hold of one of my arms. A shiver of fear ran through me. The drone metal ominous bird wings and not heard. Mary was still. My mother, who left the desk with a light, came alarmed by the cry that Mary had just heard him: this was livid.

- What is it? Asked my mother.

-That bird we saw in the fourth of Ephraim.

The light trembled in the hand of my mother, who said:

-But girl, how are you so scared?

-You do not know ... But I have nothing. Let's go, 'he added calling me with his eyes, and more serene. The bell rang and the room we were going there when Mary approached my mother to say:

-Don't go to tell my dad freaked because I will laugh.

XLVIII

At seven the next morning and had left home my father's luggage, and he and I drank coffee in costume way. Should accompany him to close the estate of the lords of M. .., which was to say goodbye, as did other neighbors. The whole family was in the corridor when the horses came to montáramos. Emma and Mary came out of my room at the time, which caught my attention. My father, after kissing one of my mother's cheeks, kissed them against Mary, Emma and each of the children up to Juan, who reminded the commission that he had made a galapaguito with holsters, guaucho to saddle a foal, it was fun in those days.

He stopped again my father in front of Mary, before going down the stairs, and said quietly, putting a hand on his head and trying in vain to get him to look.

-It is agreed that you will be very beautiful and very wise, is not it, my lady?

Maria earned him an affirmative answer, and eyes that watched the assault, she tried wiped tears slide precipitously.

I said goodbye to the evening, and being close to Mary while riding my father, so she told me that no one else would hear:

Ni-five one.

Family of Don Jerome, only Carlos was at the ranch, I was filled with pleasure, and trying to get me, from where I hugged you spend all day with him.

We visited the mill, expensively mounted, but with little taste and art, we toured the garden, beautiful work of the ancestors of the family, and finally went to the manger, adorned with precious half dozen horses.

Desktop smoked after lunch, when Carlos said:

-Apparently, I will be unable to see before we say goodbye, with your face cheerful student, to torment that you put your whim desesperador to tell some of Matilde. But after all, if you are sad because you're going, that means you'd be happy if you stay ... Travel Diablo!

'Do not be ungrateful,' I replied, since I have come back bucket doctor.

'True, man. Think you had not anticipated? Study hard to return soon. If in the meantime no one kills me tabardillo trapped in these plains, you may find me dropsy. I'm terribly bored. Everyone here wanted to go to spend Christmas Eve in Buga, and to stay had to pretend I had sprained my ankle, a risk that such conduct despopularice me among the large crowd of my cousins. At last I have to plead a business in Bogotá, even bringing soches and inserts as Emigdio ... to bring anything.

- How a woman? I interrupted.

- Takes! Can you imagine that I have not thought of that? A thousand times! Every night I make a hundred projects. Imagine: lying face up on a cot from six in the evening, waiting for blacks come to pray, to call me after you make chocolate, and then hearing conchabar desenraíces, despajes and cane planting ... At the dawn of each day, the first smell of bagazal I reached my nostrils undoes all castles.

'But you will read.

- What do I read? Who do I talk about what you read? With the butler cotudo yawning from five?

Clean-Saco in urgent need to marry, you're back to thinking you project Matilde and bring her here.

-At face value, this has happened as well. After I was convinced that I had made a blunder trying to marry your cousin (God forgive me and her), came the temptation to say. But you know what often happens? After much work and cost me solve one of those problems Barcho, imagine that Matilda is well and my wife and that is at home, loose suponerme laughter to what would be the unhappy.

'But why?

-Man, Matilde is stack Bogotá as San Carlos, as the statue of Bolivar, as the keeper Escamilla: echárseme would lose in the transplant. And what could I do about it?

'Well, make it love forever provide all possible refinements and recreations ... In short, you are rich, and she will be a stimulus for work. Furthermore, these plains, the forests, the rivers, are perchance things she has seen? Are they to be seen and not love?

'I come to poetry. And my father and campesinadas? And my aunts with their smoke and gazmoñerías? And this loneliness? What about the heat? ... What the devil? ...

Aguárdate-laughing-I interrupted, not take it so to heart.

-Let's not talk about that. Hurry much to come back soon to heal. When you return, you will marry Miss Mary, is not it?

-God willing ...

- Do you want me to be your sponsor?

-From all my heart.

-Thank you. It is therefore agreed thing.

-Do you bring my horse, 'I said after a moment of silence.

- Are you leaving already?

'Sorry, but I expect home early: you see that is very near the trip ... and I have to say goodbye today and my compadre Emigdio Custodio, who are not very close.

- Are you going to thirty precisely?

-Yes.

-You are only fifteen days should not stop you. At last I've laughed at something, even if it was from my boredom.

Neither Charles nor I could hide the grief that caused us farewell.

Amaimito forded the time I heard it calling me, and I saw my friend coming out of a forest Custodian immediately. Potron riding a roan, rein still on a chair big head: Listing wore blue shirt, pants rolled up to the knee and capisayo crossed over his lap. Followed him, mounted on a horse ridden bebeca years and four bunches of bananas, an idiot boy, the same that played in the combined functions of chagra swineherd, birder and gardener.

-God save me, compadrito-old told me when he was near. If I stubbornly to shout, I sneaks.

A home-going, buddy.

-Do not tell me. And I almost did not go out of these montarrones, giving me way to bump the handle indina already horrar again: but the mill has to pay to me all together. If I fail to pass through the gate and llanito see gualas so far would be lounging in their search. Jilo I left and said and done: half eaten and the spare car, and it seemed as bizarrote two months. Could not get the leather, which had served me with another to make a few chaps, that I have are from the sight of the dogs.

'Do not give anything, friend, that you have left over muletos and years for them to train. Let's go, then.

'Nothing, sir,' said my friend starting to walk and precediéndome-, if Cansera, time is of the bad. Take charge: a real honey, the brown sugar, not to mention, the white coming azucarita to weight cheeses, for nothing, and pigs gobbling all the corn harvest, and as if it bounced into the river. The balance of his godmother, though poor is a ringlete, do not give to candles, there is no soap cochada pay what is spent, and those garosos of guards after the sacatín that the peel ... What I tell you: I bought the master Don Jeronimo's gaudualito stubble that, but what man as tyrant! Four hundred and ten ternerotes patacones of pulled away!

- And where did the four? Soap??

- Ah! Nah, you to theme, compadre. If we broke up the bank to pay Salome.

- And Salome is as hardworking as before?

And if not, where would you water? Labra strip loin that's what there is to see, and help all to end her mother's daughter. But if I tell you that girl is me zurumbático, not lying.

- Salome? She so formalita, so demure ...

She, compadre; well as pacatica as seen.

- What?

-Nah, you is really gentleman and my friend, and I'll tell you, instead of írselo to say to the priest of the parish, I think of pure saint has no malice and he wanders the soul from the body . But I first step aguárdese and this ditch, because it does not muddy, baquía needed.

Turning Ninny, who came into the bananas falling asleep:

-Watch the road, Tembo, because if the mare atolla, gladly lose the baggy for leaving there.

The cotudo laughed stupidly and gave some grumblers inarticulate response. My friend continued:

- Nah, you know if Tiburcio, the mulatto who raised the late Murcia?

- Not that he wanted to marry Salome?

-There will arrive.

I do not know who raised him. But what if I know: I've been in your house and that of Joseph, and sometimes even have hunted together: a handsome young man.

-Wherever you see, not without good eight cows, pigs its tip, its Estancita and two good mares chair. Because Lord Murcia, although denying that scared lived, was a good man, and he left all that to the boy. He is the son of a mulatto that cost the old one rebotación of Tiricia that almost takes it because the four months of the samba in Quilichao comprao, he died, and I knew the story, because then I liked day labor Sometimes the Lord chagra of Murcia.

- And what about Tiburcio?

-Here I go. Well, sir, going for eight months I started to notice that the boy was not short of stories to come see us, but soon took the spot, and I knew that what I wanted was a chance to see Salome. One day I told him so clear to Candelaria, and she got away with it refueled maybe I had fallen in the eyes cloud and that the story was stale. I got in glimpses in the evening on a Saturday, because Saturday Tiburcio not missing at that time, and I saw Cate Nah, you meet him girl barely felt it, and I had no shred of doubt ... Yes, I saw nothing that was not legitimate. Days went by, and Tiburcio not open his mouth to talk about marriage, but I was thinking that will cateando Salome, soursop be well if he does not marry her, because there is no mechosa and housewife as no risk find that. When suddenly stopped coming Tiburcio without Candelaria girl could get to the reason, and as I have the respect due Salome, unless I averiguarle, and since before Christmas Eve looks Tiburcio not there. If Nah, you will Justinian boy friend, brother Don Carlitos?

-Not seen him since we were kids.

-Then remove the pins that has cast Don Carlos, and there you have it individually. But I wish it was like the brother is the same legs, but nice looking, what is denied. I did not know he was HERE TO Salome: agora might be that I do the swap empeñao about his father because the child that came to branding calves, and from the very day I eat a banana leaves to taste.

-That's not good.

-I, which is the risk that story with his godmother, if you know, tell me one day that is lunatic, I'm a garlero, I know what I do. But every cloud has not its cure: I have been going and digging up hitting the touch.

-Come on, buddy, but tell me before (and if there indiscretion dispense ask), what makes Salome face Justinian?

-Let me, sir, if that's what has me day and night as if I slept on pringamoza ... My friend, the girl is pitted ... Not to kill ... And I give the peels if I gets Manding ... I want, boy, that's why I tell Nah, you all to get me out with either.

- And what did you hear that she loves Salome?

- Válgame! No I have watched how her eyes dance when he sees the white boy and all she gets as azogada, if you pass water or fire, because it seems that he lives with drought, and that smoking is the only thing you have to do, for by candle and home water snuggles herding herding, and needless on Sunday afternoon at the old Dominga is not known?

-No.

'Well, I'm about to tell you is that use of the powders, and since no one will remove from head to Candelaria was the bat that he eyed the monkey so well known that both amused and a Nah, you, for the creature gasped rubbing his belly and moans like a Christian giving.

-Some scorpion that have eaten, compadre.

- Deónde! If labor cost for buffet try: convince yourself that the witch curse him, but it was there where I was going. Enanticos I went searching I found the mare in the guayabal old, who was going home, and as I walk by ear, all went to see it and I will devote itself ahead to say, "See, Na Dominga, go back, because there are the office people instead of being in converse. Van two trips with him I told you that I am shocked to see it at home. " All she began to tremble, and I saw scared me, I thought at once: this retobo not walk in anything good. He went with them and the other, but as I left church when I said, "Look I'm malicious, and if the lame to walk Nah, you wherein I rejo the skinning to, and if I do, I removed the name. "

The exaltation of my friend had gone as far. Crossing himself continued:

- Jesus, I believe in God the Father! That can Cangalla wasting a day that I bad anger journal. It's good work, white: have a good man her daughter has costao many sorrows, and not fail to embarrass whoever it one of the most loved.

My cantankerous compadre was near an access of tenderness, and I, who had not saved and chimes like his last words, I hastened to say:

-Take the remedy you found for evil, because I believe it is something serious.

Well-ory will: her mother suggested the other day my wife to send him to Salome by one week so that the girl learned to sew in fine, that's all I want to Candelaria. So could not ... I do not like agora Nah, you know.

- Compadre!

-By the Verda Christ died. Since the case is different: I want your mom to be there a few months the girl, who out there does not have to go look that bad enemy: Salome ajuiciará and will tell the same thing as wanting alborotármela that go to tip of a horn. Do you think?

-Of course. Today I will talk to my mother, and she and the girls will get very happy. I promise everything will smooth.

-God bless you, friend. Then I'll give you forms Nah, you just talk a little today with Salome, who does not want the thing: he proposes to go to his house and tells him that his mother is waiting. Nah, you then tell me what you serve, and so we will all right as groove. But if the girl is infatuated, yes I swear one of these days the fit in one of my polled, and Cali beaterio going to give, that there has not to seat me a fly, and if it does not married, praying and learning to read the book until I have San Juan bend the finger.

We passed by the stubble Custodio recently bought and he said:

- Do not see what delicacy is ground and how hawthorn monkey, which is the best sign of good soil? The only thing that hurts is the lack of water.

-My friend, 'I replied, if you can you put all you want.

-Do not tease, then I do not sell nor twice.

-My father agrees that much how much you need to take the paddocks below: I did see what you recommended and the stranger who had not asked permission before.

-But his memory, compadrito: look to the past to wait for avisármelo ... Dígamele the pattern that I appreciate in my soul, that you know that I'm not ungrateful, and here I am with all I have to send. Candelaria will be Easter: water handy for the garden, for sacatín, for Manguita ... Suppose the passing by the house is a trickle, and that revolt by my partner Rudecindo pigs, which is what hurt me the quinchas rooting and not wander, so as to clean as there are to do at home, they have to empuntar the dumb horse laden with gourds to Amaimito because to take water from the Honda, better is swallowing lye, pure vitriol he has.

'It's copper, friend.

'That will be.

The news of granting him permission to take my father to chagrero cooled water to make the point that was shone Potron the trastraba in saying it was getting into the chopper.

- Whose is this pony?, Does not have the iron for you.

- Do you like? Somera's grandfather.

- How much?

As for walking-cuffed or not gloating, I confess that Don Emigdio declined four medals, and this is a ranga gray-black in front of me, that I have it brake, and swipes the paso llano, and pulls the tail is a taste: it took me so tame, for a whole week I Baldó this arm, because there is none to beat him in canon, and a rivet in two two ... Fatter I have it, because after the last Tambarría I gave was on the spine.

We got home from Custodio, and he heel strike the foal to be traces of the patio door open. Just gave it behind us the last whimper and a blow that shook the straw ridge, my friend advised me:

-Live and gingerly Andele Salome to see what takes.

-Do not worry-I responded by extending the corridor my horse, which frightened the linen hung by.

When I tried to dismount and my buddy had covered his head with capisayo the colt, and he was holding me the stirrup and bridle. After tying the horses came screaming

- Candelaria! Salome!

Only bimbos answered.

'But neither dogs said my friend, as if they had swallowed all the land.

-Here I replied from the kitchen my comadre.

- Hu turutas!, If here is your friend Ephraim.

-Wait for me a nothing, hoodlum, it's because we're down a scratch and burn us.

- And where's Fermin? Custodio asked.

He was with the dogs to find the sheep-pig answered the melodious voice of Salome.

This suddenly looked out the kitchen door, while my friend was determined to help me remove the chaps.

Thatched cottage was the chagra and soil compaction, but very clean and freshly whitewashed: well surrounded by coffee trees, sugar apple, and other fruit trees papayuelos, no housing missing but what I was going to have on, hope so favorably had improved the mood of its owner: water and crystalline. The parlor was to trim some rawhide covered stools, a bench, a table covered with starch then on canvas, and the sideboard, where wore plates and bowls of various sizes and colors.

He covered high pink chintz curtain door leading to the bedrooms, and on the ledge of it rested a tarnished image of the Virgin of the Rosary, completing the altarcito two small statues of St. Joseph and San Antonio, placed on either side of the sheet.

He went to the kitchen my little plump reidora comadre, suffocated by the heat of the fire and holding in his right hand a cagüinga31. After giving me a thousand complaints about my inconstancy, ended by telling me:

-Salomé and I were waiting to eat.

- How so?

-Juan Angel arrived here for a real egg, and the lady sent word that you were coming today. I sent Salome call the river, because he was washing, and asked what I said, do not let me lie: "If my friend does not come to eat here today, I'll put half back."

-All of which means that I have prepared a wedding.

-I seen I do not eat a stew made with wins of my hand is still bad takes.

-Better because I'll have time to go for a swim. Let's see, Salome said stopping to the kitchen door, my compadres time entered the room was low-talking: what do you have?

-Jelly and I'm doing this he replied while grinding. If I knew what I've been waiting like bread blessed ...

'That is because I have many good things.

- A serving! Wait for me while I wash one nadita, to shake hands, but will ñanga, because as it is no longer my friend ...

That said, not looking at me squarely, and between gay and embarrassing, but letting me see, when smiling mouth sideways, those white teeth implausible, inseparable companions and loving wet lips rosy cheeks showed that in the crossbred complexion escapes certain beauty to compare. To get to and from the morbid naked arms on the stone on which he rested his waist, it showed all its flexibility, shook the loose hair on his shoulders, and stretched the folds of his white shirt and embroidered. Shaking his head thrown back to back to back hair, began to wash their hands, and acabándoselas drying over the hips, said:

-As he likes to see grind. If I knew more step-continued ground-what I have. Can not say I've been waiting for?

Positioned so that outsiders could not see it, continued shaking my hand:

-If you fail it had been a month without coming, I would have made a fine. See if my daddy is out there.

-None is. I can not make it all right now?

- And who knows?

'But do tell. You're not convinced that I will do all my heart?

-If you say no, it would be a liar, because since he took so much effort to this English gentleman came to me when he gave me the sunstroke and much interest because I encourage, I was convinced that if I had love.

'I'm glad you know.

'But is that what I have to tell is so much, so suddenly you can not, and before a miracle is that my mother is no longer here ... Listen here comes.

-Do not miss opportunity.

- Oh Lord, and I will not settle for that today go without telling everything.

'So, are you going to bathe, compadrito? Entering Candelaria said. Then I'll bring a blanket and smelling good orita same goes with Salome and her godson, before a trip they bring water, and it washes some strainers, that the journey of bananas and moved by what had to be done to Nah, you and to send to the parish, but has not been in the jar.

Upon hearing the proposal of the good woman, persuaded me that she had fully entered her husband's plan, and Salome me to neglect one muequecita expressive, so that meant me lips and eyes at the same time, " yes now. "

I left the kitchen and pacing the room while I was preparing for the trip to the bathroom, I thought my friend had good reason in celar his daughter, because any less malicious than he could come up with the face of your moles Salome , and that figure and gait, and that breast, seemed anything but certain, imagined.

Salome interrupted those considerations that standing at the door, with a half since scrape hat, said:

- Are we going?

And letting me smell the blanket that hung from one shoulder, said:

- How does it smell?

-Yours.

-A mauve, sir.

Well-mauve.

-Because I have always always many in my trunk. Walk and Do not think that is away: we will bring down the cocoa, leaving the other side, but do not have to walk a bit, and we're already there.

Fermin, loaded with gourds and strainers, preceded us. This was my godson thirteen and I had it two when he served as sponsor for confirmation, because this affection that his parents had always excused.

XLIX

We left the courtyard behind the kitchen when my relative was shouting:

-Do not go to slow, the food is estico.

Salome wanted to close the little door through which we had entered trancas the cacao, but I began to do as she told me:

- What do we do with Fermin, which is as a storyteller?

'You'll see.

-I know: let us more there, and I was unfaithful.

Cubríanos the dense shade of the cacao tree, Which Seemed boundless. The beauty of the feet of Salome, the skirt of blue pancho left visible above the ankles up, stood on the path black and dry leaves. My godson was behind us throwing shells cob and avocado seeds to Wrens nagüiblancas singers and groaning under the foliage. At the bottom of a cachimbo, Salome stopped and said to his brother:

- If the cows will foul the water? Sure, Because at this time are in the runner up. No choice but to go in a race to scare them: running, my life and See That are not going to eat me socobe That was forgotten in the Wye chiminango. But be careful About breaking the tackle or throw something. Already there.

Fermín not allowed to repeat the order: it is true I had been Given That The Most sweet and engaging.

- Vido Already? Salome asked me looking bad step and shortening branches with feigned distraction.

I've got to look after your feet as if to tell his slow steps, and I interrupted the silence we kept saying:

-Let's see, what is there and what You have ground.

-Well there you see me do not know what to tell you.

- Why?

-If That makes me very sad today as ... so serious now.

'It's what you think. Begins, Because then it has no power. I have something very good to tell you.

- Yes?, Nah, you first, then.

-As I said nothing.

- So here's the thing? Well listen, but promise me not to say what nadita ...

-Of course.

'Well, what happens is you That Tiburcio Become a Wind Vane and an ingrate and you're looking for absurdities to give me feelings now About a month ago That We have Given me bad without reason.

- None? Are you quite sure?

-Look ... I swear.

- And what did he say he has to be so after having loved you so much?

- Tiburcio? Lambido that is: he did not want me around, and at first I did not know why they put malmodoso each time, and then I realized that it was because he figured I was good the first face he saw. Nah, you tell me, is that you can endure when one is honest? First came in believing a nonsense and Nah, you walked in the dance.

- Me too?

- When going to fight!

- What think?

-To what is tell if they already contain: all because sometimes saw him coming home and because I have him fondly. Why did not I had to have, no?

- And finally became convinced that a silly thought?

-It cost me tears and good words to bring him to reason.

-Believe me I feel have been because of that.

'Do not give anything, because if I had not been with Nah, you would not have missed another who take bad judgments. Hey, I have not told you the best. My daddy he tamed the child foals Justinian, and he had to come to see a calf that was in treatment: in one of the occasions when the white wine, Tiburcio found here.

- Here?

-Do not be a fool, at home. For punishment of my sins I again found again.

-I think they're two, Salome.

-I wish I had been that alone: also found a Sunday afternoon he came to ask for water.

-Three.

'Nothing more, because although it has been at other times, Tiburcio not seen it, but to me it makes me have told that.

- And everything seems nothing in two dishes?

- Nah, you also give the same thing? And agora! Do I have to blame for that white one to come? Why is not my daddy says no again, if you can?

-Is that there are simple things difficult to do.

-Ah, well: that same I say to Tiburcio, but everything has its remedy, and that I dare not speak.

Soon-to marry you, is not it?

-If I want both ... But him and when ... and is able to believe that I am one either.

Salome's eyes were watery, and after giving a few more steps, stopped to wipe away his tears.

Do not cry, 'I said: I am certain that he does not believe this: all this is the work of the jealousy and nothing else, you'll see how to remedy.

'I do not think, unless there be tibante. Because you have said is the son of a gentleman, no one gives the ankle as conceited, and imagines that he is no more ... Gee, as if I were a black muzzle or some manumisa like him. Now tucked away where provincial, and all for kicking me, because I know him much: well I glad that Joseph Lord cast to hell.

-It must not be unfair. What is special about it is jornaleando home of Joseph? That means it takes time, worse would be to pass the days tunando.

'Look I know who Tiburcio. Less'd love to be ...

'But you seem nice because you will, in which grace makes damn, do they also seem pretty few see?

-So.

I laughed at the answer, and twisting her eyes, said:

- Velay! What does that make you ticklish?

'But do not you see you're doing the same with Tiburcio, exactly the same as it does to you?

- Good God! Did I do that?

'Well, be jealous.

- Of course not!

- No?

- What if he wanted to? To me nobody takes my head that if Lord Joseph consented, that fickle marry Lucia, and only for persons and Traffic is up with both, if they let him.

Lucia-Well Know that since I was little girl wants a brother Braulio will soon come, and you can be sure, because Transit has told me.

Salome was thoughtful. Finally arrived and the cocoa, and sitting on a log, he said with his feet hanging swinging a mop of Good afternoon:

'So say, what good do you think?

- Can I have permission to refer to what we have discussed Tiburcio?

-No, no. So Nah, you want more, do not go.

-If only I ask if you consent.

- Todito?

-Complaints without grievances.

-If every time I think of what he imagines me, I know not what I say ... See: it makes me better than to tell, because if I do not want, then I will walk tired of saying that mourn for him, and that he wanted to please.

-So, believe me, Salome, there is no way to remedy your troubles.

- Ah work! Exclaimed getting to mourn.

Come on, do not be a coward, I said brushing her hands from her face: tears from your eyes worth much so that spills profusely.

-If Tiburcio believe that, I would spend the nights I cried until I fell asleep, to see him so unpleasant for him and see that my daddy took my theme.

- What do you bet me to come tomorrow afternoon to see and be content Tiburcio?

- Ah, I confess I would not have money to pay him-I said shaking my hand in his, and bringing it to her cheek. Do you promise?

-Very unhappy and I must be stupid if I fail.

-See that I take his word. But his life is not going to tell Tiburcio well as we've been all alone and ... Because again hit the other day, and that itself was ruin everything. Now-added starting to climb the fence, flip it over there and not see me jump, or we jump together.

Scrupulous-litter, you were not much.

-If every day I catch more shame. Get on it.

But as happened to Salome, to fall on the other hand, found it difficult to not find me, he remained sitting on the fence saying:

-Look at the child, say something. Well now I have to lose if it turns.

-Let me help you, see that it's getting late and my comadre ...

- Perhaps it is like that? ... And asina, how I want to get off? Do not see that if I mess? ...

-Cut the monads and lean presenting here I said my shoulder.

Make force-therefore weight because I like ... a pen-concluded jumping nimbly. I'll put creidísima, because I know many would jump white and well talanqueras.

'You're a boquirrubia.

- Is that the same as piquicaliente? Because then I will entromparme with ustment.

- Are you going to do?

- Goodbye! ... What you do not understand?, Because I'm going to get angry. What did I do to Nah, you know how when you put good bravo? Is craving I have.

- What if you could not be content after?

- Ayayay! No I have watched it again the heart is a weed if you see me crying.

-But that's because you do not know by coquetry.

- What do I do? What's the story?

-Co-that-you-laugh.

-And what does this mean? Tell me, who really do not know ... only bad thing is ... Then I have one very guardadita, okay l'hey?

- Good deal!, While you waste it.

-Let's see, let's see: di'aquí step if he says no.

'I'll go alone-I said taking a few steps.

- Jesus, I was even able to ruffle l'water. And what dried sheet? ... Nothing, tell me what I waste. Now I will put what.

-Di.

-Will ... Is it love?

-The same.

- And what remedy? Because I want to believe that? If it were white, but very white, rich but very rich ... yes it Nah, you would want to, right?

- Do you think so? What we did with Tiburcio?

- With Tiburcio? By l'wing friend to hold out to all, we would put Butler had here and said closing the hand.

-I should be the plan.

- Why? Will not you want me to?

It's not that, but the destination that you like to Tiburcio.

Salome laughed with all wins.

We had reached the Riecito, and she then put the blanket over the lawn seat should serve in the shadows, knelt on a stone and began to wash his face. Then it was over, he would break out of the waist a handkerchief to dry, and I presented the sheet saying

'That will make you ill if you bathe.

-Nearly ... almost back to bathe, and that is as tibiecita l'water, but Nah, you cool off for a while, and pray that come Fermin, while Nah, you just, give me a dip in the pool below.

Standing and, looked at me and smirked as he ran his hands through his hair wet. At last I said:

- Do I believe that I have dreamed that it was all true what he was saying?

- What Tiburcio not want you anymore?

- Malaya!, I was white ... When I woke up, I went into a grief so great, the next day was Sunday and I did not think the parish but in the dream while it lasted Mass: Nah, you sit where washing is, brooded all week with just that and ...

Disrupted innocent confidences Salome cries of "Chinese, Chinese!" That to the side of my friend gave cacaotal calling pigs. Salome was a little frightened, and looking round, said:

And this has become Fermin smoke ... Bathe soon, then I'm going to look upstream, not wait for him to leave without.

-Wait for him here, he will come after you. All this is because you have heard from my friend. Do you imagine that he does not like us to talk the two?

Let's talk, yes, but ... as.

Jumping with great agility on the boulders of the shore, disappeared behind the lush charcoal.

The cries of compadre continued and made me think that he trusted in me had its limits. We definitely had followed distantly by between cacao, and only to lose sight had resolved to call the herd. Custodian unaware that his recommendation was already accomplished diplomatically, and the thousand charms of her daughter, no soul could be blind and deaf than mine.

I returned to the house to pass Salome and Fermin, which were laden with pumpkin zumbos: she had a bun in her handkerchief and placed it on the head about the rustic pitcher, without being supported by any hand, did not prevent the conductive body donoso hold all their ease and grace of movement.

Then he jumped Salome as the first time, thanked me with a "God bless you" and his most droll smile, adding:

-In return for this, I was throwing up side while bathing, guabitas, saithe and sturdy flowers, will you not see?

-Yes, but I thought it would be a game of monkeys up there.

-What is disengaged Nah, you, and that I take a fall ainas by getting on the guabo.

- And you're so stupid that you do not think I realized it was you who threw flowers down the river?

-As Juan Angel told me that they throw roses hacienda on the stack when bathing Nah, you will, I jumped into the water the best we had on Mt.

During the meal I had occasion to admire, among other things, the ability of Salome and my comadre grill and half-ripe cheeses, fried fritters, and to do temple pandebono to jelly. In the comings and goings of Salome to the kitchen, I put my friend in on what he really wanted the girl and what I planned to do to get them to work either. He had no taste for the poor in the body, and even a few jokes about the willingness with which I served at the table, my partner gave her a ride, which was reached after much anger her.

Past warm hours, at four in the afternoon, the house was a revolt ark of Noah, the ducks started by families go through the living room, the hens to riot in the yard at the foot of plum, where forks canoíta rested guava was eating corn on my horse turkeys strutted inflated Creoles and returning the screams of two parrots they called a corn-Benita, who was to be the cook and pigs squealing their heads trying to introduce among the sills door shut. To which we must add the screams of my friend to give orders and those of his wife shooing the ducks and hens calling. Were long goodbyes and promises I made my comadre much to commend Buga Miracle for me to do well on the trip and come back soon. Leave of Salome, squeezed my hand much, and perhaps more affectionately at me, told me:

-Nah, you look good with story. I do not say goodbye to bludgeon his way ... because even crawling, the way I see it out, if it does not come to pass. I forget ... see it or not, I do not know what to do with my daddy.

On the other side of one of the ravines between quingueadas noisy tapes down the declivio forest, I heard a loud voice of a man who sang:

While time I ask

and time gives me time,

and while he says

he desengañará me.

The singer left the trees, and was Tiburcio, with the poncho hung from one shoulder and leaning on a staff whose other end hung a small mess, entertained their way instinctively counting his troubles to loneliness. He stopped and he stopped the saw me, and after a respectful greeting and smiling told me later that I went:

- Wow! afternoon climbing and escape ... When Retinto sweats ... Where does the wind sorbiéndose well?

-You make some visits, and last, fortunately for you, Salome went home.

-And he was not going yore.

-Many have felt. And how long have not you go?

The boy, with his head down, he began to tear with the refrain one sprig of pineapple, and looked at me after responding:

She is to blame. What did he tell you?

-That you're an ingrate and a zealous and dying for you: nothing.

- Yea, all that you said? But then I saved the best.

- What do you call better?

-The party that has the child Justinian.

'Listen here: do you think I can be in love with Salome?

- What had to believe?

-For as love is Salome Justinian it like me. It is necessary you consider the girl in it is worth, that for your sake, is a lot. You have offended the jealousy, and so you go to please her, she will forgive you and love you all more than ever.

Tiburcio stood thoughtfully before answering with an accent and air of sadness:

-Look, Ephraim child, I love so much, that she did not set the crunched to me through this month. When you have your genius as to what God gave me, everything holds less than one per cipote have (your honor forgiving the bad word). Yo, I'm saying that Salome is at fault, I know what I'm saying.

-What we do not know is that today telling your grievances is desperate and cried to me sorry.

- Really?

-And I inferred that the cause of all is you. If you love her as you say, why do not you marry her? Once at home, who had to see it without your consintieras?

-I confess that if I thought about getting married, but I resolved: the first because I had always malicious Salome, and the two that I do not know if the Lord would give me Custodio.

'Well, it you know what I said, and as for my friend, I answer. You need to obres rationally, and that test I think, this very evening Salome go home, and before you understood such feelings, you make a visit.

- Wow your desire! Yea I answer all?

I know that Salome is the most honest girl, pretty and industrious you can find, and as compadres, I know you will give it gustosísimos.

-Well there you'll see that I'm encouraging to go.

-If you leave then and Salome despecha and lose, no one will have to complain.

-I pattern.

-Agreed, and it is useless to push yourself how you will warn me, because I am sure that I'll be grateful. And goodbye, they will be five.

'Goodbye, my boss, God bless. I always tell you what happens.

-Watch where you're going to sing Salome heard singing these verses were coming.

Tiburcio laughed before answering.

- Do you seem insults? Tomorrow, and tell me.

L

The clock in the hall was five. My mother and I expecting Emma walking in the corridor. Maria sat in the first steps of the bleachers, dressed in green suit that contrast was so beautiful with her dark brown hair with two braids hairstyles then with which he played John half asleep in her lap. He stood up to me dismounting. The boy begged him strolled a little while on my horse, and Mary went with him in the arms to help me put on the tortoise holsters, saying:

-It's only five, what exactly! if it were always so ...

- What did you do today with your Mimiya? I asked John after we left the house.

She is the one that has been silly today, I replied.

- How so?

-For crying.

- Ah! Why have not you satisfied?

-He would not, but I did and I brought flowers affections, but I told mom.

- What did mom?

She's contented himself hugging because Mimiya mom wants more than me. He's been silly, but do not say anything.

I received Juan María.

- Have you already watered the plants? I asked, rising.

-No, I was waiting. Talk time with mom and Emma, said quietly, and so it's time, I'll go to the orchard.

She always feared that my sister and my mother could believe that because of my affection entibiase the two, and sought his reward them with what they had taken mine.

Mary and I just water the flowers. Sitting on a stone bench, we were almost at our feet the stream, jasmine and a group of us hid all eyes except those of John, who sang his way, was stupefied embarking on leaves and passion fruit peels, beetles and chapules prisoners.

Pale rays of the sun, which was hiding behind the mountains of Mulaló half muffled by gray clouds gold filleted, played with the shadows of the willows luengas whose green plumes caressing wind.

We had talked about Charles and his quirks, my visit to the house of Salome, and Mary's lips smiled sadly, because his eyes were not smiling anymore.

Look at me, I said.

His eyes had something of languor that embellished on the nights they watched at the bedside of my father.

-John not deceived me I added.

- What did he say?

-What have you been silly today ... do not call ... you've cried and could not be content, is it true?

-Yes. When you and Dad were going to ride this morning, I thought for a moment and come back no longer deceived me. I went to your room and I was convinced that it was not true, because I saw so many things you could not leave yours. Everything seemed so sad and quiet after you disappeared in the fall, I had more fear than ever that day comes, it comes not possible and avoid ... What shall I do? Tell me, tell me what to do to make these years pass. You for they can not be watching this. Dedicated to the study, seeing new countries, forget many things for hours, and I can not forget anything ... I leave here, and remembering and hoping I will die.

Placing his left hand on my shoulder for a moment rested her head on her.

'Do not talk like that, Mary said in a choked voice and shaking my hand stroking his pale-face, not talk like that, you destroy the last bit of my courage.

- Ah! You still have value, and for days I lost everything. I was able to settle-added hiding his face with his handkerchief-I due to wear on me borrow this desire and anguish that tormented me, because by your side that became something to be in happiness ... But you go with it, and I'm alone ... and I will not be as once was ... Oh! Why did you come?

His last words made me shudder, and leaning his forehead on the palms of the hands, respected his silence, overwhelmed by their pain.

-Ephraim said in his soft voice after a few moments, look, I do not cry.

-Maria lifting her face told him, in which she had to see something strange and solemn, as still and stared at me, do not complain to me about my return, did you complain to my childhood companion, who wanted love you like I love you; cúlpate then being you ... complain to God. What have I required, you have given me and I could not be required before Him?

- Nothing! Oh, no! Why do you ask that? ... I do not blame you, but do you blame for what? ... Now I'm not complaining ...

- Do not just do it once and for all?

- No, no ... What did I say, what? I am an ignorant girl who does not know what it says. Look at me, continued to take one of my hands: do not be spiteful to me for that nonsense. I will have value because ... I will have everything I complain about anything.

Again leaned her head on my shoulder, and she added:

-I will not ever tell you that ... You have never mad at me.

As I wiped her last tears, kissed my lips first waves of hair that fringed the front, to get lost in the beautiful braids after they were rolled over my knee. Then raised his hands almost to touch my lips to defend her against the touching of them, but in vain, because they dared not touch her.

LI

On January 28, two days before the date set for my trip, I went up to the mountain early. Braulio had come to take me, sent by Joseph and girls who wanted to get my farewell at home. The mountain did not interrupt my silence during the march. When we arrived, Transit and Lucia were milking the cow Butterfly on patiecito Braulio's cabin, and rose to greet me with their usual entertainments and joy, inviting me to enter.

-Abolish before ordering novillona-I told my shotgun leaning in the arena, but Lucy and me, because I get so remember me every morning.

I took the socobe, in which snow and foam whitened background, and putting it under the udder of the butterfly, finally I managed to Lucia, all embarrassed, he had just filled. While I was doing this, I said looking at the cow below:

-Since there are over the nephews of Joseph, for I know that he has a brother Braulio more handsome than him, and he loves you since you were like a doll ...

-As another to another-I interrupted.

-The same. I'll tell Mrs. Luisa that insists to her husband to come and help the nephew, and so when I come back, you will not get all red.

- Hey, hey! Leaving said milking.

- Did not you?

-But how you want to finish, if Nah, you is so thrush? ... Has no more.

- And those two full tits? Sort them.

-This does not, if those are the calf.

- So tell Luisa?

He stopped pressing the lower teeth with their voluptuous lips to make them into a language that gestito Lucia meant "to see and how not," and on my 'do what you want. "

The calf, who despaired because he removed the muzzle, made with one end of the hobble, and tied him to a cow hand, was at ease with the milking just pull one end of the rope, and Lucia, seeing pounce the udder, said:

-That's what you wanted; cabezón more annoying ...

After which came into the house carrying on the head and looking at me mischievously socobe sideways.

I evict a creek bank a family of geese dozing on the lawn, and I began to make my headdress morning while talking with Transit and Braulio, who had the pieces of clothing that I had stripped.

- Lucia! Transit-cried; Bring the embroidered cloth that is in the little trunk pastuso.

-Comes not think I said to my goddaughter, and then I told them what I had discussed with Lucia.

They were laughing while Lucia was presented running with what had been requested, against everything we expected, and as guessed we'd tried, and that of her brothers she laughed, handed me back the cloth aside to face not see her and she saw me, and turned to Transit to make the following observation:

-Come see your coffee, because I will burn, and allow yourself to be there laughing out loud.

- That's it? Transit asked.

- Ih! time ago.

- What's that coffee? I asked.

-Well, I told the lady, the last day I was there, I taught him to do, because I put it to you fail like the chamois, and that's why we found busily milking.

That said hanging the cloth, which I had returned, in one of the palm fronds of fern picturesquely placed in the center of the courtyard.

In the house attracted attention at the same time the simplicity, cleanliness and order: everything smelled of cedar wood that were made of rustic furniture, and flourished under the eaves pots of carnations and daffodils that Mrs. Luisa had embellished the little cabin of his daughter on the pillars had deer heads and stuffed legs thereof scribbles served in the living room and the bedroom.

Transit introduced me, between smug and fearful, the coffee cup, first test the lessons he had received from Mary, but most happy test since I tried it from rivaling met anyone who knew so beautifully prepared Juan Angel.

Braulio and I went to call Mrs. Joseph and Luisa, to almorzasen us. The old man was settling in jigras arracachas and vegetables that would send the market the next day, and she running out of the oven cassava bread that would serve for lunch. The batch had been happy as demonstrated not only the golden color of fluffy bread, but tantalizing fragrance given off.

We had lunch in the kitchen all: Traffic list and played his role smiling hostess. Lucia threatened me with his eyes whenever he showed with his father mine. The peasants, with instinctive delicacy, discarded any reference to my trip, not to embitter the last few hours we spent together.

It was already eleven. José, Braulio and I had visited the new banana grove, clearing they were doing and filote cornfield. Meeting again in the parlor of Braulio's house, and sat on stools around a cast net, we put the past sinkers, and Mrs. Luisa shelled corn with girls pillar. They like me and they felt that the time had our farewell fearsome. All we kept silent. He must have something on my face that moved, because dodging me. Finally, making a resolution, I got up, having seen my watch. I took my gun and its trappings, and to hang in one of the scribbles of the room, I told Braulio:

-Whenever you hit a good shot with it, remember me.

The mountaineer had no voice to thank me.

Mrs. Luisa, sitting still, still reeling off the cob that was holding, without bothering to hide his weeping. Traffic and Lucia, standing and leaning to either side of the door, gave me back. Braulio was pale. Joseph pretended to look for something in the corner of the tools.

'Well, ma'am,' I said to the old woman appears to leaning to hug you a lot for me.

She began to weep without answering.

Stand on the edge of the door, I put together in a single embrace on my chest the heads of the girls, who sobbed while my tears rolled down her hair. When separating myself from them turned to look at me and José Braulio, neither was in the living room, I waited in the corridor.

'I'm leaving tomorrow,' he said extending his hand Jose.

Well we knew he and I would not go. Then I let go of her arms Braulio, his uncle shook me in theirs, and wiping his eyes with the sleeve of his shirt, took the path of slashing while I began to walk in the opposite direction, followed by May, and making a sign to Braulio to not accompany me.

LII

Slowly descended to the bottom of the canyon only gurríes distant song of the river and the sound disturbed the silence of the forest. My heart was saying goodbye to each of these sites, the path to each tree, every stream crossing.

Sitting on the river bank saw its currents roll at my feet, thinking of the good people who just made my farewell so many tears, and let mine drip on me fleeing waves as the halcyon days of those six months .

Half an hour after I got home and went to my mother's sewing room, where she and Emma were only. Although our childhood has passed, so we do not deny their mimes a tender mother: we lack their kisses your forehead, fades too soon perhaps, not resting on his lap, his voice not aduerme us, but our soul receives nurturing touch of his.

More than an hour had passed there, and surprised not to see Mary asked her.

-We were with her in the oratory, he replied Emma now wants us to pray all the time, then went to the bakery: will not know you're back.

I never happened to return home without seeing Mary few moments later, and much feared he had relapsed into gloom that discouraged me so much, and to conquer which had been doing in the past week continued efforts.

After an hour, during which I was in my room, called John to the door to go to eat.

When I found out Mary leaning against the railing of the corridor falling sewing.

-Mom has not called-I told the boy laughing.

- And who taught you to tell lies? 'I replied: Mary will not forgive it.

She was the one who sent me, 'said John pointing.

Averiguarle Mary turned me toward the truth, but it was not necessary, because she herself was accused with his smile. His bright eyes were the quiet joy that our love had taken away their cheeks, rosy that hermoseaba live during our childhood romps. She wore a white skirt billowing over whose graceful braids at the slightest movement of your waist or your feet, playing with the carpet.

- Why are you sad and locked? -He said: I have not been well today.

-Maybe I answered yes to have a pretext to examine it closely Approaching the fence that separated us.

She lowered her eyes again pretending to tie his laces long gro blue apron, and then crossed his hands behind her waist, leaned against a window sash saying:

- Is not it true?

-I doubted it, because as you just cheat ...

- See what a delusion! What may be good to sneak around and locked out after a night made?

-I like to see that brave. What good will let you see two hours after I arrived?

- What are the twelve hours of coming off the mountain? I've also been busy. But I saw you when you came down. For more signs were bringing no shotgun, and May had been left far behind.

-So? Many occupations, and what have you done?

-In all: something good and something bad.

-A watch.

'I prayed a lot.

'I said that every day Emma want to pray with you.

'Because I tell if I'm sad Virgin, she hears me.

- How do you know?

-In that takes away a bit this sadness and I'm less afraid you'll think. You will take your Dolorosita, right?

-Yes.

-Join us tonight at the chapel and see how true what I say.

- What else have you done?

- Are you evil?

-Yes, the bad.

- Do you pray with me tonight and tell you?

-Yes.

'But you will not tell Mom, because angry.

-I promise not to tell.

'I've been aplanchando.

- Do you?

'Well, I do.

-But how do you do that?

-A mom hidden.

-You do well to hide it.

-If I do it very rarely.

-But what need is there to spoil your hands so ...?

- So what? ... Ah, yes, I know. It was that I wanted you to wear your nicest shirts aplanchadas for me. Do not like? Yes thanks I get, right?

- And who taught you to aplanchar? How did you come to?

-One day Juan Angel returned some shirts to the servant in charge of that, because supposedly his young master did not seem good, I looked at them and I told him that I would Marcelina help to make you seem better. She believed they had no defect, but stimulated me, you were and always spotless, never happened again because the devolvieras, though I had not touched.

-I thank you very much all that care, but I figured you had to handle forces or an iron hand.

-If it is a very small, and wrapping the handle well in a tissue, it can not hurt your hands.

-Let's see how you do.

-Buenecitas then.

-Muéstramelas.

-If you are as always.

-Who knows.

-Look at them.

I took them in mine and they rubbed the palms, soft as satin.

- Do you have anything? I asked.

-As mine can be rough ...

-I am not the well. What did you do in the mountains?

-To suffer a lot. I never believed that afflict both my farewell, and I say goodbye cause so much grief, particularly Braulio and girls.

- What did they tell them?

- Poor! Nothing, because the drowning her tears too said they could not hide ... But do not be sad. I was wrong to speak of this. I remember that at the last hours we spend together, as you can see today, resigned, almost happy.

'Yes,' he said, turning to wipe her eyes, I want to be so ... Tomorrow, and tomorrow only! ... But since it's Sunday, we all day together: we'll read something of what we were reading when you were newly come, and tell me how you like You ought to see me more, to dress that way.

-As you are right now.

-Good. They're coming to call you to dinner ... Now, to the late-added disappearing.

So used to saying goodbye to me, but then we had to be together, because the same thing to me, it seemed that being surrounded by family, we were separated from each other.

LIII

At eleven twenty-nine night I left the family and Mary in the lounge. Ensure in my room until I heard the clock strike one in the morning, early in the day so long feared and at last arrived, did not want his first moments find me asleep.

With the same suit he had me lay down on the bed when struck two. The handkerchief of Mary, still fragrant with the perfume she always wore, worn by their hands and moistened with tears, received on the pillow which rolled from my eyes like a fountain that never be exhausted.

If I shed yet, remembering the days before my trip, could serve to dampen this pen to historiarlos, if it were possible to my mind only once, even for a moment, surprise my painful heart all your secret to reveal, the lines that I would be fine to draw much have cried, but perhaps unfortunate for me. It is possible to delight us with a regret forever loved: as pain, pleasure hours leave. If ever we were allowed to stop them, Mary had managed to slow that preceded our farewell. But, alas, all, deaf to their crying, blind to her tears, flew, and flew promising to return.

A nervous tremor woke me up two or three times when sleep came to relieve me. Then my eyes roamed the room and dismantled and in disarray for travel arrangements, room where I waited many times the dawns of happy days. And he sought to reconcile again disrupted sleep, because then turned to her and blushing as beautiful as the first evening of our walks after my return, thoughtful and quiet as it used to stay when I did my first confidences, in which almost nothing is had told both our lips and our eyes and smiles quietly confiding secrets and trembling child of her most chaste love, less shy to order his eyes to mine, to let me see them in exchange for his soul to show him mine ... The sound of a shuddering sob again, the evil of those who drowned had left his chest that night when we parted.

It was five o'clock when after I still pains to hide the traces of painful insomnia, I was walking in the corridor, still dark. Very soon saw light shining through the cracks of the closet of Mary, and then I heard John's voice calling her.

The first rays of the rising sun, tried in vain to tear the dense fog that as a huge, flowing veil hanging from the tops of the mountains, the plains extending to distant floating. On the western mountains, clean and blue, then yellowed Cali temples, and at the foot of the slopes which herds grouped whitened the little towns of Yumbo and Vijes.

Juan Angel, after bringing me coffee black and my horse saddled, which blackened impatient with his steps the orange foot Gramal it was tied, I expected crying, leaning against the door of my room, with leggings and spurs in their hands: the calzármelos, his cry fell in heavy drops on my feet.

Do not cry, 'I said, giving security to laboriously my voice: when I return, and you will be man, and not separate from me again. Meanwhile, all you want a lot at home.

It was time to gather all my strength. My spurs resounded in the hall, he was alone. I pushed the door ajar, the sewing of my mother, who threw the seat that was on my arms. She knew that demonstrations of their pain could make my spirit waver, and between sobs was talk of Mary and me tender promises.

All had dampened my chest with his weeping. Emma, who had been the last, knowing what I looked around me at desasirme of his arms, he pointed to the door of the chapel, and went to him. On the altar radiating its light beige two lights: Mary, sitting on the carpet, on which stood the white of his robe, gave a little cry to feel, again dropping unbraided head on the seat was reclined when the I entered. And hiding his face, raised his right hand for me to take: half kneeling, bathed her in tears and covered her with caresses, but to my feet, as if afraid that distract me and, suddenly rose to cling sobbing my neck. My heart had kept for almost all that time her tears.

My lips rested on his forehead ... Mary, shaking her head trembling, undulating loops did her hair, and hiding the face in my chest, one arm extended to point out to the altar. Emma, who had just entered the inanimate received in her lap, pleading gesture asking me to distract me. And I obeyed.

LIV

For two weeks I was in London, and one night I received letters from home. I broke up with trembling hand the package closed with the seal of my father.

There was a letter from Mary. Before unfold, I looked into it that perfume too familiar to me from the hand that had written, still preserved, in its folds was a bit of lily chalice. My eyes clouded futilely tried reading the first lines. I opened one of the windows of my room, because it seemed not enough air Serme in him ... Rosales of the garden of my love! ... American Mountains, mountains ... mine! Blue nights! The vast city, and still murmuring half muffled in his cloak of smoke, looked like sleeping under the thick curtains of a leaden sky. A gust of north wind hit my face penetrating the room. Terrified I gathered the leaves of the balcony, and alone with my pain, at least alone, wept long surrounded by darkness.

Excerpts of the letter of Mary:

"While desktops are in the dining room after dinner, I come to your room to write. This is where I can mourn without anyone coming to console, where I suppose I can see you and talk to you. Everything is as you left it, because Mom and I have wanted to be so: the last flowers to put on your table have withered and fallen to the bottom of the vase: is no longer a single, the seats in the same places, books as they were open on the table and the last in which you read, your hunting outfit, where he hung back from the mountain the last time, the almanac rack that always showing ay January 30, as feared, as frightening and as past! Right now flowering branches of roses come as your window to get you to hug me and shake again telling them.

"Where will you be? What will you do now? I gain nothing demanded many times be a map to show me how you would make the trip, because I can not figure out anything. It scares me to think of the sea that everyone loves, and my torment you always see through him. But after your arrival in London you will tell me everything: tell me how is the landscape around the house where you live, I thoroughly describirás your room, their furniture, ornaments, tell me what you do every day, how you spend your nights , what time study, in which you rest, how are your walks, and think more of what times your Mary. Restore to me to say what hours are here to there, because I forgot.

"Joseph and his family have been three times since you left. Traffic and Lucia not named without being tear-filled eyes, and are so sweet and loving with me, so fine if I talk about you, it is hardly credible. They have asked me if you come to where you letters that you write, and glad to know that yes, I have been asked to tell you a thousand things on your behalf.

"May you not forget. The day after you ran desperately up the house and the garden looking for you. He went to the mountain, and prayer, when he returned, he began to howl sitting on the hill of the climb. I saw him after lying at the door of your room: I opened it, and entered full of taste, but after finding you ferreted everywhere again approached me sad, and you seemed wondering eyes, the lacked only mourn, and I appoint you, raised his head as if to see you go. Poor! They figure that you hide from it as you did for impacientarlo sometimes, and enters all rooms walk step by step and without making a sound, waiting to surprise you.

"Last night I finished this letter not because mom and Emma came for, they think it hurts to be here when if prevented me be in your room, do not know what would.

"John woke up this morning wondering if you were back, because naming you hear me asleep.

"Our lilies bush has given the first, and in this letter is a bit. Is not it true that you're sure you never cease to bloom? So I need to believe, and I think the will of the most beautiful roses in the garden. "

LV

For a year I had two times each month letters of Mary. The latter were full of melancholy so profound that compared to them, the first I received seemed written in our days of happiness.

In vain had tried to revive her sadness saying that destroy your health, but until then had been as good as I said, in vain. "I know I can not take much for me-I see you had answered, and since that day and I can not be sad, I will always be by your side ... No, no, no one can separate us again. "

The letter containing these words was the only one who got it in two months.

In the last days of June, I presented an afternoon Mr. A. .., who had just arrived from Paris and had not seen since last winter.

-I bring you letters from home, 'he said after we embraced.

- Three-mails?

-From one. We speak a few words before-I observed holding the package.

I noticed something sinister in his face that disturbed me.

'I came,' he added after a few moments silently walked around the room, to help you to have her return to America.

- Al Cauca! I said, forgetting for a moment about everything except Mary and my country.

'Yes,' I replied, but you will have already guessed the cause.

- My mother! -I burst baffled.

-It's good replied.

- Who then? I shouted, grabbing the package were holding hands.

-No one has died.

- Mary! Mary! I exclaimed, as if she could go to my voice, and fell limp on the seat.

'Come on, trying to be heard said Mr. A. .. -, this was necessary for my coming. She will live if you arrive on time. You read the letters, that there should come one of them.

'Come,' he said, come quickly, or I'll die without saying goodbye. Finally I agree that you confess the truth: a year ago Hourly kills me that this disease that cured me for a few days. If they had not interrupted this happiness, I have lived for you.

"If you come ... Yes, you will come, because I have the strength to hold out until you see, if you come find only a shadow of your Mary, but that shadow needs hug before disappearing. If you do not hope, if a force more powerful than my will drag me without you I animes without closing my eyes, Emma let him keep it for you, all that I know you will be kind: my braids hair, the locket where are yours and my mother, you put the ring in my hand just before you leave, and all your cards.

"But, why grieve telling you all this? If you come, I will encourage, if I hear your voice, if your eyes tell me a moment alone knew what they tell me, I will live and will be as it was. I do not want to die, I can not die and leave you alone forever. "

You-me-Finish said Mr. A. ... collect the letter from my father fall at my feet. You yourself know that we can not waste time.

My father said what I had already known too cruelly. Quedábales doctors only hope of saving Mary which made them keep my back. Given this need my father did not hesitate; ordenábame precipitud return as possible, and apologized for not having prepared well before.

Two hours after I left London.

LVI

Hundíase in nebulous confines of Pacific Sun July 25, filling the horizon with flashes of gold and ruby chasing their horizontal rays until they were blue waves as fugitive to hide under the dark forests of the coast. The *Emilia Lopez*, aboard which I came from Panama, anchored in the bay of Buenaventura after having played around on the carpet caressed by sea breezes on the coast.

Reclining on the deck railing, gazed at the sight of those mountains which was reborn as sweet hopes. Seventeen months before rolling to his feet, driven by the tumultuous currents of Dagua, my heart had said goodbye to each of them, and their solitude and silence had been harmonized with my pain.

Shaken by breezes, trembling in my hands a letter from Maria who had received in Panama, which I read in the light of the dying twilight. My eyes just cross it ... Beige and still looks wet with my tears of those days.

"The news of your return has been enough to drive me strength. Now I can count the days, because each passing closer to that in which I see you again.

"Today has been very beautiful morning, as beautiful as those you have not forgotten. Emma did take me to the garden, I was in the sites that are most loved me in it, and I felt almost good under those trees, surrounded by all those flowers, watching the river run, sitting on the stone bench on the shore. If this happens to me now, how can I improve myself when I return to explore it together for you?

"I just put the lilies and roses to our picture of the Virgin, and I thought she looked me more gently than usual and he would smile.

"But they want to go to the city, because they say it better than doctors can assist me: I need no other choice but to see you with me forever. I want to wait here I do not want to leave all that you loved, because I figure that you left me and love me recommended less elsewhere. Dad beg to delay our trip, and meanwhile come, goodbye. "

The last lines were almost illegible.

The customs boat, drop anchor at the schooner, had left the beach, and was immediately.

- Lorenzo! I exclaimed to recognize a dear friend in the gallant stand mulatto came amid the Administrator and the chief of the guard.

- Here I go! Replied.

And rising precipitously scale, shook in his arms.

-Do not cry, 'said wiping her eyes with one end of his blanket and trying to smile: we are seeing and the sailors have a heart of stone.

Already half words I had said what I wanted to know more anxiety: Mary was better when he left home. Although two weeks ago I was waiting in Buenaventura, had not come to me but the letters he brought, probably because the family was waiting for me at any moment.

Lorenzo was not a slave. Faithful companion of my father in that he made frequent trips during its commercial life, was loved by the whole family, and enjoyed at home jurisdictions considerations butler and friend. In appearance and mood showed vigor and frank character: tall and strong, his forehead was spacious and tickets; beautiful shaded eyes and black curly eyebrows, straight nose and supple, beautiful teeth, beard loving smiles and energetic.

Verified visit the ship Manager ceremony, which had precipitated assuming meet him, put my luggage in the boat, and I jumped at it with the returnees, after I fired the captain and some of my co- trip. As we neared the shore, the horizon had already darkened: black waves, smooth and silent rocking passed to lose again in the dark: countless fireflies flitting about the crepe rumoroso the jungles of the banks.

The Administrator, subject to any age, obese, ruddy, was a friend of my father. Then we were on the ground, I drove home and put me in the room he had prepared for me. After hanging a hammock corozaleña, large and fragrant, left, before saying:

-I will make arrangements for clearance of your luggage, and more important and urgent to cook, because I guess that the wineries and confectionery not come very ornate *Emilia:* I found very frisky today.

Although the father was manager of a beautiful and interesting family established inside the Cauca, to take charge of the destiny that played, had not been resolved to bring it to the port, for a thousand reasons that I was given and I, despite my inexperience I found unanswerable. Porteñas People seemed increasingly cheerful, communicative and carefree, but find no serious harm in it, because after a few months on the coast, the same administrator had infected more than moderately of that carelessness.

After a quarter of an hour that I employed in my costume change to another board, the Administrator again for me: and instead brought her wedding ceremony, pants and spotless white jacket, his vest and tie had started a new season of darkness and abandonment.

-You will rest a couple of days here before continuing your journey, said filling two glasses with brandy that took a beautiful frasquera.

-But I do not need I can not rest, I watched.

-Take the brandy, is an excellent Martell, or do you prefer something else?

'I thought Lorenzo was prepared bogas and canoes for up early tomorrow.

'We'll see. So do you prefer gin or absinthe?

-Whatever you like.

-Health, for inviting me said.

And after emptying the cup of a drink:

- Is not it higher? Entrambos asked winking eyes, and producing with the tongue and palate a sound like the sound of a kiss, he added, is that you've already tasted the most stale of England.

-Everywhere burns the palate. Yea, I can get up early?

-If everything is mine jokingly replied carelessly lying in the hammock, wiping the sweat from his throat and forehead with a large silk scarf from India, fragrant like a bride. So burns huh? As the water and he are the only physicians have here, except snakebite.

Let's talk about really: What do you call your joke?

-The proposed some rest, man. Did you figure that your father is asleep to recommend me had everything ready for your departure? Going for Lorenzo arrived fifteen days, and they are ready for eight rowers and ranchada the canoe. The truth is that I had to be less punctual, and have made you that way let me ajonjear for two days.

- How much I appreciate your punctuality!

Laughed loudly hammock to be driving the air, saying at last:

- Ungrateful!

-Not that: You know I can not, I must not linger even an hour longer than necessary, it is urgent for me to come home soon ...

'Yes, yes, it is true, it would be selfish of me and said seriously.

- What do you know?

-The illness of one of the ladies ... But you would receive the letters I sent to Panama.

-Yes, thank you, in time to embark.

- Do not you say it's best:

-So they say.

- And Lorenzo?

She says the same thing.

After a moment when both we kept silence, cried Manager incorporated in the hammock:

- Mark, the food!

A servant entered to announce that after the meal was served.

'Come,' said my host standing up for hunger if you had taken the brandy would have a good appetite. Hello! -Added time we entered the dining room and heading for a page-: if they come looking for us, say we're not home. You need to go to bed early to get up early, I observed pointing the seat of the head.

He and Lorenzo were placed on either side of me.

- Devil! Exclaimed the Manager when the light of the beautiful table lamp bathed my face: what you brought bozo!, If you were not tan could swear not know say good morning in Castilian. It seems to me that I see your father when he was twenty, but I think you're taller than him: not that serious, certainly inherited your mother be with the Jewish believe the night we first landed in Pretoria . Do not you think Lorenzo?

-Same-answered.

-If you had seen my guest-continued addressing him-the desire of our Englishman then I said I would have to stay with me two days ... Became impatient to tell me my brandy burned something. Snails!, I feared that I scolded. Let's see if that's the same this red, and if we manage to make you smile. How about? He added after I tasted the wine.

-It's great.

-Trembling was that I did gesture because he is the best thing I could get to take in the river.

Manager cheerfulness did not falter for a moment for two hours. At nine allowed me to retire, promising to stand at four in the morning to accompany me to the pier. To say good night, said:

I hope that tomorrow you will not complain of rats as before: a bad night you did spend their hard expensive: they've done since deadly war.

LVII

At four good friend called to my door, and an hour earlier than I expected, and ready to go. The, Lorenzo and I had breakfast with coffee and brandy while the oarsmen canoes led to my luggage, and soon we were all on the beach.

The moon, big and in its fullness, and down at sunset, and appear under the dark clouds that had hidden, bathed the distant jungles, mangrove shorelines and the sea smooth and quiet with trembling and reddish glow, like the who spread the torches of a coffin on the marble floor and walls of a burial chamber.

- And now for how long? -I said to my manager corresponding with another goodbye hug tight.

'Maybe I will soon I replied.

- You go back, then, to Europe?

'Maybe.

This man seemed so festive melancholy at that time.

Moving away from the shore ranchada canoe, in which Lorenzo and I went, shouting:

- Have a good trip!

And to the two oarsmen:

- Cortico! Laurean! ... cuidármelo far cuidármelo just my own.

-Yes, my master answered the two black duo. Two blocks from the beach would be, and I thought to distinguish the white lump Manager, still in the same spot where he had just hug me.

The yellow glow of the moon, sometimes veiled, funeral always accompanied us until after entering the mouth of the Dagua.

I remained standing at the door of the rustic cabin, vaulted ceiling, made matambas, vines and leaves frigatebird, which call on the river ranch. Lorenzo, after having arranged a sort of bed on bamboo tables under that cave navigator, was sitting at my feet with his head resting on his knees and seemed to doze. Cortico (ie Gregorio, that this was his first name was sailing near us grumbling at times the tune of a bunde. Laurean The athletic body loomed like a giant profile over the past cloudscapes of the Moon almost invisible.

Hardly be heard singing and hoarse monotone of bamburés in shady mangrove shorelines and stealthy noise currents, breaking solemn silence surrounding deserts in their last sleep, deep sleep as long as man at last to at night.

-Take a drink, Cortico, and sings that song sadly told the dwarf vogue.

- Jesu!, My love, do you feel sad?

Lorenzo poured their chamberga pastusa more than enough of aniseed in the vogue mate introduced him, and he went on to say:

-Will the serene gave me hoarseness;-and turning to his companion: compae Laurean, the branco that if we want to clears chest alegrito cantemo a dance.

- A Try it! Replied the hoarse voice challenged and sound-: Another dance will be the one to start the escuro. Do you already know?

What mesmo-Po, sah.

Laurean tasted the brandy as knowledgeable in the field, muttering:

-Del no longer low.

- What's that dance in the dark? I asked.

Standing in his post for an answer sang the first verse of the next bunde, Cortico answering the second, after which they did break, and continued in the same way to put an end to the savage and heartfelt song.

It not Junde and moon;

Row, row.

What will my black so alone?

Cry, cry.

I take your dark night,

San Juan, San Juan.

Escura as my black

Ni ma, no ma.

The LU of mine s'ojo

Der ma, ma der.

The lightning appear,

Vogue, vogue.

He painfully harmonized singing with nature around us, the dull echoes of these immense forests repeated its plaintive accents, deep and slow.

-No more bunde-told blacks taking advantage of the last break.

- Would you like your honor poorly sung? Asked Gregory, who was the most communicative.

-No, man, very sad.

- Does juga?

-Whatever.

- Alabao! If either one when I sing and dance juga this Mariugenia black ... your honor believe me what I say to him 's'ángele sky bailala stomp with winning.

-Open your eyes and shut up, compae-Laurean said, Have you heard?

- Am I deaf?

-Well, can.

-Vamo a veil, sah.

The currents of the river began to fight against our boat. The clicks of herrones of levers and be heard. Sometimes Gregory gave a blow to the side of the canoe to mean you had to vary from shore, and we crossed the stream. Little or were becoming little dense fogs. From the sea we came the rumble of distant thunder. The rowers did not speak. A whispering flight noise like a hurricane on forests came in reach. Large drops of rain began to fall later.

I lay in bed that I had lying Lorenzo. This light would turn on, but Gregory, who saw him rub a match, he said:

-No sailing garment pattern because embarks dazzled me and the snake.

The rain lashed the roof ranch rudely. This darkness and silence were pleasing to me after the forced treatment and used the feigned kindness during my trip with all kinds of people. The sweetest memories, the saddest thoughts returned to dispute my heart at that moment to revive him or make him sad. Bastábanme and five days' journey to return to her in my arms and return life that my absence had stolen. My voice, my touch, my eyes, that had known so sweetly move her on other days, would not be able to disputársela to pain and death? That love to which science is considered impotent, that science was called to his aid, was able to do everything.

He walked in my memory what he said in his last letter: "The news of your return has been enough to drive me the forces ... I can not die and leave you alone forever. "

The family home amidst its green hills, shaded by willows elderly, adorned with roses, lit by the glare of the Sun at birth, was presented to my imagination were the robes of Mary the whispering about me Zabaletas breeze , which moved my hair, the essences of flowers grown by Mary, which I hoped ... And the desert with its aromas, perfumes and whispers was complicit in my delicious illusion.

He stopped the boat on a beach on the left bank.

- What is it? I asked Lorenzo.

-We are in the Arenal.

- Oopa! A guard who smuggled going Cortico shouted.

- Stop! Replied a man, I should be on the lookout, because that voice gave a few yards from shore.

The duo released bogas a boisterous laugh, and had not put an end to his Gregory, when he said:

- San Pablo blessed!, This itches almost Christian. Cape Ansermo at Buste going to kill a rumatismo stuck between a carrizar. Who told you I was going up, sah?

-Bellaco-ranger replied the witches. What do you wear?

-Ship people.

Lorenzo had lit light, and went out to the ranch, giving way to the black smuggler a loud slap on the back by way of affection. After openly and respectfully greeted me, he began to examine the guide, and while both Laurean and Gregory in loincloth, smiling mouth leaning out of the cabin.

Gregory's first cry to get to the beach alarmed whole detachment: two-faced guards more sleep deprived, and armed with carbines like waiting crouched low weeds, arrived on time and farewell libation. The huge chamberga Lorenzo had for all, which added that he should be willing to deal with other less contemptuous than their masters.

The rain had stopped and began to dawn, when after the layoffs and seasoned with spicy jokes laughter and something else that crossed between my bogas and guardians, we continue our trip.

From there forward the jungles of the banks were gaining in majesty and gallantry: palms groups became more frequent: one could see the spine straight pambil of stained purple in the milpesos leafy roots providing the delicious fruit and the chontadura guatle; distinguishing between all the Naidi of flexible stem and restless plumage, for I know not what flirty and reminiscent virgin seductive and elusive sizes. Most clusters with half the shell still defended that had sheltered, all with gold colored plumes, with rumors seemed to welcome a friend not forgotten. But there still remained the bejucadas of red festoons of vines fragile and beautiful flowers, the larvae silky and velvety moss of the rocks. The naguare and piáunde, as kings of the jungle, their tops towered over her to make out something greater than the wilderness distant sea.

The navigation was becoming increasingly painful. It was nearly ten when we Callelarga. On the left bank had a hut, built, like all of the river, on thick estantillos of guaiacum wood as is known, is petrified in humidity: so are the free inhabitants of the floods, and fewer family with snakes that for its abundance and diversity are terror and nightmare of travelers.

While Lorenzo, guided the oarsmen, was to have lunch at the house, I stayed in the boat getting ready to take a bath, whose excellence presage, the crystalline waters. But he had not reckoned with the mosquitoes, even though their poisonous bites make them memorable. I tormented taste, knocking him to the bathroom I took half his wild orientalism. The color and conditions of the epidermis of blacks, certainly defend these tenacious and hungry enemies, because I kept seeing that just took for the oarsmen notified of their existence.

Lorenzo brought me lunch on the boat, helped by Gregory, who fancied himself a good cook, and promised for the next day a coat.

We should arrive in the afternoon at St. Cyprian, and the boatmen did not beg for further travel, and invigorated by the red select Administrator.

The sun will not be belied summer.

When the banks permitted, Lorenzo and I, for desentumirnos or decrease the weight of the boat in danger steps confessed by the boatmen, we walked for a few short stretches of the shores, called Operation playear there, but in such cases the fear of tripping over some guascama or that any lanzase chonta is upon us, as members of that family of black snakes, plump and white collar usually what we did walk through the weeds more with his eyes than with his feet.

It was useless to find out if Laurean and Gregory were healers, because there are hardly any fashion that is not and does not carry tusks of many kinds of vipers and cons for several of them, among which are the grouse, atajasangre vines, evergreen, zaragoza , and other herbs that do not name and who kept in tiger fangs and hollowed alligator. But that is not enough to reassure travelers, it is known that such remedies are often ineffective, and dies that has been bitten, after a few hours, throwing blood through the pores, and with dreadful agonies.

We arrived in San Cipriano. On the right bank and the angle formed by the river that gives its name to the site, and the Dagua, which seems to rejoice with his meeting, was the house raised on stilts in the middle of a lush banana plantation. We had not yet jumped to the beach and Gregory and shouted:

- Na Rufina! Here I go! And then: 'Where viejota caught this?

'Good afternoon, no one answered Gregory Young black, peering into the corridor.

-I have to give inn, because I bring something good.

-Yes, sah, can rise.

- Does my partner?

-In the Board.

- Uncle Bibiano?

Asina ma-no, not Gregory.

Laurean said good afternoon and returned home to keep your silence accustomed.

While fashions and tackle Lorenzo drew the canoe, I was fixed on something Gregorio, without further comments, had called viejota: a snake was thick as a stout arm, nearly three yards long, rough back, color dried leaf and black speckled; belly that seemed assembled ivory pieces, huge head and mouth as big as the head itself, rolled up nose and fangs like cat claws. He was hanged by the neck on a pole pier and shore waters played with his tail.

- San Pablo! Lorenzo exclaimed looking at what I saw-, what big animal! Rufina, who had fallen to praise God, laughing noted that they had killed larger sometimes.

- Where did you find it? I asked.

-On the shore, my love, there in the chípero-he said, pointing to a distant green tree thirty yards from the house.

- When?

-A madrugadita that my brother was traveling, ARMAA met, and he brought her to get the counter. The companion was not there, but I saw it today and tomorrow he encounters.

The black woman told me at once that this snake hurt this way: holding on to a branch or vine with a sharp nail that has on the tip of the tail, straightens more than half of the body on the rocks of the rest: while the dam lurking no matter with distance such that only extended the entire length snake can reach it, stand still, and achieved this status, the victim bites and draws itself with an invincible force: if the prey moves away to the precise distance, repeat the attack until the victim expires: then wrapping the body wraps and sleeping well for a few hours. Cases have occurred in which hunters and boatmen are saved from this kind of death seizing the snake's throat with both hands and fighting with her to drown, or throwing a poncho over his head, but that's weird, because it is difficult to distinguish in the forest, armed resemble a slender trunk and feet and dry. While the wart is no where to grab your nail is completely harmless.

Rufina, pointing the way with admirable dexterity climbed the ladder consists of a single trunk guayacán notched, and even offered me his hand, half smiling and respectful, when would I step on the floor of the hut, made of chopped tables of pambil, black and shiny from use. She passes with braids neatly tied to the back of the head, which was not without a certain panache natural, Pancho follao blue and white shirt, all very clean, candongas of figs and blue choker same, augmented with escuditos and cavalongas I found amusing original, after leaving for so long to see women of that species and dejativo of his voice, which is grace, in people of the race, raising the tone in the stressed syllable of the word end of each sentence, so insert your waist and smiles elusive, Remigia reminded me on the night of their wedding. Bibiano, father of marriageable black, which was a fashionable little over fifty years, and disabled by rheumatism, a result of the trade, came to meet me, hat in hand, and leaning on a cane thick chonta: wearing panties yellow flannel shirt and blue list, whose skirts wore out.

Componíase the house, as it was one of the best in the river, a broker, which, in some way, then the room was because the walls of this palm, on two sides, just got up to rod and average soil, thus presenting the view of Dagua one hand and that of St. Cyprian dorrnido and gloomy on the other: the room was a bedroom, from which went to the kitchen stove which was formed by a large drawer palm tables filled with earth, on which rested the tulpas and apparatus for making fufu. Supported on the beams of the room, there was a stage that a third abovedaba, pantry species that were yellowing hartones and bananas, where he climbed a ladder Rufina often more comfortable than the patio. Cast nets hung from a beam and catangas, and were crossed over others, many levers and fishing poles. From a scribble hung a bad tambourine and an oak, and in one corner was lying the carángano, rustic music low in those banks.

Soon he was hanging my hammock. She saw lying on the distant mountains yet untrodden, that the last yellow light shone in the afternoon, and the waves of passing Dagua atornasoladas of blue, green and gold. Bibiano, stimulated by my frankness and affection, sitting near me, crezneja wove hat, smoking his congola, travel conversándome of his youth, of the deceased (his wife), of how to make fishing in pens and of their ailments. He had been a slave to thirty years in mine Iró as this, age succeeded, by dint of toil and economies, buy his freedom and that of his wife, who had recently survived its establishment in Dagua.

The oarsmen, with breeches and, chatted with Rufina, and Lorenzo, having drawn their refined edible stew to accompany Nayo was preparing us Bibiano's daughter, had come to lie quiet in the darkest corner of the room.

It was almost dark when they heard screams of passengers on the river: Lawrence hurried down and returned a few moments later the mail saying it was coming up, and had taken news that my luggage was in Mondomo.

Soon we rounded the night with all its pomp American: the nights of Cauca, the London, the last at sea, why were not as majestic as those sad?

Bibiano left me, believing me asleep, and was to rush food. Lorenzo candle lit table and prepared the house with the furniture of our wallet.

At eight o'clock all were, good or bad, accommodated sleeping. Lorenzo, after I had settled with almost maternal care in the hammock, lay in his.

Rufina-Taita said from his bedroom to Bibiano, who slept in the room with us-: your mercy hear the singing in the river warty.

Indeed, that side was heard something like a chicken cochlear huge.

Laurean lis-warn them-the girl continued to spend the morning with mannitol.

- Have OITE, man? Bibiano asked.

'Yes,' said Laurean sah, who must have been awake Rufina's voice, because as I realized later, was his girlfriend.

- What is this big flying here? I asked Bibiano, to figure out next and it would be a winged snake.

The bat, little master replied, 'but he has not foundered fear sleeping in the hammock.

The bats are real vampires such bleeding in a short time to let available who reaches the nose or fingertips, and actually save your sucking sleeping in the hammock.

LVIII

Lorenzo called me in the morning: my watch and saw it was three. In favor of the moon, the night seemed a dull day. At four, entrusted to the Virgin in the bridal Bibiano and his daughter, we embarked.

-Here he sings the warty, Laurean said to compae Cortico then we had sailed a short distance-kick Just outside, lest ARMAA ta.

All the danger for me was that the snake entered the canoe, as was advocated by the roof of the ranch, but she grabbed by one of the boatmen, the wreck was likely.

We happily, but, truth be told, none quiet.

Lunch that day was a copy of the above except the capped increase Gregory promised, stew prepared by making a hole on the beach, and once placed in him, wrapped in banana leaves, meat, bananas and others should compose the stew, covered with earth and above all lit a fire.

Amazing that the navigation was more painful onwards that we had done up there, but it was, in Dagua is where most properly be said that nothing is impossible.

At two in the afternoon, when we took a haven sweet, Luareán refused, and went into the forest some steps to bring back some leaves: after a matte estregarlas full of water until the liquid was stained green, slipped it into the crown of his hat and took it. Leaf juice was stinking, only antidote to fevers, terrible on the coast and in those banks, which effectively recognized as blacks.

The levers, when the river is low serve thousand times to avoid stellation are generally less useful for uploading. From Fringe, at every step and fell into the water Gregorio Laurean, always after the usual warning strike, and then the first cabestreaba by taking her canoe galindro, while the other drove her astern. So climbed cabezones jets or inevitable, but to get rid of the most furious had small canals called arrastraderos, practiced on the beaches, and more or less short of water, which was up the canoe hull skimming pebbles in the riverbed and sometimes teetering on the rocks more outgoing.

The condition worsened dumps afternoon: as more and more were taken down streams as we approached the little jump, the oarsmen impelled to change simultaneously shore up the canoe while a jump on it, to wield the levers; and leaving them at the moment, after crossing the river, prevented us snatch the stream, enraged at having let slip a dam and yours. After each set of this species, it was necessary to throw the canoe water had entered, the oarsmen operation executed instantly and feinting to step back to bring the foot forward into the firm, which went out of the way water plumadas thereof. Such developments and marveled executed gymnastic prodigies Laurean, although he, his height, with a wreath of branches sticking, would have passed for the god of the river, but made by Gregory, who saved his always smiling face, seemed to present the figure cut his companion, his legs that were walking almost an 'o', and whose feet were bent inward rather than feet, shrink instruments, those miracles of agility caused terror.

Overnight stay in the little jump that day, poor and bleak village despite the movement that gave their cellars. There's an obstacle to navigation, and is usually the end of the trip coming bogas del Puerto, and those who went up the little jump came only to jump, and at this point it down the boards daily.

The afternoon dragged my canoe overland bogas, and no ranch, to lay on the beach where he was embarking on the following day. The little jump to jump, the dangers of the trip out of the area of any weighting.

In the jump had to be repeated creep of the canoe to overcome the last obstacle that there deserves the honor of the name.

Forests were taking as we pulled away from the shore, all that majesty, gallantry, ink diversity and abundance of aromas that make the inland forests set indescribable. But the plant kingdom reigned almost alone: was heard from time to time and in the distance the singing of pauji; very rare pair of panchanas sometimes crossed over almost perpendicular mountains encajonaban the plain, and some spring flew stealthily under the dark vaults formed by Guabos crowded or the reeds, chontas, and chiperos naceredos on which rocked the arched guaduas their plumage. Kingfishers, waterfowl habitadora only those banks, bordered by the backwaters rarity with wings, or sink into them to get a little fish in its beak silver.

From the little jump find as many canoes down, and the most capable of them have eight yards long, and scarcely a wide.

The couple who ran bogas each canoe, rocking forward and constantly shrinking, sitting on the stern sometimes, always quiet, only to descend spotted amid a revolt distant jets, it disappeared and then happened very quickly by near us, to return to be down and distant and, as running on the foams.

The steep cliffs of the Viper, with its clean Delfina creek flowing from the heart to the mountains seems timidly after their current mix with the rushing of Dagua, and collapsed of Myrtle, were being left. There was no need to do to get a higher lever because Laurean had broken his last spare. It was a time that nurtured a downpour accompanied us, and the river began to bring foam tape and some weeds Petite.

-She said Cortico tá jealous when arrimamos to the beach.

I thought he was referring to a sad and like muffled music that seemed to come from the neighboring hut.

- What child is this? I asked.

Pepita-Pue, my master.

Then I realized he was referring to the beautiful river of that name joins Dagua Meeting the people below.

- Why are you jealous?

- Do not see what sumercé low?

-No.

-Growing.

- Why is not the jealous Dagua? She is very nice and better than him.

Gregory laughed before answering:

-Dagua has a temper. Pepita and growing, because the river does not drop yellow.

I went to the ranch while the boatmen made their preventions, eager to see what instrument played there: was a marimba, keyboard chontas small bamboo jars lined up on high to low, and that is sounded with small bobbin aforrados in calfskin.

Having gained the lever and filled the indispensable condition that was of biguare or cueronegro, continue climbing with better weather and longer without jealousy hiciesen Pepita importunate.

The bogas stimulated by Lorenzo and gratification that I had promised them for their good management, endeavored to reach me from day to Boards. Shortly after we left to the right of sombrerillo campiñita, whose greenery contrasts with the harshness of the mountains that shade south. It was four o'clock when we at the foot of the cliffs of Crescent sour. We left shortly after the dreaded Creed, and finally gave implausible happy end to a beach jumping Navigation Meeting.

The friend D. .., former dependent of my father, I was waiting, warned by the correísta overtook us in San Cipriano, that I should come that afternoon. I drove home, where I was to wait for Lorenzo and bream. These were very happy with "me," as Gregory. They were up early the next day, and said goodbye to me in the most cordial and wishing me health, after two glasses of cognac rush and having received a letter to the Administrator.

LIX

As we sat at the table stated to D. .. I wanted to continue the journey the same evening if possible, begging expires drawbacks. He seemed to see Lorenzo, who was quick to answer that the beasts were in town and that was a moonlit night. I gave order to prepare our march without delay, and in view of the way it worked out, D. .. did not observe any kind.

Soon after Lorenzo introduced me to mount the harness, manifesting at how low it was pleased that no pernoctásemos on Boards.

Arranged ensure that D. .. conducting pay my luggage there and put it on the way back, we took leave of him and rode good mules, followed by a boy, gentleman in another, leading to a pair of saddle cuchugos small way with my clothes and some accoutrement to quickly put in them our guest.

We had won more than half of the rise of the door, when the sun was hidden and in the times when my horse took a breath, I could not but see with satisfaction the hollow of which had just come out, and breathed with delight the vivifying air of the mountains. And looked at the bottom of the deep vega Meeting people with their thatched roofs and Cinderellas: the Dagua, luxurious with light then I bathed, fringed islet of the village, and hastily rolled away into the revolt of the Creed, mirrored far away on the beaches of hat.

For the first time since I left London I felt absolutely my own will to close the distance between me and Mary. The certainty that I lacked only done two days to complete the trip, it would have been enough to make me burst during these four mules as they rode. Lorenzo, experienced resulting from such endeavors in such ways, tried to get me something moderate pace, and with the fair grounds guide, I was placed in front of it was nearing time to coronáramos slope.

When we got to the nest, only the moon showed us the path. I stopped because Lorenzo had dismounted there, which had alarmed the house dogs. Leaning it on my mule's neck, he said, smiling:

- Do you feel good that we sleep here? This is good people and no pasture for the cattle.

-Do not be lazy, I replied: I have no sleep and mules are fresh.

-Not especially eager-eyed me pulling my stirrup: I just want to vent these judas, lest we be so ovachonas achajuanen by. Just comes with my mules continued descinchando Joint-mine-and he told me that boy who met at the door, must toldar Santana tonight, if it fails to reach leaves. Where we find it, we make chocolate and go to bed a little while out there where you can. Do you like it?

Of course: it is necessary to get to Cali tomorrow afternoon.

-Not so much: turning seven in San Francisco we will enter, but going to my step, because otherwise, give thanks to reach San Antonio.

Speaking and doing, bathed the backs of mules with mouthfuls of aniseed. He took fire and lit his cigar link; threw reprimanded the boy, who had been lagging behind, because supposedly his mule was leathery, and started going wrong again gozques redundant in the cottage.

Although the road was good, ie dry leaves could not reach but after ten. On the plane whitened crown slope one awning. Lorenzo, noting mules browsed on the edge of the road, said:

-That's right, because we walk the drummer and Frontino, never desmanchan.

- What people is that? I asked.

For male-mine.

Deep silence reigned around the caravan arriera: a cold wind swung the cane fields and neighboring mandules of skirts, sometimes fanning the embers damped two immediate to the tent stove. Next to one of them slept curled black dog that barked and growled to feel in recognizing strangers.

- Hail Mary! Lorenzo shouted, thus giving carriers the greeting between them to get used to an inn. Calla, Chins! He added, addressing the dog and dismounting.

A tall thin mulatto emerged from the barricades of pouches of snuff, which tapiaban the two sides of the tent where it did not reach the floor: Justo was the foreman. Ponytail shirt wore a short blouse with pretensions, baggy pants, and had his head covered with a scarf tied at the neck.

- Olé!, Lord Lorenzo said his employer recognizing it, and he added: this is not the child Ephraim?

Correspondimos their greetings, pampeo Lorenzo with a back and a chanzoneta, I more fondly than spoiling let me.

-Continued-Apéense-corporal; bring a tired mule.

-Yours will be the tired-Lorenzo replied as ant come to pass.

'There will not. But what they're doing at this hour?

-Walking while you snore. Cut the conversation and send the script we stoke embers to make chocolate.

The other carriers were awake, and that should stir up the black. Just lit a candle, and then placing it in a banana bored, handed a clean cobijón on the floor for me to sit.

- And hast'onde go now? He asked Lorenzo drew their supplies bearings to accompany chocolate.

-A Santana replied. How are crutches? Garcia's son told me to leave boards that you had the Rosilla tired.

-Is the only maulona, but keep with ten, here he comes.

-Do not go get them load bales.

- Tan crook that was me! And what good will come out of the doomed: Chamomile yes I did in Santa Rosa one of toditicos Devils: who looks so tasajuda and is the most filática, but now is giving: to bring it from Platanares atillos.

The boiling chocolate olleta came on the scene, and each more ready muleteers offered their waist matecillos for what we took.

- Válgame! -Just as I said that chocolate tasted arrieramente made and served, but the more appropriate that came into my hands. Who would know the child Ephraim? When Lord will burst Lorenzo right?

Instead of warm water gourd and gave to his servants Just good brandy, and prepared to leave.

-The eleven will be raising the foreman said to see the moon that bathed with white light of the lofty hills and Bitaco Chancos.

I saw the clock and it was eleven effectively. We said goodbye to the carriers, and when we had half a block away from the tent, called Just Lorenzo: I hit it a few moments later.

LX

The next day at four in the afternoon I arrived at the top of the Crosses. Apeéme to tread that ground from where I said goodbye to my native land badly. I saw that valley of Cauca, hapless beautiful country as I ... Had so often dreamed spot it from the mountain, that after having it in all its splendor before, looked around to convince me that at that moment was not a dream toy. My heart was beating fast as if foreseeing that soon he was going to rest on Mary's head, and my ears eager to collect in the wind lost her voice. My eyes were fixed on the hills lit the distant foot of the mountain, where bleached my parents house.

Lorenzo had the clever catch me bringing a beautiful white horse he had received Tocota for me to do it the last three miles of the day.

'Look I said as he prepared to ensillármelo, and my arm was showing the white point of the mountains which I could not stop looking-morrow at this hour we'll be there.

- But there to do? Replied.

- How!

-The family is in Cali.

-You did not tell me that. Why have they come?

Just last night, told me that Miss was very bad.

Lorenzo in saying this I looked, and I thought moved.

I rode the horse trembling he had saddled me already, and the spirited animal began to descend rapidly and almost cheap by the rocky path.

The evening went off when I turned the last blade of montañuelas. A violent wind from the west buzzed around me in the rocks and weeds cluttering the abundant horse's mane. At the edge of the horizon to my left and not bleached my parents house on the slopes of the mountain dark and on the right, far away, under a turquoise sky, were discovered the massive sudden flashes of Huila half wrapped by floating mists.

Who raised what I said I can not destroy even the most beautiful of his creatures and what he wanted me more love. And again stifled sobs in my chest I drowned.

Since leaving my left the neat and pleasant valley of the Rock, worthy of its beautiful river and fond memories of my childhood. The city had just rest on its green and padded bed: as huge flocks of birds that nest looking cernieran, divisábanse on it, brightened by the moon, the leaves of the palm trees.

I had to gather all the rest of my courage to knock on the door of the house. A page opened. Apeándome flanges Throw your hands in the hallway and walked hurriedly and part of the corridor that separated me from the entrance to the hall: it was dark. I had advanced a few steps when he heard a scream and felt embraced.

- Mary! My Mary! I cried to my heart shaking that head delivered to my touch.

- Ah, no, no, God! -Interrumpióme sobbing.

And getting rid of my neck immediately fell on the sofa: it was Emma. She was dressed in black, and the moon had just bathed her face pale and watered with tears.

He opened the door of my mother's room at that moment. She, feeling my stammering and with kisses, arms pulled me in the seat where Emma was silent and motionless.

- Where is it, where is it? I yelled getting up.

- Son of my soul! Exclaimed my mother with the deepest tone of tenderness and shake again to her breast: 'in the sky.

Something like the cold blade of a knife penetrated my brain missed my chest and my eyes light air. It was death that hurt me ... She, so cruel and relentless, why did not know hurt? ...

LXI

I could not realize what had happened to me, one night I woke up in a bed surrounded by people and things that I could hardly distinguish. An evening lamp, whose light became more opaque curtains of the bed, spread through the quiet room indecisive clarity. I tried in vain to sit up: I called, and I felt one of my hands shook; contemptible to call, and the name was to answer faintly uttered a sob. Turned me to the side of where it had come out and recognized my mother, whose eyes filled with tears anhelosa and was fixed on my face. I was almost in secret with his voice softer, a lot of questions to make sure if I was relieved.

- So it's true? I said when the memory still confused about the last time he'd seen, came to mind.

Without answering, leaned his forehead against the pillow, thus uniting our heads.

After a few moments I had the cruelty to say:

- So I cheated! ... How did I come?

- What about me? - I broke my neck moistening with tears.

But his pain and tenderness corriesen not getting some of my eyes.

It was, no doubt, to avoid me any strong emotion, for a little while after my father went silent, and shook my hand as he wiped his eyes shadowed by sleeplessness.

My mother, Eloise and Emma took turns that night to ensure near my bed, then pulled the doctor promising a slow but positive replacement. Vainly exhausted their sweetest them care for me sleep. So my mother slept rendered by fatigue, I knew I was doing something more than twenty-four hours I was at home.

Emma knew all I needed to know: the story of his last days ... his last moments and his last words. I felt terrible to hear these confidences, I lacked courage, but I could not control my thirst for painful details, and asked many questions. She only answered me with the accent of a mother making her son sleep in the crib:

-Tomorrow.

And stroked my face with his hands or playing with my hair.

LXII

Three weeks had run since my return, during which he held me beside him and my mother Emma, advised by the doctor and apologizing for his tenacity with the poor state of my health.

The days and nights of two months had passed over his grave and my lips murmuring a prayer not talk about it. Sentíame even without the strength to visit the abandoned mansion of our loves, to watch the tomb that hid my eyes and refused to my arms. But in those places she should wait: there were the sad farewell present for me, who had flown his last farewell and receive their first kiss before death froze his lips.

Emma was slowly squeezing my heart all the bitterness of the last to confidences of Mary for me. So, recommended to break the dam my tears, did not wipe them later how, and mixing theirs to mine those hours spent painful and slow.

On the morning after the evening when Mary wrote his last letter, Emma, after having searched in vain in his room, he found her sitting on the stone bench in the garden: dabase see what had wept: their eyes on the current and enlarged by the shadow that surrounded, still moist with tears despaciosas some pale and emaciated those cheeks, once so full of grace and freshness: exhaled sobs and weak echoes of others in their pain had filed.

- Why did you come alone today? Emma asked hugging her: I wanted to go with as yesterday.

'Yes,' he answered, she knew, but wanted to come alone, I thought I would have the strength. Help me to walk.

He leaned on the arm and headed Emma rose in front of my window. Then they were close to him, Mary saw him almost smiling, and removing the two roses cooler, said:

-Maybe it will be the last. Look how many buttons: you shall to the Virgin to be the most beautiful opening.

Bringing his cheek flowered branch, said:

- Goodbye, my rose, emblem of constancy dear! You tell him that I took care of him while he said, turning to Emma, who wept with her.

My sister wanted to get her out of the garden saying:

- Why so sadden you? Did not Dad agreed to delay our trip? Back every day. Is not it true that you feel better?

-Estémonos still here replied slowly approaching the window of my room: the forgotten Emma was watching, and then leaned to release all of his kills favorite lilies, my sister saying: Tell him never stopped blooming. Now let's go.

He stopped at the edge of the stream, and looking around her forehead within Emma murmuring

- I do not want to die without seeing him again here!

During the day she was seen sadder and quieter than usual. In the afternoon he was in my room and left in the vase, together with a few strands of her hair, the lilies that had taken in the morning, and there was Emma to look after dark. He was leaning on the window, and disordered loops of hair almost hid his face.

-Mary-Emma said after having watched in silence for a moment-do not you do wrong this night wind?

She, surprised at first, replied taking her hand, pulling him and making him to sit beside her on the couch:

-Nothing can harm me.

- Do not you want to go to the chapel?

Not now: desire estarme here yet, I have to tell you so much ...

- No time for me to say them elsewhere? You, as obedient to doctor's prescriptions, so you make fruitless all their care and ours: two days ago are not as docile as before.

-You do not know that I will die, 'said Emma hugging and sobbing into his chest.

- Die! Ephraim? Die when going to get there? ...

-Without seeing it again, I will tell ... die without being able to wait. This is awful, shuddering added after a pause, but it's true: never access symptoms have been like I'm feeling. I need you to know everything before I say it is impossible. Hey: I want to leave as I have and has been kind. Put in the casket when I have her letters and flowers dry, this locket where your hair and my mother got me this ring on the eve of his trip, and fold them in my blue apron my braids ... Do not worry so he continued his cold cheek closer to my sister and I could no longer be his wife ... God wants rid of the pain of finding myself as I am, trance to see me expire. Alas, I could die under, giving my last goodbye. Estréchalo for me in your arms and say that I struggled in vain not to leave ... I dreaded his solitude more than death, and ...

Mary stopped talking and shaking in the arms of Emma; overlaid it with kisses and his lips found her stiff, he called her and said nothing, he cried out and ran to his aid.

All medical efforts were unsuccessful access it again, and in the morning the next day was declared powerless to save her.

The old parish priest happened at midnight to the call was made.

Waterfront Mary's bed was placed on a table adorned with the most beautiful flowers in the garden, the chapel crucifix, two candles lit and blessed. Kneeling before that altar humble and perfumed, the priest prayed for an hour, and rising, gave one of the candles to my father and another Mayn to approach them to the bed of the dying. My mother and my sisters, Luisa, his daughters and some slaves knelt to witness the ceremony. The minister said these words in the ear of Mary:

My daughter, God comes to visit you: will you receive it?

She went silent and motionless as if deeply asleep. The priest looked at Mayn, who, realizing instantly that look, his pulse to Mary, saying quietly followed:

-Four hours at least.

The priest blessed and anointed. The sobs of my mother, my sisters and daughters accompanied Highlander prayer.

An hour after the ceremony, John had approached the bed and tiptoe to catch a glimpse of Mary, weeping because he rose. Tomolo my mother in his arms and sat him on the bed.

- Are you asleep, right? Asked the innocent head resting on the same pillow where Mary rested, and taking him in his hands one of the braids as they used to sleep.

My father stopped that scene exhausting the strength of my mother and sorrowed attendees witnessed.

At five in the afternoon, Mayn, who stood at the head constantly pressing Mary stood up, and his eyes moistened understand my father left that agony was over. Her sobs made my mother Emma and precipitasen on the bed. It was as if asleep, but sleep forever ... Dead!, Without my lips had drawn his last breath, but my ears had heard his last farewell, without some of the many tears shed for me later on his grave, had fallen on his face!

When my mother was convinced that Mary was dead before his body bathed in the light of the afterglow of the evening that penetrated into the room through a window that just opened, cried hoarsely from crying, kissing one of those cold and unfeeling hands:

- Mary ... Daughter of my heart! ... Why did you leave us so? ... Ah, and you'll never hear me ... What answer to my son when I ask you? What will my God! ... Dead!, Exhaled dead without a complaint!

Already in the chapel, on a table in mourning, dressed in white gro and lying in the coffin, his face showed some sublime resignation. The candlelight shining on his forehead and on his broad smooth eyelids, cast the shadow of the lashes on the cheeks: those pale lips seemed to have frozen while trying to smile, could not believe that even encouraged. Sombreábanle throat half braids wrapped in a veil of white gauze and hands, descansándole on his chest, holding a crucifix.

Just saw Emma at three in the morning, when approaching the most terrible comply Custom Mary.

The priest was praying on his knees at the foot of the coffin. The night breeze, scented roses and orange blossoms, stirring the flames of the candles, and worn.

"I thought, 'said Emma, that cutting the first braid was so sweetly at me as if I used reclined her head on my lap I combed her hair. Púselas the foot of the statue of the Virgin and the last time I kissed cheeks ... When I woke up two hours later ... Was not there! ".

Braulio, Jose and four pawns more people led to the corpse, across these plains and low lying in the woods where Mary spent a happy morning beside me lover and beloved wedding day Transit. My father and the priest remained humble step to step the convoy ... Alas!, Humble and quiet as the Nay!

My father came home at noon and only slowly. Alighting made futile efforts to stifle the sobs that choked him. Sitting in the lounge, in the midst of Emma and my mother and surrounded by children who waited in vain for his touch, gave vent to his grief, making it necessary to give my mother a conformity procurase that she could not have.

"I-I told him cursed author of that trip, I've died! If Solomon could come to me for your daughter, what would I say? ... And Ephraim ... and Ephraim ...

Ah! Why do I call? So will fulfill my vows? '.

That afternoon left the hacienda of the saw to go to sleep in the valley, where they were to embark on a day trip to the city below.

Braulio and Traffic inhabit the house agreed to take care of it during the absence of the family.

LXIII

Two months after the death of Mary, the 10 September, Emma I heard the end of that relationship she delayed as long as he could. It was night already and John slept on my lap, he had contracted habit since my return, perhaps because I sensed instinctively sought partly replace him love and maternal care of Mary.

Emma gave me the key to the cabinet where they were kept in the house saw the dresses of Mary and all that she had recommended most especially for me will be saved.

In the early hours that followed that night I set off for Santa R. .. where it remained for two weeks my father warned after leaving everything to my return to Europe, which was to undertake the eighteen of that month.

The twelve to four in the afternoon I said goodbye to my father, who had been led to believe that he wanted to spend the night on the farm of Charles, to be that way earlier in Cali next day. When I hugged my father, he had his hands in a sealed package, and handing it to me said:

-A Kingston: contains the last will of Solomon and his daughter's dowry. If my interest in you, he added in a voice that was tremulous emotion made me stay away from her and perhaps hasten his death ... you know apologize ... Who should do it if not you?

Heard that the response was deeply moved paternal gave that excuse given humbly as tender as I shook his arms again. There remains in my ear his accent when pronouncing that goodbye!

Leaving the plain of ... forded after the Amaime, Juan Angel waited to tell him to take the mountain road. Looked at me as scared with the order received, but seeing me bent on the right, I followed as closely as he could, and soon lost sight of him.

We began to hear the noise currents Zabaletas, could see the tops of the willows. Detúveme leaning on the hill. Two years earlier, on an afternoon like this, then harmonized with my happiness and now was indifferent to my pain, had seen from the spot lights that with loving home where anxiety was expected. Mary was there ... We closed the house and its surroundings lonely and silent: the love that was born then and I love without hope! There, a few steps from the path that the program began to clear, he saw the wide stone seat that served us so many times in those happy evenings reading. He was, at last, the garden immediately confident of my loves: pigeons and thrushes chirping and fluttering foliage moaning in the orange: the wind blew leaves on the pavement of the grandstand.

I jumped off the horse, leaving it to his will, and without strength and voice to call, I sat in one of those steps where agasajadora many times his voice and his eyes told me goodbyes lovers.

A while later, almost dark now, I heard footsteps near me: it was an old slave who, having seen my horse loose in the manger, came to know who owned it. May laboriously followed him: the sight of that animal, my childhood friend, loving companion of my days of happiness, my chest started moaning: introducing me head for a treat, licking the dust off my boots, and sitting at my feet howled painfully.

The slave brought the house keys while Braulio and told me that they were on the mountain Transit. I entered the room, and taking some steps in it without my bleary eyes could distinguish objects, I fell on the couch where I was sitting with her forever, the first time I spoke of my love.

When I lifted his face, complete darkness surrounded me. I opened the gate of the house of my mother, and my spurs resounded mournfully in that room and smelling cold grave. Then a new strength in my pain made me plunge the oratorio. I was going to ask God ... Ni could want and return it in the ground! Where would search had narrowed my arms where my lips first rest upon his forehead ... The light of the moon rising, penetrating through the lattice ajar, let me see what all he had to find: pall rolled half of the table where the coffin rested: the remains of the candles that had lit the mound ... Dull silence my moans, mute eternity before my pain!

Light in the room I saw my mother was that Juan Angel had just put a plug in one of the tables: I took it, sending him with a gesture to leave me alone, and went to the bedroom of Mary. Some of his perfumes were there ... ensuring the latest clothes from his love, his spirit was estarme waiting. The crucifix still on the table: the dead flowers on his sentence: the bed where he died, and dismantled: still stained with the last few drinks potions given him. I opened the closet: all flavors of the days of our love are combined breathed it. My hands and my lips touched those dresses so familiar to me. Pull the drawer that Emma had told me, the precious casket was there. A cry escaped from my chest, and eye shadow covered me in my hands to unwind those braids seemed sensitive to my kisses.

An hour later ... My God, you know. I had walked the garden calling, upon request to the foliage shade we were given, and the desert in the echoes only returned me his name. At the edge of the abyss covered with roses, on whose background report and whitened dark mists and the river thundered, criminal thinking stalled for a moment my tears and cooled my forehead ...

A person I hid the roses, gave me my name near: Traffic was. At aproximárseme should make you fear my face, then stood stunned for a few moments. The answer I gave to the appeal that made me to leave that place, he revealed his bitterness perhaps with all the contempt that I had such moments in life. The poor girl began to mourn without insisting for the moment, but revived, mournful voice faltered with a whiny slave:

- Neither wants to see Braulio or my child?

Do not cry, Transit, and forgive me, I said. Where are they?

She clasped one of my hands without even wiping his tears, and led me into the hall of the garden, where her husband was waiting. After Braulio got my hug, got on my knees Transit a precious child of six months, and kneeling at my feet and smiled at his son looked pleased me cherish the fruits of their innocent love.

LXIV

Unforgettable and last night at the home where he ran the years of my childhood and the happy days of my youth! As the bird by Hurricane impelled to try in vain scorched plains bias their shadowy flight into the native forest, and worn feathers and return to it after the storm, and vainly seeking their love nest tree hovering around shattered and my soul is downcast within hours of my dream to wander around the former home of my parents. Lush orange and green willows Gentiles You grew me, how you have aged! Roses and lilies of Mary, who will love them whether there! aromas of lush garden, I will not aspiraros! Whisperers winds murmuring river ... I will not hear you!

Midnight found me in my room watching. Everything was there as I had left it, only Mary's hands had removed the indispensable, adorning the room for my return: withered and eaten away by insects remained in the vase of lilies last she got. Given that table I opened the package of letters that I had returned to die. Those lines erased by my tears and was traced as far as to believe that would be my last words to her, those rumpled sheets within it, were deployed and read one by one, and looking through the letters of Mary's response to each of which I had written, Collate this immortal dialogue dictated by hope love and interrupted by death.

Taking my hands braids Mary and lying on the couch in that Emma had heard his last to confidences, the clock struck two, he had also measured the hours of that night of anguish, the eve of my trip, he should measure of the last I spent in the home of my ancestors.

I dreamed that Mary was and my wife chaste delirium that has been and should continue to be the only delight of my soul wearing a floaty white dress, and wore a blue apron, blue like it was made from a scrap of heaven was that Apron so often helped him fill of flowers, and she knew so cute and carelessly tied around his waist restless, one in which I had found her hair wrapped: carefully parted my bedroom door, and trying not to make even the most slight noise with his robes, knelt on the carpet at the foot of the couch: after half sonreída look at me, as if afraid that my dream was faked, touched my forehead with his lips soft as velvet lilies Paez less fearful because of my deception, forsaken me suck a moment his breath warm and fragrant, but then waited in vain to oppress my lips with yours: sat on the carpet, and as I read some of the pages scattered her cheek was on one of my hands hanging over the cushions: she felt that hand animated, his eyes turned to me loving, smiling as she alone could smile, pulled her head on my chest, and recline so my eyes as he looked fringed forehead I silky tresses or inhaled with delight the fragrance of basil.

A cry, cry me, interrupted that dream: reality disturbed him jealous as if that moment had been a century of that. The lamp had burned, by the cold wind penetrated the window in the morning, my hands were yertas and oppressed those braids, only spoil its beauty, only truth of my dream.

LXV

In the afternoon of that day, during which he had visited all the places I was loved, and that he should not see again, I was preparing to take a trip to the city, through the parish cemetery where the tomb of Mary . Juan Angel and Braulio had gone ahead to wait on him, and Joseph, his wife and daughters around me and for my farewell. I followed the invitation of the oratory, and all knees, crying all, pray for the soul of her whom we both loved. Joseph broke the silence that followed the solemn prayer to recite a prayer to the protector of pilgrims and navigators.

Back in the corridor, Transit and Lucia, after receiving my goodbye, covered his face and wept sitting on the pavement, Mrs. Luisa had disappeared; Jose, becoming the face aside to hide her tears, I expected to have the horse Halter at the foot of the stands; May, wagging his tail and lying on the Gramal, was watching my every move as if in his days of vigor went out to hunt partridges.

Faltóme voice to say a last kind word to Joseph and daughters, but they also would have had to answer the.

A few blocks from the home I stopped before beginning the descent to see again dear that mansion and its environs. From hours of happiness that she had passed, I carried only the memory, of Mary, the gifts that I had left on the brink of the grave.

Then May came, and fatigued stopped at the edge of the stream that separated us: ford tried twice and both had to back down: sat on the grass and howled so piteously as if their cries had something human, as if they wanted Remember how much I had loved, and reproach me because I left in his old age.

½ When I dismounted the cover of a sort of garden, isolated in the plain and palisade fencing, which was the village cemetery. Braulio, getting the horse and taking part of the excitement that I discovered in my face, pushed a door leaf and went further. I crossed through the middle of the weeds and the crosses of wood and bamboo that rose above them. The setting sun crossed the tangled branches of the neighboring forest with some rays, which yellowed over the bushes and the leaves of the trees that shaded the tombs. As I turned to a group of tamarinds was stout in front of a white pedestal and stained by rain, on which stood a cross of iron: I approached. In a black iron poppies and hid half, began to read: "Mary" ...

A monologue that terrible soul before death, the soul that asks, that the curse ... he asks, that the flame ... gave eloquent answer too cold and deaf that grave, my arms and my tears bathed oppressed.

The sound of footsteps on the leaves made me get up in front of the pedestal: Braulio approached me and handed me a crown of roses and lilies, a gift of the daughters of Joseph, remained in the same place as to tell me it was time to from.

Púseme to hang up the cross, and went to hug to her feet to give Mary and her grave one last goodbye ...

He had already assembled, and clasped his hands Braulio one of mine, when the commotion of a bird passing overhead and gave a sinister croak known to me, interrupted our farewell saw fly into the iron cross, and inn and one of his arms, flapped repeating his awful singing.

Shaken, I went galloping down the middle of the lonely prairie, whose vast horizon darkened night.

THE END

Made in the USA
Monee, IL
18 October 2021